THE LAIRD'S SECRET

LINDA TYLER

Print ISBN 978-1-913942-18-2

For my sons, the original Nicholas and William.

CHAPTER 1

Aberdeenshire, Scotland, 1953

Christina could hear the presenter's enthusiastic voice on the wireless, talking about the Queen's coronation only a month away, as she popped her head round the open kitchen door.

'Do you mind if I go for a walk on the beach while the twins are sleeping, Vanessa?'

'Of course not.' Her friend straightened up from sliding a batch of scones into the oven and wiped her hands on her frilly apron. 'You're on holiday.'

'Thanks, Van.' Christina pulled on her beret. 'I won't be long.'

'Take your time,' Vanessa said, 'although you might want one of the scones while they're still warm.'

Christina let herself out of the cottage door and into the May sunshine with a small sigh. Her friend was so very kind, but she needed to be outside, to walk off the restlessness she felt.

Cheerful violas basked in their tubs by the stone wall. Spring was her favourite time of year, she thought, not simply for its new colours, but for the light and a hint of promise in the air.

This was what she wanted: simplicity and a sense of hope for the future.

She set off along the rough path to the beach. The warmth of the afternoon had brought out the coconut smell of the gorse. Bees buzzed around the bright yellow flowers. She turned the corner and drew in a deep breath. Sparkling in the sun, the North Sea rolled onto the long stretch of sand. There was nothing like this in London, she thought with a wry smile.

The beach was empty, as it had been on the previous day when she'd first walked here. She sat on a rock and removed her ankle boots. Glancing quickly around, she lifted the hem of her pleated skirt to unclip her stockings. With the nylons rolled down and slipped off, stockings and boots in her hand, she strolled along the beach. There was only the low roar of the waves and she felt the tension ebbing away through her bare feet on the warm sand.

Christina heard the dog before she saw it. She was not, after all, alone in this perfect coastal wilderness. Excited barking came as she scrambled down the dune, half-sliding on the fine, soft sand, her skirt flapping about her knees. A golden Labrador came lolloping round the bay and its paws sent up small clouds of sand. It made straight for her, its tail wagging furiously as if she were an old friend.

'Hello there!' Laughing, she bent to stroke the dog, puppy-like in its delight. As she straightened up and neatened her fitted jacket, she searched the beach for its owner. All she could see were orange fishing nets, draped high across poles to dry under the blue sky.

Christina bent again to the dog, now dancing round her to regain her attention. 'So you want to play?' She looked for a stick to throw, spotted one still wet from its journey on the North Sea tide and, picking it up, swung back her arm.

'What are you doing?' called a masculine voice.

She whirled round, almost dropping the stick.

The man had crested a low dune. Shielding her eyes from the sun, Christina watched as he strode towards her. It was an isolated spot and her heart began to thump.

She stepped back as he reached her. At the same time, she saw a livid scar running across his forehead and down to one eyebrow. His dark eyes pinned her with an accusing stare.

Christina conjured up a friendly smile. 'I was going to throw this stick for the dog.'

He drew his brows together and the scar puckered a little. 'Aye, well don't you know that Labradors have soft mouths, which a stick can harm?'

'I...' He seemed to carry a sense of authority and she felt herself hesitating.

'Wasn't thinking?' he finished.

She felt the colour tingling over her face. 'No, I was going to say I didn't know that. About the dog's mouth, I mean.'

'Obviously.'

He looked like an outdoor type, strong and tanned, perhaps in his late twenties. He might have been good-looking if it weren't for his solemn expression. His dark hair ruffled in the breeze.

'Well,' she found herself saying, as her cheeks burned, 'I have to wonder why you don't keep better control of your dog, instead of allowing it to run about wherever it likes.' The words flew from her mouth before she could stop them.

His eyes registered faint amusement. He glanced at her bare calves and feet, the ankle boots and stockings gripped in her hand. Had he seen her sliding down the dune?

'I – and my dog – have every right to walk freely on this beach,' he said carefully. 'And nor is she undisciplined, I might add.'

'Do you always speak like this to perfect strangers?'

'Only to *perfect* strangers...'

She felt a frown crease her forehead as the ghost of a smile formed on his lips. His gaze took in her fair hair escaping from under her beret and she knew how untidy she must look. Why couldn't he act like a normal person? It must have been clear she meant no harm. Her heart raced and she didn't trust herself to speak again, so she said nothing.

He nodded slightly, pushed up the sleeves of his thick cream jumper and turned to the dog. 'Tess, heel.' A moment later he was away along the sand.

She watched him go, the Labrador trotting obediently beside him.

Christina stood for a few moments and considered the retreating figure with its easy stride. Her cheeks were hot with a mixture of embarrassment and fury. She had never answered a man back like that before. What had got into her? And who did he think he was? Everyone else she had met so far on this holiday in Scotland had been pleasant and welcoming, but this man... he acted as though he owned the place.

What had she seen in his eyes? They hadn't looked as angry as his words.

Christina realised she was still holding the stick and threw it down. She took a deep breath and sighed, her anger going with it.

What did it matter what they had said in that short exchange? She'd probably never set eyes on him again. He was gone and she needed to get back to her friend's cottage.

Christina stuffed her stockings into her jacket pocket, brushed the sand from her feet and slipped on her boots. Turning, she took the rough path from the beach and pushed the dark-eyed stranger from her thoughts as David crowded into them. It was David's fault – he'd made her feel hostile, wary.

She counted her blessings that she had Vanessa for a friend. When Vanessa had heard about David's death, she'd immediately suggested that Christina come to stay with her and the children in Aberdeenshire.

You need to get away – a holiday. And you haven't visited us here yet, she had written to Christina. Even Vanessa's familiar scrawl on the blue notepaper made Christina long to see her again. *The boys are three years old now and a lot of fun. Besides, Callum's frequently working away from home – you know how war damage has meant a lot of work for civil engineers – and I'd love the company. You'd be doing me a favour, really.*

Dear Vanessa. They had been war children together and had a special bond. 'Really, Van,' Christina had murmured to herself as she read the letter, 'I'm fine. Honestly.'

But the ache that she woke with every morning finally persuaded her. She needed a change of scenery, somewhere new, with the time to heal. And, as her friend pointed out, Christina hadn't yet visited since Vanessa, her Scots husband and twin boys had left Surrey a year ago for their new home in the north-east of Scotland.

Stay as long as you like, Vanessa said, but Christina planned for a fortnight only, three weeks at most. She didn't want to outstay her welcome. When the time came for her to leave, she wouldn't return to her old life. She hadn't renewed the tenancy on her bedsit in London and had given in her notice at the studio where she worked. A new opportunity would turn up, she was sure. Everyone needed a photographer for special events, didn't they? And there were magnificent locations to capture everywhere. Perhaps one day she would have a one-woman exhibition, her own studio…

As he strode away, Alexander MacDonald let his thoughts linger on the girl on the beach. He pictured her sparkling blue eyes and thought of her spirited response to his comment. Eight years since the war had ended and he still didn't know how to deal with people. He suspected he'd deserved her retort.

Who was he trying to fool? It wasn't 'people' he couldn't deal with, but this attractive young woman. And she was attractive. It wasn't just her spirit he admired, but her hesitant smile, the way she blushed so quickly, her tousled blonde hair. He wondered what she was doing here.

He knew everyone who lived in this area and he hadn't seen her before. She must be here on holiday, probably staying at the Boat Inn. He might pop in later for a pint and see if Gordon had any tourists up from south of the border.

He laughed at himself. What was he thinking? He had to get back to Craiglogie. On Home Farm, the oats had to be planted, the calves fed and the old bull moved into the low field. There were always jobs to do, which was as he liked it. No time to think too deeply, not even about pretty English lassies.

He reached his Land Rover parked on rough ground above the beach, lifted up the tailgate and folded down the lower section. 'In you get, Tess.'

The dog jumped into the car, settling herself on an old blanket. Alex rubbed her ears and sighed. He loved the farm and the estate, was grateful every day for what he had, but sometimes it seemed he was merely repeating the same tasks according to the season. And he was well aware of the expectations associated with being the laird.

He slammed the boot doors shut. As long as he got on with things, he'd get through.

He climbed into the car and drove the few miles home, trying not to think of how inadequate he was at small talk. Worse than that, he'd been impolite, which is not the way he'd been brought up. And then there was that, 'Only to *perfect* strangers'. He flushed at the memory of his words. What on earth had made him say that? It was out of character for him to even attempt to flirt. He touched the scar on his forehead, felt the raised skin, and then remembered how she had stepped back when he'd got closer to her.

As he passed between the stone pillars and caught a glimpse of Craiglogie House at the end of the driveway, Alex felt the usual surge of pleasure in the MacDonald family home. He loved the old granite house with its large windows and high, ornamental turret.

He pulled up in front of the house, climbed from the seat and walked round to the back of the car. As he let out Tess, he smiled at her excitement at being home again, as if she had left it months ago and not an hour or so earlier. The dog bounded around him, before bursting in through the open door of the house, colliding with the slim figure of his sister coming out to greet him.

'Hello, Tess!' Fiona laughed, bending down to stroke the Labrador's head.

Fiona turned to him as she pulled off her hat and gloves. 'I just dropped in to see Vanessa. She has a friend newly arrived from England staying with her for a few weeks. I didn't meet the friend, Christina, as she was out for a walk, but I've invited them both to dinner tomorrow evening.'

Alex felt a rush of something he could not identify, attached to a memory of blue eyes. He swallowed hard.

'Is that all right with you, Alex?'

He shook himself and met Fiona's gaze. 'It's fine. I'm looking forward to it.'

In spite of his misgivings, he thought perhaps he might be.

By the time Vanessa's cottage came into view, the May sunshine and the warm breeze in her hair had bolstered Christina's spirits. She pushed open the wooden gate and made her way along the short path. As she turned the handle on the front door and pushed it open, the scent of freshly-baked scones wafted out from the kitchen to welcome her.

The kitchen door was standing ajar and through it Vanessa called out, 'You timed that well!'

Christina entered the small, brightly-painted room, its shelves crammed with assorted pottery. It was so cosy that she had instantly felt at home. Vanessa smiled at her, turned off the wireless, took the kettle from the stove and poured boiling water into the teapot warming on the hotplate.

'The fresh air and sea breeze are clearly good for you,' said Vanessa. 'Your cheeks are glowing and your eyes have quite a sparkle in them.'

Christina had told herself not to think again of her encounter with the obnoxious man, but as she pulled off her hat, unbuttoned her jacket and slid into a chair at the table the words were out of her mouth before she could stop them.

'So,' she said as she finished her story, 'my eyes aren't sparkling – they're fiery! All because of that man I met on the beach. I swear he acted as if he owned the place.' Her face flushed, she slipped off her jacket and hung it on the back of her chair.

'This man wouldn't happen to be about six foot tall, muscular, with dark hair, would he?' said Vanessa, handing her a cup of tea. She laughed at the look on Christina's face. 'Well, my dear, that's probably because he does! That would have been Alexander MacDonald, the Laird of Craiglogie. His family own a large stretch of the beach as well as much of the land around here.'

Christina put down her cup and saucer with a clatter. 'So I was trespassing on his property?' She looked out of the window to try to hide her dismay. 'Will this cause a problem for you and Callum?'

'Of course not. Whatever makes you think that it would?'

'Because he's your neighbour.' She turned back to Vanessa. 'You know, he was awfully prickly about my throwing a stick for his dog and I'm afraid for once I was just as rude back.' She took a sip of tea. 'He has no manners.'

'Don't you think you're being a bit unfair?' said Vanessa. 'You've only met him once. Alex can behave in a rather superior way at times, I suppose, but he doesn't mean it. It's just an act. Probably something to do with the life he's had – being the first born, fighting in the war, the death of his father and his mother living abroad. He's used to taking charge.'

'He had a scar on his forehead,' Christina said, running a finger across her own forehead and down to her right eyebrow. 'Is that from the war?'

Vanessa nodded. 'He was hit by a piece of flying shrapnel, I've been told.'

Christina felt a stab of pain for the man. 'Do you know him well?'

Vanessa rose from the table to stir the contents of a saucepan on the stove. 'I'm friendly with his younger sister, Fiona. Both she and Alex have a lot of charm when you get to know them.'

Charm! David had plenty of that. But before Christina could insist to Vanessa that she was never again going to allow herself to be impressed by a man's charming ways, the twins burst in from the garden demanding to know what was for dinner.

'It's not dinner time yet, boys, but we'll be having stovies.' She turned to Christina. 'See what a Scottish cook the children and Callum have turned me into. Before I moved here, I would never have dreamed of producing a meal of potatoes, onions and minced beef all stewed together into a kind of mess, but they love it.'

As if to prove this, the little boys chanted, 'Stovies, stovies, stovies.' They each snatched up a warm, buttered scone from the plate on the table and ran back outside.

Christina smiled. The twins were so full of life.

Vanessa turned to her with a mischievous grin on her face. 'Anyway, you're about to see more of Mr Alexander MacDonald.'

'Oh?' said Christina, as the colour rushed from her cheeks.

Vanessa frowned. 'Are you all right, Chrissie?'

Christina took a breath and met her gaze. 'I'm fine. Just tired from all the fresh air, I suppose.'

'Good.' Vanessa dropped back into the chair. 'Because Fiona popped round while you were out. I mentioned that I had a friend staying and she's invited us both to a small dinner party at Craiglogie House tomorrow.'

The strong desire not to see the man again flooded over Christina and she couldn't hide it.

'You will come, won't you?' said Vanessa, seeing the look on Christina's face. She slid the plate of scones across the table towards her. 'It's quite something to go to the big house for dinner.'

Christina conjured up the image of Alex MacDonald on the beach, when he'd given that half-smile, once he seemed to have forgotten how cross he'd been a few minutes earlier...

'Chrissie? You're not going to turn down a dinner date from Fiona based on a two-minute conversation with her brother this afternoon, are you?'

Christina felt a pang of guilt at the dismay on Vanessa's face, but still found herself saying, 'Would it cause a problem for you?'

'No, I suppose not – but I've already accepted for both of us. And you know you were telling me only this morning that you were going to move on with your life. If you survived almost maiming his dog and you still got an invitation to dinner, I don't think you have anything to worry about–'

'But he wasn't the one who invited me.'

'He never invites anyone. He leaves that up to Fiona.'

'He'll not want to sit making polite conversation with me.'

'It won't be just us. We can sit at the opposite end of the table from him. He probably won't recognise you from today, anyway. Some make-up and a dress will transform you, like Cinderella. Go on, it'll be a night to remember, I guarantee it.'

'All right,' she said reluctantly, taking a scone and putting it on her plate. 'I'll come and I promise to be a pleasant guest.'

What on earth was she thinking, agreeing to spend an evening at this man's home? Still, it was Fiona who'd made the invitation. As if it would have come from the unpleasant brother.

He might not even be there. That was possible, surely. He

must have as little desire to see her again, as she had to see him. Christina gave an inward sigh. She couldn't offend Vanessa. This man was, after all, the brother of her friend. No, she couldn't back out, she would have to go to the dinner party.

She looked across the table and saw the quizzical look on Vanessa's face. Leaning across, she took her friend's hand. 'It's really good to see you again, Van. It's been too long and I've missed you.'

Vanessa squeezed Christina's hand. 'I've missed you too. I'm sorry this is the first time we've managed to get organised for your visit. I've hardly had a moment to myself since the move up here and with the twins being so active. And you, you've been busy with moving to London, your work, and then wrapped up with David–'

She broke off with a horrified look. 'Sorry, Chrissie. I didn't mean...'

Christina bit her bottom lip to stem the tears that threatened to flow. All she could think, when it happened, was how could other people be walking about, living their lives as usual, when David was no longer there?

She swallowed back the tears. You've cried enough, she told herself. She wouldn't let David – or this dark-eyed laird – spoil her holiday with her friend.

'I'm fine,' she said, 'but I'd prefer not to talk about him. If you don't mind, that is.'

Vanessa nodded. She refused Christina's offer of help with making the apple crumble for pudding, so Christina curled up with Nicholas and William on either side of her on the sofa and read *The Biggest Bear* to them in front of the sitting-room fire.

The following morning the weather was warm and sunny, so Christina decided to take a trip to the next village along the coast. She'd been here only a few days and already felt more at peace than she had for a long time. The isolation of Vanessa's cottage, the vast expanse of white, empty sands and the high tussocky dunes soothed her.

'I thought I'd visit the castle ruins you mentioned the other day,' she'd told Vanessa, who was busy getting the boys ready for a birthday party in the village.

'Sure you'll be okay?' Vanessa asked as she wrestled Nicholas into his jacket. 'There's only one bus in each direction on that route every day, so if you miss it coming back, you'll be stranded. I can easily take you in the car this afternoon.'

'I'm twenty-two years old, Van, not one of your children.' Christina snatched a small coat off its peg and caught hold of William's hand. 'I'll be fine.'

Fond as she was of her friend, she knew they couldn't spend all their time in each other's company and she didn't want Vanessa to feel she had to entertain her. She managed to get William's jacket on his squirming body and buttoned him into it. 'I'll keep an eye on the time, I promise.'

Vanessa wrinkled her brow. 'You won't get carried away taking photographs?'

'No, I'll leave my camera behind this morning.'

'Good,' said Vanessa as she opened the door and bustled the boys outside. She turned and smiled. 'You're on holiday, after all.'

Christina was the only passenger on the blue country bus, so after she'd paid the driver, she took the seat closest to him.

'You're lucky with the weather,' he said as he pulled away. 'It's not always this warm in May.'

'I'm making the most of it,' she said.

'You're away to see the castle ruins, then?' he said over his shoulder.

'Yes. I've heard they're worth a visit.'

'You'll find them interesting, right enough,' he said cheerfully. 'Mary Queen of Scots spent a night there, they say.'

'Did she really?'

'All the locals swear it's true.'

'And what do you think?'

'I think it brings the visitors in and that's good for the area.' She heard him chuckle as he navigated a bend in the road.

'Then I'll pass on that bit of history and recommend this place to my friends when I go back south,' she said.

'That would be a fine thing to do, lassie.'

Christina turned her head to look at the passing scenery. Earlier in the year the news had been full of the heavy storm which had lashed the east coast of Britain, and she could see the damage it had caused in this part of the country. Some of the farm buildings were missing their roofs and debris had been caught in the fences and hedges bordering the fields.

'It looks like the storm was really bad here,' she said.

'Oh, aye, terrible. Folk here won't forget it in a hurry. The last night of January and the next morning, it was. Mind, the coast along the Moray Firth was the worst hit. Fisherfolk in the wee village of Crovie had to flee as houses were swept into the sea.' He shook his head.

The bus wound its way along the narrow coast road bordered with yellow gorse bushes. The scene Christina looked out on was peaceful, idyllic. In the fields lambs trotted after their mothers and the sun danced on the sea.

'That's Craiglogie House we're coming up to now.'

She started, her ears pricking. 'Craiglogie House?' Wasn't that where she and Vanessa were invited to dinner? The family home of Alexander MacDonald. She caught herself fidgeting with the sleeve of her jacket. Stilling her hands, she turned to look in the direction the driver indicated.

'Aye,' he said, 'where the Laird of Craiglogie stays. They're good people, him and his sister. Well liked around here, you'll find.'

That's what Vanessa had said, but Christina wasn't convinced. The bus rumbled along the road, following the high drystone wall that encircled the Craiglogie estate. She saw a pair of stone pillars and huge wrought-iron gates standing open. Leaning forward, she caught a glimpse of a driveway bordered by beech trees, before it curved out of sight and the bus passed by. A little further along the road, above the tops of the trees, a turret rose majestically into the pale-blue sky.

'It certainly seems imposing,' she murmured. Immediately, Christina knew she wanted to see the house, the gardens, the grounds, and to photograph them. For the moment, her professional interest brushed away her dislike of the owner. Craiglogie promised to be both impressive and intriguing, with an element of excitement. She could picture Alexander MacDonald living in a place like that.

The bus slowed down.

'This is the spot you'll be wanting.' The driver pulled to the side of the narrow road and stopped.

'Thank you.' Christina scrambled out and looked around, unsure where to go.

'Down the path till you reach the signpost, lassie. You'll not miss it. I'll be back in two hours, so be sure to be here,' he called, before the folding doors hissed closed. She lifted her hand to wave as she watched the bus trundle away and then she set off in search of the sign.

A small wooden fingerpost bearing the hand-painted words *Craiglogie Castle* pointed to a grassy path heading down towards the sea. The path was springy under her feet as she picked her way along it. Round a corner there came into view the remains of a round tower, its window spaces staring blankly. The roof had gone and grass grew from the stones at the top of the structure.

She paused to read the date engraved on the granite

lintel:1565. Stepping cautiously under it, she entered the ruin and wandered through what remained of the rooms. High vaulted ceilings and huge empty fireplaces. She imagined the inhabitants of the castle going about their daily lives almost four hundred years ago. In the kitchen, bakers would have been sliding flat loaves into the bread oven, cooks roasting meat over the open fire and at night the servants would have settled down on straw close to the embers to keep warm as they slept.

In the great hall, she pictured the laird and his lady in their fine velvets, colourful silks and soft wools, entertaining friends and family at a long table laden with local produce, laughing and chatting in the light of the flames burning brightly in the grate. Would it be like this at Craiglogie House? Christina smiled to herself, and the images from long ago disappeared abruptly.

She climbed the circular staircase, placing her feet with care on the worn, irregular steps, her fingers touching the damp stone walls. The rooms here were smaller with moss-covered flag-stones on the floor. At the top of the castle was nothing but the wide-open sky – and the view was incredible. A patchwork of fields, the sea sparkling in the distance... and the roofline of Craiglogie House clearly visible in the trees. Was there no escaping the place? she thought with a small sigh.

Christina checked her wristwatch. An hour had gone already, but she had enough time to walk on the dunes before catching the bus back.

Strolling down the steep, empty road to the beach, she thought of her annual visits to the seaside as a child in England. Her parents always went to the popular south coast resorts. She smiled as she remembered her younger self believing that all seaside towns began with a B. Brighton, Bognor Regis, Bournemouth. Her world was small and untroubled then, just as she had been, swinging on the arms of her parents as they saun-tered along the promenade.

Now her life felt very different. Turbulent, like the stretch of sea before her. Yet this north-east coastline was much more than that. It was also beautiful and wild. The image of Alexander MacDonald's dark eyes and windswept hair came back to her and she caught her breath.

She shook her head, pushed aside the image and made her way onto the beach. Miles of empty sands and grassy dunes stretched away in both directions. Standing with her face tipped briefly towards the sun, she breathed in the tangy sea air. Then she turned to watch the white-flecked, ice-cold white horses rolling in to crash on the shore, a reminder that life here could be harsh.

Christina found a sheltered place to sit on the sand, her back against a rock, and saw four children come running along the beach towards the upturned wreck of a wooden boat. It must have been there a long time, as its hull was covered with barnacles and seaweed. Poor little abandoned boat, she thought. I will come back soon and photograph you.

The warmth of the day and the shimmering water combined to make her relaxed and sleepy, and she let her eyelids close, just for a moment. The moment stretched into a minute, the minute into two, until the roar of the sea and the sounds of the children as they called to each other faded into the background.

She thought of David. She thought about him without crying for the first time since she had discovered the truth. Three months ago; had it only been three months?

It was supposed to be easier not to think of him here, hundreds of miles away from London and its memories and heartbreak. But still the image of David, with his fair hair and green eyes, came painfully back to her. The night they met, dancing to the big band at the Lyceum in the West End; their feelings for each other quickly growing over the next few months.

She could almost feel the touch of his fingers stroking her

hair, his warm breath on her cheek. 'I do love you, you know that, don't you, Chris?'

Her heart welled up and a soft sigh escaped her.

'To match your bewitching blue eyes, my darling,' he'd said, slipping the ring with its turquoise stone onto the third finger of her left hand. His arm slid round her waist. She tasted his soft kisses…

Christina felt a stab of anguish as the reality hit home once more that he would never hold her close again. David was dead.

When he died no one came to tell her – because no one in his other life knew of her existence.

A gull shrieked overhead and she shivered, opening her eyes to the bright day, almost expecting to see him there, smiling tenderly at her. Suddenly cold, she rubbed her arms through her woollen jacket to bring back some warmth. She wanted to hold close the precious memory of his loving her, but the ache was too painful and it was pointless. She rubbed the empty ring finger with her left thumb. She'd loved David and trusted him completely. How could he have deceived her?

She would never forget her wait at Croydon Aerodrome for his return flight from a business trip to France and her thumping heart when she discovered that he was not on the plane. There followed her desperate attempt to find out what had happened, but she had no phone number or address for him. She had been too much in love to realise what that meant. Or why they always met outside Aldwych station on the same two days of the week, before he'd take her dancing or to the pictures, where they snuggled against each other.

After an unbearable few days when she could neither eat nor sleep from worry, she'd spotted the small funeral notice in the *Evening Standard*. David had never even made the business trip, but had died of a heart attack the day before he was due to fly to Paris. Further shocking news was still to come. At David's grave-side, among the mourners had been his wife and little daughter.

Christina's face burned with shame at the memory. 'Never again will I trust a man,' she repeated to herself fiercely.

The sound of the children calling to each other on the beach jerked her out of her thoughts. Drying the tears she felt on her cheeks, she climbed to her feet and brushed the sand from her skirt. The sun was warm on her face, the sea breeze tousled her hair and a sense of peace again crept over her. This place was perfect for her to begin to heal.

She reached down and picked up a pebble, smoothing her fingers over its hard, sun-warmed surface. Then she threw it as far as she could into the water. Men were not worth the heartache, she told herself. If that was what happened when you fell in love, she wanted no part of it.

CHAPTER 2

*A*lex walked in through the back door and kicked off his boots. The cattle had been fed and watered for the morning and now he had a few hours to himself. He strode into the kitchen, rolling up his sleeves, and made for the sink.

As he lathered soap over his hands and forearms, he tried to work out exactly how a simple thing like a small dinner party could have caused him to feel so unsettled.

The corners of his mouth lifted as he remembered Christina's warm smile when she first spoke to him, one that had forced a brief smile onto his own lips.

Their encounter had been short, but it was long enough for him to have admired her shapely legs, the way her jacket fitted to her slender waist, her womanly curves beneath the blue wool. He winced at what he'd said to her and regretted that he had sounded so pompous.

He held his hands and arms under the tap to rinse off the soap suds and stared out of the window. He let his eyes travel over the neat kitchen garden.

It had been a long time since he'd noticed any woman in that way. He was so used to the emotional numbness he'd felt since the war, that most of the time he went through each day as if none of his life was real. But this girl, the way she'd looked in the sunlight, with strands of hair escaping from her ponytail and blowing about her face, and those blue eyes… they'd tied his tongue.

'Alex?'

He turned to see Fiona had entered the kitchen and was staring at him.

'What on earth are you doing? There'll be no water left in the well if you keep running the tap like that.'

'Sorry. I wasn't thinking.' He turned it off, crossed to the Aga, water dripping from his broad hands, and pulled a towel from the drying rail.

'Honestly,' Fiona said, 'I hope you intend to pay better attention to our new guest this evening.' She looked up into his face and gave a sisterly grin. 'You never know, Alex, you might like her.'

By the time Christina returned from her excursion, Vanessa was back at the cottage after dropping off the children. There was a pile of neatly folded clothing on the kitchen table.

'Did you have a good time?' said Vanessa, looking up from pressing the creases out of a navy-blue dress.

'Yes, thanks.' Christina slipped out of her jacket and dropped it over the back of her chair. 'The castle ruins were really dramatic in that setting.' She sat down and smoothed the pleats in her skirt.

'What is it?' said Vanessa. She eased the dress onto a coat hanger and hung it on the back of the door.

'Nothing, not really.' Christina shrugged. 'I was just going to say that I caught a glimpse of Craiglogie House this morning.'

'Of course – you would have seen the tower from the bus. It's quite something, isn't it?' Vanessa stood the hot iron on the side of the stove and collapsed the legs of the wooden ironing board.

'It seems very grand,' said Christina. 'All the trees around it meant I couldn't actually see the house, but I got an idea of the place. I'm afraid I've only brought two frocks with me and neither of them is very dressy.'

'The house *is* grand, but the evening won't be that formal. I'd offer you one of my dresses, but since I had the twins you and I are no longer the same size.' Vanessa pulled a rueful face.

Christina laughed and motioned towards the low-necked dress on the hanger. 'I bet Callum loves this new, voluptuous you. And in that dress, you'll look like Jayne Mansfield.'

Vanessa gave a hoot of laughter. 'Not quite. But I intend to look more like a film star than I usually do. You know,' she added, 'I may have something to fit you at the back of my wardrobe. Would you like me to have a look?'

'Don't worry about it. But if you've got a spare evening shawl, do you think I could borrow that?'

'Of course you can. I've one in a soft pale blue that will suit you.'

Christina thought about her two dresses hanging in the small wardrobe upstairs. It didn't matter what she wore, as long as she looked presentable. After all, she wasn't dressing to please that man. 'It's kind of Fiona to include me in the invitation,' she said.

'You'll like her and you'll enjoy yourself,' said Vanessa, putting the ironing board in the cupboard and closing the door. 'There's always wonderful food and an interesting mix of people.'

Christina wasn't sure that a dinner party was what she wanted right now. She didn't really want to spend the evening making polite conversation, but she couldn't let Vanessa down. Her friend would enjoy the break from her usual cares of household and children. Christina was sure Vanessa could easily go on her own, but she was equally sure that if she excused herself it would embarrass her friend in front of Fiona and upset the seating arrangements. Alexander MacDonald would either be there or he wouldn't; there was nothing she could do about it.

'Fiona wants to discuss a couple of things with me before tomorrow's meeting about the village's annual dance,' continued Vanessa, 'so you and I are to arrive a bit earlier this evening than the other guests.'

Christina straightened the freshly laundered handkerchiefs on top of the ironed pile. 'Do you know who else will be at the dinner?' she said, keeping her voice light.

'I'm afraid I didn't ask,' said Vanessa. Seeing Christina frown, she added, 'Don't worry, you'll look gorgeous, whatever you wear.'

Christina laughed and shook her head. She decided on the white *broderie anglaise* dress, with its fitted bodice, narrow waist and full skirt, and hoped it would be smart enough. Her hair she could pin up with the diamante clip her grandmother had given her, leaving a few tendrils to frame her face. It was a look David had loved...

'Let me make lunch today,' she said quickly. 'And you can tell me about how you and Fiona became friends.'

Vanessa sank into the old armchair. 'Bliss. Someone else preparing lunch and the children staying with friends until tomorrow morning. Morag is such a saint.' She swung her legs in their slacks over the side of the upholstered chair. 'Let's see now. I've been friends with Fiona almost since we moved up here. I'm sure I've mentioned her in my letters to you.'

Christina nodded agreement. 'Scrambled eggs okay?'

'Mmm, lovely. We've got plenty. Fiona keeps me supplied from their hens. The eggs are in the box there.' She pointed to a square wooden box on the counter. 'We met in the local shop. I'd gone in for eggs, but they hadn't got any that day. There'd been a run on them, because the Rural were all entering the baking competition at the agricultural fair.'

'The Rural?' Christina set a pan on the stove and dropped in a knob of butter.

'The Scottish Women's Rural Institute, to give it its full name,' said Vanessa. 'Well, Fiona took me back to her house. Callum had taken the boys out in the pushchair, so I was able to stay for coffee and a chat. I made one of my sponges for her as a thank you and it went from there. Now let me see, what else can I tell you?' She thought for a moment.

'Oh, her mother lives abroad, in Portugal; says the climate there is better for her arthritis. Imagine; hot, sunny days in a villa looking out over a warm sea...' Vanessa drifted off for a second or two. 'Anyway,' she said, coming back to their conversation, 'it means Fiona is used to playing hostess.'

Christina nodded and cracked eggs into a bowl.

'And there's Fiona's older brother, Alex, whom you met the other day.'

'Yes,' said Christina, beating the eggs.

'Every woman around here moons over Alex, you know,' Vanessa went on. 'I have to confess I'd go for him myself, but Callum wouldn't like it!' She giggled. 'Alex is handsome, wealthy, thirty-one and unmarried. Quite a catch for some lucky girl, wouldn't you say?'

Christina had a sudden image of those smouldering eyes. 'No, I wouldn't say so.' She was surprised by the vehemence in her voice. 'There needs to be more to a man than that.'

Vanessa stopped swinging her legs and stared at Christina. 'Chrissie, sorry. There I go again.' She gave a small sigh. 'Rabbiting on about the most eligible bachelor in the area, as if you'd be interested.'

Christina tipped the egg mixture into the sizzling butter. Lifting the wooden spoon, she stirred the mixture in the pan.

In the weeks after David died, she'd seen his image everywhere – laughing at her as she looked for unusual images to photograph, holding her close as he kissed her tenderly, promising marriage and a wonderful future.

'Chrissie, the eggs!'

She smelled burning, looked down and whisked the pan off the heat. 'I'm sorry, Van.' Peering at the contents, she gave a tentative poke with the spoon. 'I think they're still all right to eat.'

'I'm sure they are.' Vanessa's voice was soft and full of concern. 'It's you I'm worried about, Chrissie. I thought going over to Craiglogie would lighten your mood, shake you out of yourself for a bit.'

'Things are getting better, honestly.' A dreadful thought struck Christina. 'You've not said anything to Fiona about–'

'David? No, of course not. I knew you wouldn't have wanted that. I've only told her that you're here on holiday from the depths of London.'

'Thanks, Van.'

'That, and the fact that you're single,' said Vanessa, her face colouring.

The evening sun cast long shadows over the fields as Christina set out with Vanessa in her friend's Morris Minor.

'How lovely it is here,' Christina said. They drove past a pretty little house with wisps of smoke rising from its chimney. 'I almost feel as if I've come home.'

'Glad to hear it.' Vanessa smiled. She glanced at Christina and added, 'You know you really are welcome to stay for as long as you like. It doesn't have to be only a fortnight or so.'

'You are kind, Van, but I will need to make some permanent arrangements before too long.'

'I mean it. I enjoy having you – and so do the twins.'

'That was some game of hide and seek we played yesterday afternoon in the garden,' Christina said, and they laughed at the memory. The boys' idea of hiding was to stand together behind the same tree every time; and their seeking involved openly watching the adults' attempts to be a bit more creative. 'At least they counted to ten,' Christina added with a grin.

'Even if they forgot six, seven and eight!'

She felt a wave of sadness at the thought of leaving. It would be hard to say goodbye to Vanessa and her family. 'I love being here, Vanessa, but I need to work. Mum said I can stay with her in Surrey, although to be honest that would seem like a backwards step.'

Vanessa murmured her understanding and they drove on in silence.

'Here we are, at Craiglogie.' Vanessa's voice broke into Christina's thoughts.

They turned through the tall granite pillars with its open gates she'd seen that morning. And now, instead of peering through the bus window, she was bowling down a driveway lined with beech trees and hundreds of cheerful daffodils. As the drive curved round to the left and away from the canopy of trees, she caught her first sight of the house.

Craiglogie House stood large and imposing against the soft evening sky. Set in what looked like substantial grounds of neatly mown grass and purple flowering rhododendron bushes, it made Christina think of a more pleasant version of Thornfield Hall. She'd brought *Jane Eyre* with her to read on holiday. Yes, imposing, she thought, with its turret, tall windows and granite tinged with pink in the low, golden sunlight, but not forbidding as she had expected. Smoke rose from a few of its chimneys. She gazed at it all in delight and a thrill of excitement and nervousness washed over her.

Vanessa brought the Morris to a stop on the gravel in front of the house and pulled on the handbrake. Christina felt the butterflies in her stomach start to dance and she put up her hand to check her neat chignon was still in place.

The huge oak door stood open to the warmth of the evening.

'Craiglogie *is* something, isn't it? Sure you haven't changed your mind about not wanting to meet the laird?' Vanessa teased.

Christina shook her head, unable to speak for a moment. The house was so romantic, she couldn't stop herself thinking of David.

'Come on,' said Vanessa. 'I'm going to enjoy this evening. I'll just have one sherry as I can't be bleary-eyed with the children tomorrow, but what a treat it will be.'

Christina opened the car door and climbed out. Drawing in a breath, she followed Vanessa, crunching across the gravel towards the house.

'Hello.' A young woman appeared at the entrance, a broad smile lighting up her face. 'I thought I heard the car.'

Fiona MacDonald was dark-haired and attractive, but there the resemblance to her brother ended, Christina thought. The young woman was warm and friendly. Christina was sure she would like her.

Fiona came down the stone steps to meet them, her well-cut black dress softened by a small emerald brooch. 'It's lovely to see you again, Vanessa.' Fiona leaned forward and kissed Vanessa on the cheek. 'And you must be Christina. I'm very pleased to meet you,' she said, holding out her hand.

Christina smiled and shook the proffered hand. 'Hello, Fiona. It's good to meet you, too, and thank you for inviting me.'

'We're happy you could join us.'

Us? thought Christina, as their hostess turned back towards the house and led them up the steps into a square, tiled hall. So Alex would be at the dinner. Of course he would be – he lived there. She managed to keep a polite smile on her face as she told herself everything would be fine.

'Come this way,' said Fiona.

They were ushered through a pair of glazed double doors and into a large main hall, as the butterflies in Christina's stomach resumed their hectic fluttering. She only had time to notice a grand central staircase, and at the top of the first flight a glorious stained-glass window, before being led into the drawing room.

Decorated in pale blue, it was large with a high, ornate ceiling. Christina's eyes travelled round the room. Looped-back curtains framed the long windows, with a view of a terrace and of lawns stretching away in the slanting rays of the evening sun. A highly-polished grand piano stood in one corner and on top of it sat a bowl of deep-purple hyacinths, their scent filling the room.

Fiona noticed Christina's expression and smiled. 'I see you approve. I'm glad. It's my favourite room, mine and Alex's.'

'I can see why. It's stunning.'

'Thank you,' said Fiona. 'Can I get you something to drink?'

'A small dry sherry, please.'

'Vanessa?'

'Same for me, thanks, but make it a large one.'

Fiona poured glasses of pale amber liquid from a decanter on a tray on the sideboard. She handed one glass to Christina and the other to Vanessa. Vanessa took hers and sank with a sigh into one of the deep sofas loosely arranged in front of the fire.

Christina accepted her glass and allowed her gaze to stray to the large, framed, black-and-white photograph above the fireplace, depicting a castle deep in snow.

'Do you like it?' said Fiona.

'It's Balmoral, taken by George Washington Wilson, isn't it?'

Fiona's eyes widened. 'How on earth did you know that? I mean,' she said, recovering herself, 'not many people know his work.'

Vanessa laughed. 'I should have told you that Christina is a professional photographer.'

'How exciting!'

Christina felt the colour creep into her cheeks as Fiona appraised her. 'I've been working for a small photographic studio, but I'm hoping to start my own business…'

'You must see Alex's collection of Wilson's work while you're in the area,' said Fiona.

'I'd love to.' Christina took a sip of her sherry.

'I know,' said Fiona, 'why don't you take a look now, while Vanessa and I have our chat? It's in the library. The other guests won't be here for another half an hour, so you don't need to rush.'

Christina stiffened. What if Alex was in the library? She hadn't seen him since she'd arrived. 'I wouldn't want to disturb your brother.'

'You won't. Alex was called to a problem at Home Farm and isn't back yet.'

Christina took a gulp of her drink and set down the glass. 'Then I would love to see the collection,' she said, getting to her feet.

'I'll show you the way. We'll take the servants' staircase,' said Fiona. 'It's more direct.' She indicated a door set into panelling at the side of the fireplace.

'Alex will be very pleased to meet you, Christina,' added Fiona, as she pushed open the door.

That's very unlikely, Christina thought, following Fiona through the doorway.

'These were the servants' stairs when the house was built, but there are no live-in staff any longer. It makes the house feel so empty,' said Fiona.

She led the way up a plain, wooden staircase, chattering as she went. Christina hardly noticed what she said. Her heart was beating loudly at the realisation that Alex would soon be here, in this house. She pictured his dark eyes and imagined how they would harden with displeasure when he recognised her.

Fiona pushed open a door at the top of the stairs and stood to one side. They had reached a thickly-carpeted corridor and Christina guessed they were back in the main part of the house.

'The library.' Fiona opened the double doors and flicked on the light switch.

Cosy side lamps lit the room. In the centre stood a large desk and dotted about were chestnut-coloured leather chairs, looking well-used and comfortable. Two walls were covered from floor to ceiling in books and a third wall was swathed in heavy curtains drawn against the coming night.

'This room is delightful too,' she said, her eyes drinking it in.

'If you don't mind, I'll leave you to it,' said Fiona. 'I must have that chat with Vanessa.'

'A meeting before a meeting?' In spite of her nerves, Christina smiled.

'It does sound rather secretive, doesn't it? But it's just that the third person on the committee is Mrs Telfer and she can be – well, rather too much. She likes to argue about everything, so Vanessa and I prefer to have as much as possible agreed before she's involved. A united front and all that. I know it sounds mean, but honestly we have to do it for sanity's sake.'

'Are there just the three of you on the committee?'

'No, the fourth person is Jean Greig, the minister's wife. She's really nice and is happy to go along with what is decided. So, can you find your own way down in about half an hour?'

'Of course,' Christina said. 'And thank you, Fiona. I really appreciate being able to have this private viewing.'

Fiona nodded and closed the door.

Left alone, Christina's nervousness gradually diminished as she walked about the room. She wandered around the desk and ran her fingers along the edge of the warm wood. But her attention was held by the collection of old framed photographs covering the entire fourth wall.

Some she recognised immediately – historic prints by Wilson, the Victorian pioneer photographer whose work she had admired downstairs. She stopped in front of a perfectly composed image. Weather-beaten men in rough waistcoats and caps stood in a wet, cobbled street, as smoke rose from chimneys set in thatched roofs on the bleak dwellings. On the other side of the picture, sea spray had been caught in mid-arc, crashing over a high stone wall. Behind it all, a mountain rose grandly.

A second print showed a group of women seated on the ground. They wore headscarves and thick full skirts, woollen shawls pinned across their chests, as they mended a tangle of nets spread before them.

A third photograph captured children in a classroom, indoors yet warmly-clad, seated on long wooden benches in rows. Like the adults in the other photographs, they stared solemnly at the camera. A boy and a girl stood at a large blackboard, chalking up something which must have been rubbed away more than one hundred years ago.

So, thought Christina, what do these pictures tell me about Mr Alexander MacDonald? That he is interested in photography, certainly, but also perhaps that he cares about people, ordinary people doing their best to get on with their lives. Yet the way Alex had spoken to her on the beach didn't fit in with this thoughtful man.

She walked slowly on, stopping to examine some valuable plates of work by either Wilson himself or his studio. Interspersed with Wilson's masterpieces, there were other photographs that Christina could not identify at all, fine modern work. She wandered along, absorbed, until she was drawn to a group of four small portraits all posed by the same model.

The woman was strikingly handsome, bold, overtly provocative. She stared directly out of the frame at the photographer, with an expression of knowingness and arrogance that Christina felt sure any man would have found challenging and seductive. Christina recognised the influence of Antony Beauchamp and Norman Parkinson, with their images of Marilyn Monroe and Ava Gardner, the actresses' heads tilted slightly back with sultry, half-closed lids. Christina turned from the woman in the portraits in front of her, as uncomfortable as if she were intruding on a private moment.

She glanced at her watch. Almost half an hour had passed since she'd entered the library. It was time to get back to the others. It would be embarrassing if someone were sent to find her. Hurriedly, she turned off the lights and let herself out of the room, closing the door behind her.

There were panelled doors along the passage in both directions, but which one led to the stairs back to the drawing room? She'd allowed her thoughts to wander when Fiona had brought her upstairs and now she was unsure which way to turn. She couldn't open a door at random, but she couldn't stand here all evening, either.

It could only be left or right. She made a decision, turned to the right and followed the corridor to the end. Placing her hand on the brass doorknob, she turned it – and a deep voice she recognised resonated down the corridor.

'Can I help you?'

CHAPTER 3

*C*hristina halted in her tracks. Dropping her hand, she turned slowly, dreading what he would think, what he would say.

Alex MacDonald leant against a closed door, arms folded across his chest, stretching the dark fabric of the sleeves of his jacket.

'Here you are again,' he said, as he dropped his arms and pushed himself away from the door to stand upright a few feet from her.

Christina fixed her eyes on his. 'Do you always sneak up on people?' she said, shocked at the words as they left her mouth. This was no way to speak to her host.

'I never sneak up on people.'

He was tall, surely over six feet; taller than she'd remembered from when they met on the beach.

Christina found she was staring at the purple scar on his forehead and she tore her gaze away.

'May I remind you,' he said, 'that on both occasions when we have been fortunate enough to meet, I have merely been walking on my own property. And what are you doing, if not sneaking a look into another person's room?'

'I–'

'Surely you're not going to deny it, with your hand already poised on the door handle.'

'It's not what it looks like,' she said. Her gaze fell to the floor. 'Your sister invited me to dinner and I was trying to find my way back to the drawing room.'

He laughed. 'You're lost! Why didn't you simply say so?'

She jerked up her head and frowned. 'You didn't give me a chance!'

'I think you'll find I did, but you were too busy being cross again.'

Before she could form a suitable reply, he took a few quick strides towards her. She went to step back, but found she was already against the door.

'Tell me,' he said, drawing his dark brows together. His eyes took in her painted lips. 'Tell me, do you ever smile?'

Do *you*? she was about to say, when she realised he already was. A dimple appeared in his left cheek as his smile grew. It transformed his face and she found she wanted him to keep smiling. Christina felt the colour creeping into her face at the unbidden thought and she looked down at her skirt as her fingers nervously smoothed the fabric.

When she looked up at him again, his smile had disappeared. He was standing close and she was very aware of the masculine cedar scent of his aftershave.

He held out his hand. 'Let me introduce myself – I'm Alex MacDonald. And you, I believe, are Christina Camble.'

'I am,' she said, taking his hand. For a moment she was lost in the dark pool of his eyes and she felt the warm strength of his palm against hers.

'How do you do.' She shook his hand quickly and slipped her fingers from his grasp.

'You were in the library?' he said.

Christina nodded.

'You haven't told me what you were doing in there.'

She couldn't resist a little mischief. 'You haven't asked me.'

A smile tugged at the corners of his mouth and then it faded away. 'My query, "Can I help you?" was merely a polite way of asking what you were doing.'

Christina felt her brow wrinkle. Perhaps she had been too familiar. She composed her features and said in a more formal manner, 'Your sister was kind enough to say I could look at your collection of photographs.'

'Did she, indeed? Well, that's Fiona for you – always helpful, never mind the consequences.'

'Consequences?' She *had* overstepped an invisible mark…

'Only that I might have left private papers on the desk, for example,' he said.

'I didn't see any–'

'Oh, were you looking?'

'No, of course not! I only meant that I wasn't aware of any…'

'I'm teasing.'

The smile that spread on his face caused her pulse to climb. He looked down at her, searching her face for – what? Embarrassed, she broke away from his gaze.

'I'm sure you looked only at the photographs,' he said, serious again. 'What did you think of them?'

She said, with perfect honesty, 'I think you have some really interesting images.'

'George Washington Wilson, a north-east man,' he said. 'His company was once the largest and best known photographic and printing firm in the world.'

'Yes, I know.' She smiled at his obvious pride in his fellow Scotsman.

'You know? You're interested in photography, then?'

'I am. I've seen some of his photographs, but not the plates showing the fishing community. Where were they taken?'

'St Kilda, in the Outer Hebrides. The island is abandoned now, but it was inhabited until some twenty years ago. After the First World War, the population fell to a little under forty.' He gave a shrug. 'With such a pitifully small number, the community could no longer continue.'

'That is sad.' She watched his face, which couldn't disguise the emotion he felt. It was clear his country's history meant a lot to him.

He nodded. 'At their request, knowing their way of life was over, the people were taken to the mainland. When they departed that morning, they followed the tradition of leaving an open Bible in each house. Although by that time they were living in impoverished conditions, St Kilda was still their home. At the severing of their ancient ties, they crumbled. Every one of them, young and old, was reduced to tears. I don't blame them. I think I would have done the same.'

The husky timbre of his voice and the gentleness in it took her by surprise. She pictured the sun rising out of a sparkling sea, the boat drawing away, its passengers with heavy hearts watching their island home growing smaller and smaller until it disappeared below the horizon.

'That's the way of the history of Scotland,' said Alex. 'Displacement, loss, betrayal.' He cleared his throat. 'But tell me, what did you think of the other photographs?'

'The portraits?'

He shifted his stance. 'Yes.'

Christina smiled. 'They are good, too.'

He relaxed a little. 'Perhaps. But stand them against a professional photographer and they are just second-rate snaps.'

'That's a harsh comment to make and not an accurate one.'

'Being interested in a subject is not the same as being able to create art in it.'

'Who took the photos?' she said.

'They're my effort, I'm afraid. Fiona says they're quite good and I just need a few lessons. Perhaps she's right. But there are simply not enough men to do all the necessary work around here, so I must put my shoulder to the wheel with the rest of them.'

'Well, you are being a hard critic.' She felt a strange sensation in her stomach and a rush of conflicting emotion. She had formed the view that he was cool and measured, but here, talking about photography, that opinion was slipping from her. Perhaps there was more to Alex MacDonald than she had first thought.

'How do you know that I am a harsh critic?' he said.

'Because I'm a photographer.'

'It's a fulfilling hobby, don't you think?'

'Yes, it is. But I don't do it as a hobby any longer. I turned professional a year ago.'

'Ah.'

At that, she glanced quickly at him, thinking he was being flippant. But the admiring look he gave her made Christina blush from her toes to the roots of her hair.

'Excuse me,' she said hurriedly. 'Your sister will be wondering where I am.'

She started to move away. His fingers lightly touched the bare skin of her arm. A jolt of electricity went through her and she flinched. A frown flashed across his face and he dropped his hand.

'I should return the way I came, but I'm not sure which door it is,' she said, trying to sound matter-of-fact.

'You were, and still are, going the wrong way.' He turned and strode back to the door where he'd been leaning minutes earlier.

He opened it and with relief she saw the servants' stairs in front of her.

'You can use the main staircase, you know,' he said.

'These stairs are fine. Thank you.' She stepped forward with as much dignity as she could muster. Her footsteps seemed loud on the wooden staircase and she felt a fool for insisting on this route. She didn't hear the door close and knew that the Laird of Craiglogie was still standing at the top of the stairs, watching her.

At the bottom she slipped round the corner, out of sight, and sagged against the wall. What had just happened between them? She shook her head. Nothing. Nothing had happened.

Letting out a long breath, she pushed open the door and emerged into the drawing room. The other guests had arrived and all eyes turned to her.

Fiona and Vanessa had been joined by a stocky young man in a tweed three-piece suit and a tall, elegant woman.

'Christina,' said Fiona, 'I'd like you to meet Helen Farquharson, an old friend of mine.'

The woman was stunning. She looked about the same age as Alex and, with her stilettos, must be almost the same height. Her glossy, chestnut hair was in the latest Italian style, with short curls cut close to the head. Pink pearls hung from her ears and round her neck. She wore a calf-length red dress, one side of the skirt split to the thigh. Despite Christina's pinned-up hair and pretty dress, she felt young and *gauche* beside this sophisticated creature.

'Less of the *old*, if you don't mind.' Helen laughed and her eyes fixed on Alex as he sauntered into the room.

He strolled over to where they all stood in a little group. Helen laid a hand on the sleeve of his jacket, her red-painted fingernails bright against his dark suit. Her gesture and gaze flashed the message: *This man is mine.*

'And this,' said Fiona smoothly, seeing the awkwardness of the moment, 'is Fraser Cameron, the estate factor we couldn't do without. Fraser, Christina is staying with her friend Vanessa for a holiday.'

'Pleased to meet you, Christina.' Fraser shook her hand and smiled. She returned his smile, liking immediately the freckle-faced, earnest-looking young man. He'd attempted to smooth down his red hair with Brylcreem. 'Where are you from?' he asked.

'England, *obviously*, from the accent,' put in Helen, before Christina had a chance to reply.

'Yes, I could tell that,' said Fraser, his cheeks turning pink. 'I meant what part of England.'

'Surrey,' Christina said. 'Kingston-on-Thames.'

'I was there once,' Fraser said, 'some years ago–'

'Alex, darling, do you think I could have another drink?' Helen smiled charmingly at their host and held out her empty glass. He gave a nod and moved to the drinks set out on the sideboard.

The conversation continued along polite, general lines until the mantel clock struck the hour. Still a little nervous from her encounter with Alex, overawed by her surroundings and intimidated by Helen's elegance, Christina had said little. She was relieved when Fiona declared dinner was ready and ushered them through the hall and into the dining room.

The mahogany table was set with sparkling crystal, gleaming silver and lighted candles. It was all so sophisticated. She drew in a deep breath and waited to see where Fiona would seat them. Wherever she was placed, she suspected dinner would be an ordeal.

'Alex, you're at the end as usual,' said Fiona. 'Christina, you're on Alex's right, Helen on his left. Vanessa on my right and Fraser on my left. There! Now I just need to pop to the kitchen. I won't be a moment.'

Christina felt the colour rise to her cheeks as Alex stepped forward and pulled out her chair.

'Thank you,' she murmured.

'My pleasure,' he said, just as quietly.

She was aware of him moving to hold Helen's chair and Fraser doing the same for Vanessa. As Alex went round pouring glasses of Bordeaux, Christina took the opportunity to look at the room. It was as grand as the drawing room, with the same high ceiling and tall windows, but here the walls were painted in a pale green and, as in the library, the heavy curtains had been drawn against the dusk.

Fiona returned with plates of smoked salmon on a tray. Alex helped his sister to serve their guests, before he took his seat at the top of the table.

Christina's eyes were drawn to his. Over his glass of ruby red liquid, he held her in a thoughtful gaze. Her stomach lurched and, dropping her eyes, she fussed with arranging the napkin in her lap.

'Alex,' Helen's voice broke in. 'You haven't told me how your day went.'

Christina looked across the table at Helen. Her curls shone in the candlelight and she smiled at Alex, not taking her eyes off him. There was something about Helen that looked familiar. The angle of her head, the confidence of her gaze... At once Christina realised that this was the provocative woman in the photographs she'd seen in the library. Her hair had been longer, but it was undoubtedly Helen.

'Just the usual,' said Alex, snapping open his napkin and laying it over his lap. 'Did some jobs on Home Farm. Took a few photographs round and about when I got the chance.'

'I wish you wouldn't work on the farm, Alex,' Helen said, wrinkling her nose. 'You have men to do that.'

'Yes, but not enough since the war,' said Alex, his voice growing quieter. 'We all know there is more work to do than there are men to do it.'

In the silence that followed, Christina glanced at Alex and thought he looked strained all of a sudden.

Helen brightened. 'Well, I think your pictures are all really good. Excellent, in fact. And I should know, I've been in front of the camera enough times to tell the difference. Some of them in particular stand out.' She looked at Alex through her lashes and gave him a sly, intimate smile.

'You're too kind.' Alex put down his knife and fork. 'Christina, forgive us. We're chatting on as if you weren't here. You know, of course, that Craiglogie House is part of the family estate. I'm sure Vanessa has told you that much. But perhaps she didn't say that it includes Home Farm where I like to keep myself busy.'

Her eyes flickered to his broad shoulders and again she noticed how snug his jacket was around the biceps. She brought her gaze back to his face. 'I didn't know that you ran a farm.'

'You sound surprised.'

'No,' said Christina, as she lifted her napkin to dab her mouth, in an effort to hide the rising colour in her cheeks.

'There is nothing that surprises *me* about Alex,' drawled Helen. She showed Christina perfect white teeth, before turning it into a dazzling smile for Alex.

'Fiona and Helen have been friends since Helen was evacuated from London to this area,' Alex said.

'We are *such* close friends. Alex always insists on my spending as much time as possible at Craiglogie, whenever I come up. He's a generous host.' Helen said with a little sigh, 'Do you remember when news came of the peace, Alex? The popping of the champagne corks! How you waltzed me across your drawing room! What times. *What* memories we share.' She shot a sideways glance at Christina.

Christina had no intention of taking part in this silly game, but Vanessa continued, 'Did you know that Christina is a photographer by profession?' It was a statement rather than a question.

'Yes,' said Alex, drawing a glare from Helen.

'She's taken quite a few images of the area already,' continued Vanessa.

'There's some spectacular scenery to photograph,' said Alex.

'Yes,' said Fraser, turning his head to join in the conversation. 'What about Bullers of Buchan, Alex? It's a collapsed sea cave, Christina, and very dramatic.'

'And Slains Castle sits on the cliffs nearby,' said Alex. 'Bram Stoker stayed there and used it as inspiration for his novel, *Dracula*.'

'I thought it was set in Whitby,' said Christina.

'Ah, but the author was inspired by Slains. He used to come to the coast here for his summer holidays and that's where he started writing the book,' said Alex. 'I'll take you to that stretch of coastline when the sky is moody enough for some interesting photographs.'

'The locals call Bullers of Buchan the Pot,' added Fraser.

'The Pot?'

'It's an almost circular chasm, some 100 feet deep, so it seems an appropriate name,' said Alex. 'Close by this, there's another cave. Apparently, in the Edwardian period people used to form parties to dine in it. Mind you, they had to be sure to get back out before the tide came in.'

'I'd love to visit,' she said.

Eventually, Christina managed to extricate herself from the conversation, glad to leave Helen and Alex to each other's company.

She forked up the remains of her salmon. Even as she realised that Fraser had spoken to her, she could feel the heat of Alex's gaze on her skin. With relief, she laid her cutlery on the plate, blotted her mouth with her napkin and turned her attention to Fraser.

'I'm sorry,' she said. 'I missed that.'

'I was asking if you are staying in Scotland long.'

She found herself looking into his friendly blue eyes. 'I'm not sure yet, but I still have at least ten more days.' She smiled at Fraser.

'Then perhaps I could show you round one or two places?' he said, his voice eager. 'If you'd like to, that is.'

'Thank you, I'd love to see more of this part of the country. I've been relaxing for the few days since I arrived, so all I've really done so far is walk on the beach.'

A deep, muffled laugh came from her left. She glanced across the flickering candles and saw Alex's eyes crinkle at the edges as they briefly met hers. Helen stopped talking and stared at Christina.

Christina felt confused and awkward under Helen's cold gaze. I should never have come to dinner, she thought.

'Tell me about your work, Fraser,' she said, turning back to him. 'What does a factor do?'

'Basically, I'm the manager of the farm and the estate,' he said. 'Business, financial and legal management. That's ordering supplies, dealing with the sale and purchase of animals and land, collecting rents, giving practical advice on crops and livestock, and so on. Estates are little towns, really.'

She laughed. 'I like the idea of a little town, so very different from the sprawl of where I live.'

'I say little town, but in fact the estate covers a fairly large area. One thousand acres in all.'

'One thousand acres!' She couldn't keep the surprise out of her voice.

'We don't farm all of it,' Fraser hastened to add. 'There are some tenanted farms on the estate. Alex is mainly concerned with Home Farm.'

'Nevertheless, that sounds like a lot of responsibility for you. From the way Alex was speaking earlier, I thought he did most of the work.'

Fraser smiled. 'Aye, well, Alex works hard, too.'

∾

Alex heard Fraser mention his name, and saw Christina was laughing. What was he telling her that could make her laugh like that? He watched her as she and Fraser talked. She seemed relaxed and happy in Fraser's company, unlike when she was with him. What was his factor doing that he, Alex, wasn't?

Alex narrowed his eyes and tried to discern what they were saying, but a cluster of fine blonde strands nestled in the soft nape of her neck, distracting him. He wished he could see inside her head, know what she was thinking. He laughed at himself.

'What's amusing you?' said Helen, leaning one elbow on the table and resting her cheek on a slim, elegant hand. 'Tell me what you are thinking.'

Thinking? He barely knew what he was thinking. He certainly had no idea what had produced that ridiculous comment to Christina upstairs earlier, about her wandering on his property. He'd said it and then seen a chink of vulnerability in her eyes.

There had been a time when he could charm girls without effort. That had been before the war, before the bomb fell on the gun emplacement, before everything changed.

'Alex!' Helen's voice broke in on his thoughts. 'You're not listening to a word I've said.'

He forced a neutral expression onto his face and turned to her. 'I'm sorry, Helen. You were saying something about tennis in the morning?'

'I was wondering if you'd like a game.'

'Yes, let's play tomorrow.' He raised his voice across the table. 'Did I hear my name mentioned just now?'

'Only in a compliment.' Fraser grinned. 'Are you planning to work tomorrow on the farm?'

'Helen has suggested a game of tennis for the morning.' Alex took a sip of wine and said in a casual voice, 'Why don't you play with us, Fraser – and Christina, too? There's a court in the grounds and spare racquets, Christina. We can make up a four-some.' He felt a pressing need to see her again.

'An excellent idea,' said Fraser.

Christina forced herself to smile. 'Are you sure you have the time?' she said to Alex. 'I thought you would be rather too busy.'

'Tomorrow is Saturday. All work and no play makes Jack a dull boy.'

'I'm afraid I've never really played tennis, just knocked a ball about with a friend.' She shrugged. She wasn't keen to spend any more time with either Alex or Helen. 'You would find it a very boring game with me.'

'I'm sure it would not be boring with you,' Fraser said.

Christina sent him a grateful look.

Alex said abruptly, 'I can teach you how to play.'

As Christina hesitated, Helen took from her clutch bag a packet of Sobranie Cocktails, removed one in pastel red and slid it into a cigarette holder. She held the long holder to her lips and waited for Alex.

Christina watched, fascinated, as he took a matchbox from his pocket, struck it and leaned forward to light her cigarette. She drew in the vapour and expelled it through her nostrils, narrowing her eyes at Christina as she did so.

'Of course,' Helen said, 'you must both join us.'

Christina didn't miss the emphasis on *us*.

Vanessa turned from her conversation with Fiona. 'I'll be driving over here tomorrow morning, Chrissie, and I can give you a lift. Fiona and I will be going to the meeting about the village dance.'

It might be fun to learn to play tennis properly, Christina thought, but not with Alex as her tutor.

'Do come, Christina,' said Fraser, so keenly that she couldn't help smiling. 'It'll be more fun if you're there.' Not only was Fraser easy company, he was, she couldn't help noticing, about her height. There was something intimidating about a tall person; and Alex and Helen were both much taller than she…

They were all watching her and her heart began to pound. The words just popped out.

'All right.'

∽

'Fire!' he shouted, as the German bomber overhead was caught in the searchlight. The men below waited, holding their breaths. Death had come for someone tonight. The gunfire lit up the sky like fireworks to the deafening sound of their ack-ack. His last conscious thought was that there were men in that plane. It dropped its bomb. Pieces of metal flew through the air. He was thrown upwards, up, up, into the sky. He crashed into the crater. Rubble fell everywhere, burying him. He tried to scream.

Alex trembled as he opened his eyes. His heart pounded in his chest, the sheet clung to his perspiring body, and it took a few moments for him to realise that he'd been dreaming. The explosion, his hurtling into the air, being buried alive – none of it was real. At least, no longer. It had happened years ago and yet still he relived it.

He'd been lucky. He told himself this for the thousandth time as he lay in the damp, tangled sheets. Aware of the wetness on his face, he wiped away the sweat – or was it tears? The latter, he suspected. He'd survived, unlike two of his men that night and thousands of others during the war itself. He mustn't complain, even though these nightmares, these fearful memories, made him less of a man.

As the terror of the nightmare faded, he became aware of the sun streaming through the gap he always left in his curtains and his thoughts turned to the day ahead. He remembered that soon he would see Christina again, but he no longer felt confident that it was a good idea.

Helen knew about his shell shock, the nightmares. She had been there when he'd first come home. She'd told him to push these memories from his mind and that had helped him. Not showing his feelings meant that people didn't ask what had happened and he didn't have to explain.

He sighed, threw back the sheet and sat up. Was Christina looking forward to their game of tennis as much as he had been? Last night it seemed to him that there was some sort of connection between them when their eyes met, but now he wondered if he'd been imagining it. In the light of morning, he was forced to admit that it was Fraser who had persuaded Christina to play. She obviously enjoyed Fraser's company.

As Alex climbed out of bed, the sun caught the angry weal around his right biceps. He disliked seeing this scar, but the wound on his forehead was worse because it was so visible. Last night, outside the library, Christina had averted her gaze from the ugly scar on his forehead. She must have been sickened by the sight.

He crossed to the mirror and looked at himself in the glass. He tightened the muscles in his biceps and saw the right arm strain against the scarring. An ugly, purple wound on his biceps and a deep, livid gash on his forehead. No young woman, much less someone like Christina, would ever look at him.

Why was he thinking of her? Christina was an innocent, a charming innocent. She had looked so pretty in that white dress yesterday evening. The last thing she needed was a man like him in her life. A broken man. She deserved better.

hen Christina woke, it was with a start and a vague sense of anxiousness. Through the curtained window the sun was shining and it promised to be another heavenly day. She stretched luxuriously in the bed and then remembered her foolish promise to play tennis. Fraser was a lovely young man and she would be happy to see him again, but as for the other two, Helen clearly disliked her and, well, she didn't know what Alex thought.

Sighing, she turned onto her side. She couldn't work him out. There was something troubling him, that was obvious, yet when he allowed himself to smile it was strangely pleasing. She pictured his dark hair, the way the candlelight had made his eyes shine last night, the strength in his broad shoulders. His eyes holding hers…

Christina turned and pummelled the pillow. A little breathless, she lay back down staring at the ceiling. Would her thoughts always be tangled into knots? She didn't want to be attracted to Alex; she had enough difficulty dealing with her emotions about David. The pain of losing him, to death, to his family.

Perhaps David had never loved her at all. No, he had loved

her, she was certain. But he hadn't loved her enough. He was already married and had a child. How could he do that to her? How could he do that to them?

Round and round went her thoughts. She felt like a child with a daisy, pulling off the petals one by one as she chanted, *He loves me, he loves me not*. She hated and loved David in equal measure. He had been the love of her life for six wonderful months and then had shattered her dreams. She couldn't push away the memories of him but she ought to, needed to. She knew she had to face the reality that even though he'd loved her, he'd loved himself more.

Perhaps she wasn't ready for that new start, after all.

Christina listened to the sounds of the cottage. The twins calling to each other downstairs, dishes clattering in the kitchen, and outside, the distant drone of a tractor.

Her thoughts drifted back to the events of the previous evening. The little party had returned to the drawing room for coffee and arranged themselves on the sofas by the log fire. The dog basked in front of the crackling flames. Helen soon established herself as the centre of attention, relating anecdotes about her modelling assignments. Every now and again she paused. With cool politeness, through her cigarette smoke and eyes narrowing like a cat, Helen asked Christina if she'd understood the meaning of a particular Scots word or if she was managing to follow everyone's accent. Christina felt like an outsider, just as Helen intended.

What was the relationship between Alex and Helen? Christina couldn't make it out. Helen had sent her a clear *Hands off* message, but Alex showed no obvious attachment to Helen.

As Helen had chattered on, Christina caught a glimpse of Alex watching not Helen but her, his brows drawn together. Was he angry that she – an outsider – was there, disrupting one of their usually pleasant, intimate dinner parties? She'd thought so before the invitation to play tennis, but now she wasn't so sure. The game had definitely been his idea, at least inviting her to join them had been, judging by Helen's reaction to the suggestion.

The focus of attention shifted when Fiona asked Alex to play something on the piano.

'Oh yes, *do*,' said Helen.

'I don't need much persuasion,' said Alex with a quick smile, getting to his feet.

He took his seat on the piano stool, while Helen and Fiona called out suggestions. The light from a floor lamp shone on his hair, as he turned the pages of the music book resting on the stand.

'Debussy,' he announced. 'I'll play a couple of pieces from his *Suite Bergamasque*.'

The sweet sound filled the room. Christina focused her attention on the music, but she was aware of his strong profile with its dark lashes, his long fingers on the keys, his body swaying with the music as he played. She found her own body swaying in time with his and stopped instantly, clasping her hands in her lap.

The last notes died away and Alex lifted his fingers from the keys to a ripple of applause. He swung round on the stool, stood and gave a mock but elegant bow. The buzz of conversation began again and Christina watched, the blood rushing in her ears, as Alex crossed the room towards her.

'That really was charming,' she said, looking up at him with a smile. '*Clair de Lune* and *Passapied* are two of my favourite pieces.' She knew her face was warm, but told herself it was from the sherry and then the wine during dinner. 'The French are very romantic.'

'And the Scots aren't?' he said, lowering himself next to her on the sofa.

Flustered, she tucked a lock of hair behind her ear. Their eyes met and suddenly he seemed as lost for words as she. The seconds ticked by.

Alex opened his mouth to say something.

'Let's have a game of Knock-out Whist,' had come Helen's abrupt voice.

Now, lying in bed on this Saturday morning, Christina smiled, remembering the look on Alex's face as Helen had almost pulled him from the sofa.

Christina's amusement faded. She sighed and thought how different she'd be feeling today if she hadn't agreed to the game of tennis. There was too much confusion in her head.

Pulling herself upright in bed, she wished for a sudden fierce downpour, even though the sunlight blazing in through the curtains told her there would be no such luck. The game would not be cancelled. Never mind, she thought, once today was over she wouldn't have to see Helen or Alex ever again.

Christina climbed out of bed, washed in the bathroom and returned to her room to dress. She drew on her white, short-sleeved blouse and blue shorts, and a pair of whitened canvas shoes she'd borrowed from Vanessa. Catching sight of herself in the bedroom mirror, she decided she didn't need to reveal quite so much of her bare legs until it was absolutely necessary, so she slipped on the only other dress she'd brought with her, a pale-yellow cotton which buttoned down the front. She went down the stairs, gathering her hair up in a high ponytail as she went.

Vanessa had already collected the twins from their overnight stay with friends and now the four of them piled into the Morris Minor. She drove the few miles to Craiglogie House, with the children bouncing up and down in the back seat of the car.

Christina tried not to think about Alex, and even less about Helen, but as they drew near to Craiglogie she felt her stomach began to churn. She must distract her thoughts.

'What time is the meeting this morning, Vanessa?'

'Half past ten. Behave, boys,' called Vanessa to the twins, not taking her eyes off the road. 'Honestly, you need eyes in the back of your head. Or a rear-view mirror.' She laughed. 'Jean Greig, the minister's wife, has arranged for her sister to look after the twins until the meeting finishes, which should be about half past twelve. Then we'll be back at Craiglogie House in time to return home for lunch.'

'Fine.' Christina nodded. Only a little over two hours at Alex's house; she could manage that.

They drove through the open gates onto the long driveway. The house came into view and once again the main door stood wide open. On the gravel in front of the house, two Land Rovers and a small red sports car were parked.

'Looks like Fraser and Helen are already here,' said Vanessa, pulling up next to one of the Land Rovers and turning off her engine.

Christina paused with her hand on the car door. 'I thought Helen was a house guest.'

Vanessa gave a short laugh. 'She'd like us to think that, I'm sure.'

Christina opened the door, slipped from her seat and turned to thank Vanessa for the lift. A scrunch of footsteps on the gravel made her spin round.

Alex was walking towards her, dressed in white shorts and sports shirt, his limbs tanned and firm. 'Good morning,' he said.

Christina forced herself to meet his gaze instead of staring at his muscular thighs.

'Stop that, you two,' came Vanessa's sharp voice, and Christina started guiltily, her face beetroot red. She turned to glare at Vanessa for embarrassing her. One glance at the car showed her Vanessa twisting over the back of her seat, trying to sort out some disagreement between the twins. Christina hoped Alex hadn't noticed her confusion.

'Uncle Alex!' shouted the boys, spotting him.

'Can they come in for a moment?' said Alex, bending down to

speak to Vanessa through the open window. 'Fiona's not quite ready.'

'Yes. It'll do them good to stretch their legs for a few minutes.' Vanessa took Alex's hand as he assisted her out of the car. She blew her fringe from her forehead. 'They always have far too much energy.'

Grateful for the distraction, Christina helped Nicholas out of the back seat. He sped across the gravel and through the main door. Alex leaned into the car and helped out the second twin.

William ran towards the house, followed more sedately by the adults, but before he reached it he set up a wail. 'I've forgotten my teddy!'

Vanessa groaned. 'Where is it? Don't say you've left it at home.'

'It's in the car.' The little boy skipped back towards the Morris.

'Be careful with the car door! Wait for me!' called Vanessa, dashing after him.

When Christina and Alex reached the main hall, Nicholas had opened the grandfather clock and was investigating the pendulum inside.

'And how's my favourite Nicholas?' Alex gently closed the door of the clock's casing, squatted down in front of the child and smiled. Nicholas giggled, suddenly shy. Alex laughed, ruffled the child's hair and rose. He looked at Christina and was about to speak, when Vanessa returned with William clutching his teddy.

'Found it, thank goodness,' she said. 'It had fallen on the floor between the front and back seats.'

'And here's my favourite William,' said Alex, winking at the boy.

'You're silly, Uncle Alex,' said William. He contorted his face in an effort to wink back.

'William!' scolded Vanessa.

Fiona appeared through a doorway which Christina thought

must lead to the kitchen, judging by the delicious smells which wafted out.

'I wanted to check the arrangements for lunch.' Fiona smiled enquiringly at Christina and Vanessa. 'You will be able to stay and eat with us?'

'We'd love to.' Vanessa shot an apologetic glance at Christina, one which said that a meal made by someone else was too good a gift to refuse.

Christina's heart sank at the prospect of having to spend even longer here.

'Good,' said Fiona. 'That will give Christina time to see the gardens and the pond.'

Vanessa nodded. 'Are you ready, Fiona? We'll be off, then. See you both later.'

She and Fiona shepherded the chattering twins out the door. Christina was left with Alex and a fluttering in the pit of her stomach.

'Perhaps we could begin the tennis lesson,' she said, more primly than she'd intended.

She saw his mouth twist in amusement, before he motioned to the open main door. 'Certainly. This way, please.'

He stepped aside, the fresh scent of his soap lingering in the air causing her to feel a little unsteady.

Christina didn't attempt conversation and neither did Alex. Self-consciously, she walked beside him along a path leading from the house, trying not to think how close he was. She was relieved when at last she heard the thwack of a tennis ball. They passed behind a high screen of privet and there stood the hard court. Helen and Fraser were already knocking a ball to and fro. Alex pushed open the gate.

'So you're back at Craiglogie, Christina.' Swinging her racquet by her side, Helen strolled towards Christina and Alex. Her chestnut hair and make-up was as immaculate as the previous evening. She wore a low-cut black silky top and tight shorts which emphasised her voluptuous figure. Giving Christina a brief, cool smile, she turned to Alex.

'What kept you so long, darling?' She almost purred.

'Hardly that long.' Alex gave an embarrassed laugh.

Helen watched his face, looking like a silky black cat wanting to be stroked.

'Morning, Christina,' said Fraser, bounding up.

She smiled. 'It's nice to see you again, Fraser.'

He darted forward and picked up a racquet from the bench at the side of the court. Releasing it from the wooden press, he held it out to her. 'Try this Wisden.'

'I'll take over with the instruction, Fraser, thanks,' said Alex, relieving him of the racquet. 'You and Helen continue with your game. We'll join you shortly.'

Helen pouted like a disappointed child, then cast a sunny smile towards Alex, before she went off with Fraser.

'Let me first show you how to hold a racquet correctly,' said Alex. 'Grasp the end of the handle, like this.' He stepped closer to Christina. 'With the racquet held side-on, this centre line on the handle should sit in the vee between your thumb and forefinger.'

For a moment her eyes lingered on his strong brown hands with their neatly-trimmed nails, and she forced herself to concentrate on his words.

'Now you do it.' He passed the racquet to her and she took it, placing her hand as he had demonstrated. 'That's good. Now, to hit the ball properly, turn from the waist and put one leg in front of the other. You need to bring the racquet back in a swing before you hit the ball. No, like this.'

Suddenly he was standing behind her and she felt his warm body against hers, his arms around her. His hand closed over hers on the handle. He gently guided her arm up and forward in a graceful sweeping curve. The short sleeve of his polo shirt rode up and she saw the edge of a dark purple weal around his biceps. Involuntarily, she stiffened.

'I know what to do,' she burst out, snatching away her hand, still clutching the racquet, and turning to face him. He was standing too close; heat flooded her.

He frowned. 'But you told me you knew almost nothing about tennis.'

Her heart thudded. 'I just meant that I think I can hold a racquet.'

Christina moved towards where Fraser and Helen were playing, determined to ask Fraser to give her instruction instead. She had not gone far when Alex grabbed her free hand and drew her back. She caught a fleeting image of Helen's hard stare and felt the rush of air as a tennis ball just skimmed her head.

'Take care, Helen,' shouted Alex. 'That shot almost hit Christina.'

Helen lifted her racquet in response.

'Thank you,' murmured Christina. She threw him a glance. 'I'm sorry for what I said. I know you only wanted to help me, but well–'

'I was standing too close for comfort?'

'Perhaps we should just get on with the game.'

She realised her hand was still held in his firm grip and she was tipped into a memory of walking hand in hand with David on a day as sunny and warm as this one. She bit her lip quickly to stop it trembling at the bittersweet memory.

Alex was staring at her, concern on his face. 'I'm sorry, I didn't mean to upset you. We don't have to play if you'd rather not.'

Christina swallowed hard. 'No, I'd like to play.'

'If you're sure?' said Alex.

She nodded.

'Then come on to the other court.'

At that moment she wanted nothing more than to go back to Vanessa's cottage and wait for the return of her friend and the children.

Helen and Fraser had resumed their game and it was punctuated by the steady thud of ball on strings. Christina trailed after Alex. When they reached the second court, he turned to her.

'If you don't mind,' he said, 'I'll check that the handle is the right size for you. If it's not, I have got another racquet you can try.'

He took her hand holding the racquet and turned it over, his touch impersonal. 'Yes, it's fine. Now we can begin the game.'

He glanced at her flushed face. 'You look rather warm. Do you want to change before we get started?'

'Oh, yes, of course.'

As she walked to the bench and began to unbutton her cotton dress, she could sense his eyes lingering on her for a moment. Hastily, she slipped off the dress and draped it over the back of the seat.

When she turned round again, he said, 'That's better.' His voice was neutral, his eyes unreadable.

He showed her the correct way to hit the ball, using basic forehand and backhand, making her aware of the placement of her feet as well as her arm. Alex was a good player and she couldn't help admiring his easy grace. She hit a few balls and missed many more.

Christina was surprised when he said, 'I think an hour's long enough for a first session. I don't want to put you off.' He shot her a glance and she detected a softening of his expression. 'Would you like to see the gardens? We have time before lunch.'

'I'd love to,' she said. She really did want to see the gardens. Perhaps later she could ask Fiona for permission to photograph them before the holiday was over.

Alex took her racquet and placed it with his on the bench. As she slipped her dress back on and buttoned it up, she was aware out of the corner of her eye his pulling on a pair of grey flannels. He called to the other two. 'I'm taking Christina to see the walled garden.'

'We'll come,' said Helen quickly, lowering her racquet.

'No, you mustn't let us disturb your game,' said Alex. He ushered Christina through the court's gate, shut it firmly behind them and raised his voice. 'Fraser looks like he could do with the practice.'

Christina couldn't hear Fraser's good-natured reply for Alex's burst of laughter as he led her along a path.

'Stay close to me. I don't want you getting lost again.' He gave a sudden grin. The dimple in his cheek was plainly visible and she resisted the urge to touch her finger gently to it.

He caught hold of her hand when they reached a wrought-iron gate set into a high stone wall. 'The steps here can be a little difficult if you're not used to them.'

The old stone steps had an uneven tread, and were worn in the middle from countless feet over the years. She let her hand lie in his as she stepped carefully down into the walled garden.

Clusters of orange marigolds and white alyssum bordered the neatly-manicured lawn. Against the far wall, fanned apple trees were dusted with pale-pink blossom. A stone fountain stood in the centre of the grass, its water gently splashing. The patterns of light and dark, sun and shade, playing across the garden were crying out to be captured on film.

They made their way down the central path, past the fountain, to a long wooden seat with a high carved back. 'Please sit,' he said. 'From here you can enjoy the view.'

She slid onto the seat and he joined her. Her gaze travelled over the garden. 'It's exquisite. When was the garden planted?'

'It was laid out in the seventeenth century, along the lines of the great gardens of France.' He leaned back in the seat, his posture relaxed, his focus forward. 'I love it here, it's so peaceful.'

Secretly, she studied his strong, tanned forearms, resting on his thighs; the way the sun caught the fine hairs. For a moment she wondered what it would be like to run her hand over that warm, bare skin. And then she wondered how he might respond.

Gentle, tender, urgent perhaps… The thought of it made her dizzy.

What was happening to her? She'd convinced herself – hadn't she? – that she had no interest in him, yet here she was fantasising about him. What was it about Alex MacDonald that moved her? She reminded herself, whatever it was, she was not ready for such emotion.

He turned to her and smiled, the sun lighting his face, making her insides churn. For a few moments their eyes locked – until, over the soft splash of the fountain, Christina heard a long, liquid warble high overhead. She broke away from Alex's gaze, looked up and saw a small brown bird rising steeply. It hovered effortlessly in the wide blue sky, still singing from its great height.

'A skylark,' said Alex, following her gaze. 'He can hang in the air above his territory, singing, for as long as an hour.'

'He?' she said.

'Yes. The song-flight belongs to the male. He's looking for a mate.'

They watched for several minutes.

'You are fortunate,' she said, 'to have all this beauty around you.'

'For a moment, I thought you were going to say I'm fortunate I don't have to do that.' He pointed up at the skylark. At once it parachuted back down to earth. 'You're right, of course,' he said, his tone serious again. 'I know I'm a very lucky man.'

She felt her brow creasing and wondered what caused his sudden bouts of – what? Sadness? Perhaps he was embarrassed by his scars. She had a sudden longing to ask him about them, to see if she could help in some way. Then she remembered that Alex was none of her business.

She smiled and stood. 'Would you mind if we walk on a bit? I'd like to see the pond your sister mentioned earlier, while we still have time.'

Alex got to his feet and indicated the way. The path turned

into a rough track, away from the house and through a little copse. They reached the other side of the trees and she saw a large pond which glimmered in the sunlight. Huge blossoms of red and pink rhododendrons hung heavily over the water, their colour reflected in the depths below.

A little breeze came up and ripples crossed the water, disturbing the peaceful image.

'It's a fire pond,' Alex said, 'constructed to provide water to extinguish any fires in the house.'

Her eyes were fixed on the shivering reflection. 'Has it ever been used?'

'Not that I know of. Probably just as well, as it's quite far from the house and a fire might have taken hold before the water could be carried there.'

She turned towards him, her foot slipped on the bank and instinctively she cried out.

'Take care,' he said, catching hold of her elbow. 'You are near the edge of the water.' He drew her back.

'Thank you,' she said a little breathlessly as he let go of her.

His lips curved into a smile. 'I have saved the life of my enemy.'

'Your enemy?' She frowned. 'What do you mean?'

He lifted an eyebrow and she saw the scar on his forehead pucker a little. 'Don't you know your Scottish history? The Massacre of Glencoe?'

'I'm sorry,' she said. 'I really don't know what you are talking about.'

'The MacDonalds – the oldest of all the Scottish clans – were betrayed and murdered at Glencoe by the Campbells. Your surname, Camble, is a derivation of Campbell.'

Christina stared at him. She had a Scottish name and Scottish roots? Was that why she felt an affinity with this country? 'I had no idea. What happened?'

'It's a simple enough tale, although not a pleasant one. The

MacDonalds refused to pay allegiance to the new monarchs, William and Mary. The king secretly ordered the Campbells to arrest the MacDonalds. The Campbells billeted themselves in the MacDonald houses in Glencoe and for a fortnight accepted traditional Highland hospitality. Then, in the early morning of that harsh winter in 1692, the treacherous Campbells slaughtered thirty-eight MacDonalds as they slept. Even more MacDonalds died of exposure in the snow when they tried to escape. So you see,' Alex said, 'the reason for the feud between the two clans.' He shook his head, but there was a smile around his mouth. 'As I said, I have saved my enemy.'

'But that was so long ago,' she said. 'I mean, it's a shocking story, but more than two hundred and fifty years is a long time to hold a grudge.'

'Nothing is dismissed as too long ago in Scottish history. I think it's fair to say that the Campbells remain under something of a cloud for their part in the massacre of the MacDonalds.' He folded his arms across his chest. 'Perhaps the MacDonalds still want to conquer in some way.'

She felt a sting of anger. 'People want to remember their history, that's only natural. But there's a difference between being aware of important events in the past and allowing them to become a conflict continuing into the present day.'

The breeze teased at her hair, whipping loose strands across her cheeks. His eyes flickered with an emotion she couldn't read.

'What I mean is,' she said, 'that the Campbell–MacDonald feud should be over.'

Before he could reply, the sound of a gong travelled out from the house and floated across to where they stood by the pond.

'We're being summoned to lunch.' Alex grinned down at her, the laughter lines around his eyes suddenly deep in his handsome face. 'Let's call a truce.'

CHAPTER 5

$\mathscr{A}$lex saw that on the terrace the table had been covered with a white cloth and lunch set out.

'*There* you are,' said Helen.

She and Fraser were seated on a large blanket spread on the lawn. Helen's eyes followed him and Christina as they made their way back across the grass. 'We were beginning to wonder if something had happened to you both.'

'We were wondering no such thing,' said Fraser, his embarrassment clear in the colour on his cheeks.

'As you see,' said Alex, choosing to ignore Helen's tone, 'we are unharmed.' He checked his wristwatch. 'And we are not late. Fiona and Vanessa should be joining us shortly.'

Helen and Fraser had changed out of their tennis clothes. He was in a white shirt and dark trousers, while she had pulled on a black skirt that hugged her curves like a second skin.

Helen patted the blanket beside her and looked at Alex.

Tess had been gambolling on the grass nearby and she took that as an invitation. She bounded over and flopped down heavily next to Helen.

'Mind my new skirt!' Helen flicked a bare foot with red-painted toenails towards the dog. It caught Tess on the muzzle.

Tess looked surprised and stole over to Christina. 'You poor thing,' she said, bending down to fondle the dog's ear.

'That dog,' said Helen. 'Honestly, I hardly touched it.'

'Tess is trying it on,' said Alex. 'She's had worse bumps than that running through the woods and never so much as flinched.'

He stifled a laugh as Tess flopped onto her back and waved her paws in the air. The dog drew back her lips and seemed to smile at Christina. She looked at Tess and raised an amused eyebrow.

'It is fatal to let any dog know that she is funny, for she immediately loses her head and starts hamming it up,' said Alex.

'What do you mean?' said Helen, wrinkling her brow.

Christina laughed. 'It's a quote by P. G. Wodehouse.'

'Ah.' Alex smiled. 'So you're a fan of his, too?'

He was about to assist Christina onto the blanket, when voices carried through the open French windows. He heard Vanessa say, 'Poor George. He'll have to come, of course.' She and his sister stepped out onto the terrace and Vanessa's face was grave.

Alex stepped forward. 'Is there a problem? Can I help?' The words were out of his mouth before it occurred to him it was a personal matter and Vanessa might not welcome his intervention.

'What's wrong?' asked Christina, glancing at Vanessa and Fiona in turn.

'Vanessa has had some bad news,' said Fiona.

Christina's face paled. 'Van, what's happened?' she said quickly. 'Are the children okay?' She looked round for them. They were nowhere to be seen. She sent Alex a touching, silent plea.

'They're fine, don't worry,' said Vanessa. 'They asked to have their lunch in the kitchen with Mrs Morrison.'

'Thank goodness.' Christina's shoulders relaxed a little.

'Our housekeeper might be tetchy with us, but she's a lamb with the twins. I'm afraid she rather spoils them,' said Fiona.

'Then has something happened to Callum?' asked Christina quickly.

'No, it's nothing like that. It's his father.' Vanessa waved the telegram she held in her hand. 'He needs someone to look after him for a while.'

'Come and sit down,' said Alex, guiding Vanessa over to the table.

Lunch had been set out with slices of pork pie, devilled eggs, crusty bread and fruit. They stared at the pineapple upside-down cake in pride of place in the middle of the cloth. A chunk was missing.

'It looks like Mrs Morrison has already taken a couple of slices for the twins,' said Fiona, with a smile.

Helen and Fraser joined the table and Alex poured glasses of white Beaujolais for everyone as they took their seats.

'Van, is there anything I can do? Do you need me to look after the boys while you go to see Callum's father?' said Christina, taking Vanessa's hand in her own.

Vanessa squeezed Christina's hand and looked at her. 'I'm so sorry, Chrissie, but I'll need your room.' She bit her lip. 'You know Callum's father is a widower and lives alone? He's been ill and he asks if he can stay with us for a bit, just until he feels better. He wants to come on Monday. I feel awful as I'd promised you a holiday and now... But I can't let George down.'

Alex saw disappointment flash across Christina's face before she smiled, a convincingly reassuring smile. 'Of course your father-in-law must have the room. It's perfectly all right. I can easily return south and stay with my mother.'

He knew immediately that he didn't want Christina to go. The tightening in his throat told him so. He should do something. He could ask her to stay, couldn't he? Would that seem out of place? Surely not. He'd just be helping Fiona's friend.

He'd have to put Christina in the room next to his sister. She must be far enough away from him that she wouldn't hear if he screamed during his sleep. It was bad enough that Helen knew of the nightmares, but if Christina found out…

'Christina,' said Fiona, 'why don't you move into Craiglogie for the remainder of your stay? We have plenty of rooms and it would be lovely to have you here.'

Bless her, thought Alex, sending a grateful smile towards his sister. Above the clatter of the others helping themselves from the dishes on the table, she gave him a barely perceptible nod.

'I couldn't possibly,' said Christina, flushing, 'but it's very kind of you to ask.'

He must speak, before it's too late. 'I have a suggestion to make.' He looked at Christina, who had turned her gaze to fix on him. He swallowed hard; she was so alluring.

'Remember yesterday evening, when I mentioned to you that I could do with some instruction in taking better photographs? Well, as you are a professional photographer, I wonder… Would you consider moving into Craiglogie and teaching me?'

He ploughed on, unable to keep the excitement from building in his voice. 'I know you're on holiday, but it could serve a purpose for both of us. I will get the teaching I obviously need without having to be away from the farm for long, and you will be able to stay in the area and add to your portfolio. We could work together, an arrangement of mutual benefit. Of course, I'd pay for your time.' He took a breath and added, 'It wouldn't be kindness, as you put it, but a working relationship.'

Stay here? In Craiglogie? Christina's heart fluttered. She looked at Vanessa, then at Fiona. The house was magnificent and Fiona had been nothing but hospitable, but she would have to see Alex every day. Not just see him, but talk to him, spend time with him, teach him what she knew about photography.

Would that be such a bad thing?

All morning she'd felt an awareness of him – when playing tennis, standing by the pond, the glance that had passed between them when laughing at Tess's antics. Christina couldn't make sense of the way she felt, or the way he seemed to feel about her. He'd never actually flirted with her and sometimes she was convinced that he didn't even like her. Yet, what she thought she had seen in his eyes contradicted this.

She had seen, too, the look that passed between Alex and his sister, but it was too quick for her to know what it meant. Whose idea really was it that she stay? That he might want her there seemed unlikely, despite his sudden desire for tuition. It didn't mean he'd been thinking about her in any special way, did it?

Christina brushed the thought aside. It was simply a business relationship. She'd be employed by him and that was all she had to concern herself with. There was also the fact that she needed to start earning money again soon. And although she would no longer have the little pleasures she'd enjoyed staying with Vanessa and her boys, and the cottage where she felt safe, she would still be able to see Vanessa and the twins for the remainder of her holiday.

Through her spinning thoughts, she heard Vanessa's enthusiastic response. 'Fiona, that's an excellent idea.'

Christina couldn't stop herself; she glanced at Helen. The other woman's face was tense under the make-up she must have reapplied when changing after tennis. It was clear she thought that Alex didn't need any help with his photographic skills. When Christina remembered the portraits of Helen in the library, she was of the same opinion. He'd clearly managed well so far. She was sure from Helen's sultry expression in the portraits that Alex had been more than simply the man behind the camera.

'So you like taking pictures, do you?' Helen made it sound as if Christina took holiday snaps of tourists on the beach for a living.

'I love my work,' Christina said as politely as she could. 'I get tremendous pleasure out of capturing something special, whether it's a place or an event. And there is also the satisfaction of developing my own photographs–'

'I'm sure it's fascinating, standing in a darkroom with trays of liquid,' drawled Helen. She turned a dazzling smile on Alex. '*Your* photos are definitely something special, Alex. I don't see why you think you need any sort of tuition.'

'Thank you, Helen, but I do,' said Alex, his voice firm. 'I'm sure there is much Christina can teach me.'

He turned to her. 'Christina, perhaps you could also show me how to develop my photographs.' He ignored the scowl on Helen's face. 'What do you think?'

Christina knew she would enjoy the teaching aspect of the work he proposed. There were certain techniques she could show him that would be easier to learn first-hand than from a book. But could she spend so much time with him?

He must have seen the uncertainty on her face. 'At least say you will think about it,' he urged.

Christina knew her expression told him she wasn't convinced – and that Helen's face showed there could be trouble ahead.

'What are you going to do about Alex's job offer?' said Vanessa, tying on her apron as they prepared dinner at the cottage.

Christina looked up from the kitchen table where she was peeling and chopping potatoes. She added them to the bowl of prepared carrots and laid down the knife.

'I'm not sure. It's tempting, of course, and I have no work at present. My savings won't last very long.'

'I'm so sorry about this, Chrissie,' said Vanessa. She paused in the act of dipping slices of Spam into breadcrumbs. 'George is a lovely old man and I would usually be happy to have him to stay. But I'm so sorry about throwing you out.'

'You're not throwing me out, Van. I would feel awful if I thought that was on your conscience and spoiling your father-in-law's visit. Please don't think any more about it. I can't stay here indefinitely, anyway, and I really do need to think about the future.'

'Oh, the future. Meat off rationing would be a good start.' Vanessa laughed and set the prepared slices of tinned chopped pork on a plate. 'But seriously, teaching would be good experience, another string to your bow.'

'So you think I should do it?'

'Absolutely. I don't want to say goodbye to you so soon.'

'It's just that I feel strange about living in the house with...' She caught herself in time. 'With people I don't know.'

'You know Fiona.' Vanessa picked up the bowl of chopped vegetables and tipped them into the pan of boiling water. 'And Alex–'

'Yes...'

'Let's think who else there is.' Vanessa put lard to melt in a frying pan. 'There's Mrs Morrison, the housekeeper-cum-cook. Mrs Morrison's husband, the gardener-handyman, and the farm workers, but as they are busy on Home Farm you probably won't see much of them.'

'What about Alex and Fiona's parents? You mentioned earlier that their mother lives abroad.'

'Yes, Sylvia has a house in Portugal. She spends most of the year there.' Vanessa arranged the slices of Spam in the sizzling fat. 'She went off as soon as she could after the war. That's made Alex and Fiona close.'

'What happened to their father?'

'He died towards the end of the war. A heart attack while he was working on the harvest.'

'I'm sorry to hear that,' Christina said. 'So Alex wouldn't have been called up, because he was a farmer?'

'No, Alex went to war. He was barely seventeen when war broke out. Fiona told me he joined up as soon as he was eighteen.'

Suddenly things began to fall into place. Christina had assumed Alex had been in the reserved occupation, but it seemed he'd spent most of the war fighting and enduring goodness knows what horrors. Something bad, very bad, must have happened – something that caused the raw grief she had seen in his eyes.

At once she remembered his scars and how Vanessa had told her he'd been hit by flying shrapnel. Her heart missed a beat. For the first time since she'd met him, she began to realise that he might have reasons for being the way he appeared to be. Her preconceptions about Alex began to shift.

Vanessa turned the Spam slices in the frying pan. 'Fiona babysits for us sometimes. The boys can't wait to start school. Imagine, being taught by your babysitter, neighbour and friend.' She set down the spatula. 'Dinner will be ready in ten minutes.'

'Smells good,' said Christina. Out of the window she could see the boys digging in a little patch of bare soil and smiled. 'Looks like they are aiming for Australia.'

Vanessa joined her at the kitchen table. 'Do you remember when we were little we used to think that? Dig far enough and you would come across kangaroos?'

'Yes, and I was worried that I might accidentally hit one on the head with my spade!' Christina sighed. 'Life was so much simpler then. No difficult decisions to make.'

'Make the decision now,' said Vanessa. 'Either to go to work at Craiglogie House with free food and lodging and the charming–'

Christina frowned and Vanessa amended '– and the laird, or go back to Surrey, move in with your mother and look for a job.'

'I'll have to do that eventually, anyway.'

'Yes, but at Craiglogie you'll have time to look for something suitable while enjoying all that the place has to offer. It's a great opportunity.'

Christina nodded slowly. The opportunity to produce a portfolio of work for a future employer. Or even, as she hoped to do one day, impress future clients in her own studio. This job would give her the experience and the confidence she needed to start her own business. 'Okay, I'll write to him this evening.'

Nicholas burst into the kitchen, trailing soil. 'I heard a kangaroo!'

'Really?' said Vanessa with a smile. 'What noise did it make?'

Nicholas screwed up his face and roared as loudly as he could.

'I heard the kangaroo first,' cried William, running in behind his brother.

'Well, there's a surprise,' said Vanessa. 'You can both carry on digging tomorrow, but now let's get your boots off and your hands washed. After dinner, if you're good, you can help me make a cake for tomorrow.'

'Is it a birthday cake?' asked Nicholas.

'No, but it is a special cake,' said Vanessa, turning to wink at Christina. 'Aunty Chrissie has got a new job.'

'*Dear Mr MacDonald,*' Alex read, standing in the hall, holding the letter which had been hand-delivered earlier through the letter box.

Thank you for your offer of employment and accommodation. I have thought about it and, if you are sure I can be of some help, I would like to accept. If this is satisfactory, I can come tomorrow afternoon. I would be grateful if you could collect me from Vanessa's house any time after lunch.

Yours sincerely,
Christina Camble

A suitably formal response to a job offer, he thought. So that is how he would play it – a formal employer–employee relationship. She was coming here to work. Good, it would be less complicated that way.

Knowing she would be here soon, he found himself smiling.

Alex and Fiona went to church as usual on a Sunday, then he kept himself busy seeing to the animals for the remainder of the long morning. Lunchtime came round at last and he went indoors.

After he and Fiona had eaten in the kitchen, Alex waited impatiently until he felt an acceptable period of time had passed. When he went outside, Tess sat by the Land Rover, anticipating him.

'Not this time, old thing.' He smiled, bent down and fondled her ears. 'Christina will be here soon, though, and you'll like that, won't you?'

The dog smiled and thumped her tail. Alex laughed, scratched under her chin and jumped into his car. He started the engine, wound down the window and turned out of the courtyard, onto the driveway.

A gentle breeze came through the window as he drove, bringing with it the sweet smell of the countryside. A shaft of sunlight broke through the clouds overhead and it seemed to him the first really happy day he had known for a long time. How was it possible that one person – Christina – could make his heart feel lighter?

∽

Christina was packed and ready when Alex arrived at the cottage, earlier than she had expected. The twins burst from the garden into the kitchen when they heard him arrive.

'Hello, Uncle Alex.' They threw their arms around his legs.

'Boys, let the poor man sit down,' said Vanessa. 'Cup of tea, Alex?' She put the kettle on the stove.

'Please,' he said, smiling at the boys as they released him. He slipped off his jacket and hung it on the back of the chair.

His clean white polo shirt emphasised his biceps, sending a spark through Christina's body, and she flushed and turned away. 'Let me make the tea,' she said quickly.

'Thanks,' said Vanessa. 'I would have given Christina a lift to Craiglogie myself, Alex, but I've promised to take the boys to visit a friend and she lives in the opposite direction.'

'It's no trouble,' said Alex.

'Goodness, look at the pair of you,' said Vanessa, noticing the twins' grubby hands and faces.

She ushered them out of the kitchen. Their protestations of, 'Mummy, we washed this morning,' gradually faded.

As Christina moved around the kitchen, laying out the tea things, she felt his gaze on her. The kitchen seemed small with Alex in it, in a way it never did with Vanessa and the children.

'Let me.' He stood to take the laden tray from her and a trace of his masculine scent made her legs feel weak.

She watched as he leaned forward to put the tray on the table. The muscles in his back shifted under the soft cotton of his shirt. She wished she could stop noticing him in that way. It was unsettling – and pointless. She wasn't interested in falling for any man. What if she found more rejection, more hurt? If only she could stay here with Vanessa, then everything would be all right.

With a small sigh she took a seat.

He put a cup and saucer in front of her and sent her a quick look. 'You haven't changed your mind, have you?'

'No, of course not. After all, I can't stay here.' She saw a frown dart across his face and she added, 'I mean, you and Fiona have been so kind, allowing me to come to Craiglogie, but I'm concerned that I'm... a bit in the way.'

He slid into the seat opposite her. 'You're not, Christina.'

Caught in his steady gaze, her pulse quickened. She felt awkward, so close to him. The sound came through the door of the boys singing and laughing as they made their way down the stairs.

Alex smiled. 'We used to sing that song,' he said to Christina, 'Fiona and I, about the coo's mou'.'

'The coo's moo?'

'It's Doric and means the cow's mouth.'

She returned his smile and for a moment there was only him in the world.

The children exploded back into the kitchen. 'That's done,' said Vanessa, following more calmly. 'Right, boys, sit nicely at the table and you can each have a piece of shortbread and a glass of milk.'

'How is Callum's father getting here tomorrow?' Alex asked Vanessa when the boys were settled. 'Can I be of assistance?'

'That's kind of you,' said Vanessa, pouring out the tea, 'but I've already arranged to collect George from the station in Aberdeen.'

'Thanks.' Alex helped himself to shortbread from the plate Vanessa offered him. 'When is Callum back?'

'He'll be home on Wednesday. I've written to tell him about his dad coming here. Callum will be pleased to see him.'

Before long, the twins had finished their milk and biscuits and were demanding answers to questions about their grand-dad's visit, Uncle Alex's dog and Aunty Chrissie's new job.

Eventually Alex rose and said, 'We should be off now, Vanessa. You'll have some things to do before your father-in-law arrives.'

Vanessa nodded. She smiled encouragingly at Christina. 'See you whenever your boss gives you time off.'

'Hardly a boss,' said Alex, with a grin. 'I like to think we will each be helping the other in some way.'

Christina got slowly to her feet. Alex picked up her bags.

The twins threw their arms around her waist. 'Bye, Aunty Chrissie.'

She tousled the sandy curls on their heads. 'I'll see you soon, I promise.'

'Bye, Uncle Alex.' They ran to him and clutched his knees.

'Heavens, boys,' said Vanessa, with a laugh, 'they are only going up the road.'

With kisses and hugs, best wishes and promises between all, Christina and Alex finally went out the door.

Christina followed Alex to the Land Rover and accepted his hand to climb in. He placed her bags on the back seat, slid into the driver's seat, turned the key in the ignition and put the vehicle into gear. They set off, bumping along the uneven track.

She threw him a sideways glance. His eyes were trained on the road ahead and there was something about the set of his jaw which betrayed… irritation? He hadn't looked at her since they'd got in the car and Christina couldn't blame him. She'd as good as said that she was going with him because she couldn't stay with Vanessa. Of course, that was true, but it could have been put with more care. She bit her lip, remembering the frown that had crossed his face at her thoughtless comment. It would have been much better if she had said it was a wonderful opportunity to complete a portfolio. She just hoped she was good enough at her work to justify Alex's trust.

Secretly, she studied his broad hands on the wheel. Her gaze slipped down to his thighs as he pressed the clutch. Drawing in a silent breath, she clenched her hands tight as if they might reach out to slide along the warm muscle.

Christina lifted her eyes to his face. His lips were pressed together in concentration and she moistened her own.

'Thank you for the lift,' she blurted out, above the sound of the engine.

He shrugged. 'That's okay.' He turned off the cottage track and accelerated along the road. As if he could sense her gaze on him, he glanced across at her. 'I was going to ask if you were all right with dogs, but I know the answer to that.' There was amusement in his voice.

'Yes.' She felt the smile creep onto her lips. 'Especially Labradors.'

When Alex drove between the stone pillars and down the driveway, she felt her stomach lurch as his house came into view. Despite her determination not to feel intimidated, there was no getting away from the fact that the house was decidedly grand and the family barely known to her. More importantly, Christina was aware of the need to compose herself when she was with Alex and perhaps to be on her guard against Helen.

CHAPTER 6

*A*lex pulled up on the gravel outside Craiglogie House and turned off the engine. He jumped out, walked round and opened her door. 'Make yourself at home. Fiona's indoors, waiting for you. I'll bring in your bags.'

Christina just had time to notice Helen's little red sports car parked a short distance away, before the main door was thrown wide, Tess bounded out and Fiona followed close behind.

'I'm so glad you could come, Christina,' she said, giving her a quick hug.

'Hello, Fiona. Thank you for having me.' The butterflies had gone, to be replaced by nausea.

'Come on,' said Fiona, slipping her arm through Christina's. 'I'll show you to your room.'

She led the way across the flagged hall, up the wide staircase and along the landing. Christina remembered the last time she was here, on this landing. It seemed like weeks had passed, so much had happened, but it was only two days ago.

Fiona stopped and opened a door. 'I do hope you like it.'

Christina's bedroom was full of light and she immediately liked it very much. The large bed was covered with a cream-and-yellow candlewick bedspread, the dressing table held a vase of bright daffodils and a deep armchair sat under the window. There was a small writing desk with a chair, too.

She smiled at Fiona. 'I do like it. It's lovely.'

Christina crossed the room and looked out of the window. She saw the formal garden and in the distance the copse, and knew beyond the trees was the pond where Alex had told her about the clan feud.

Fiona had left the door open, and Alex entered and put Christina's bags on the floor by the bed.

'We'll leave you to it,' said Fiona. 'There's a bathroom along the corridor. We're having an early dinner this evening, about five o'clock, as Helen has to catch a train.'

A wave of relief passed over Christina at this news. She would not have to cope with Helen for very long, after all.

As soon as she was alone, Christina decided to unpack and have a bath. She laid her hairbrush and the few other belongings on the dressing table and hung her clothes in the wardrobe. The bathroom was large and cold, but thankfully the water was hot. As the heat of the water began to relax her, she lay back in the bathtub and closed her eyes. She had been worrying unnecessarily; she was here to do a job and would do it to the best of her ability.

When the water had cooled she climbed out, wrapped a white, fluffy towel around her, hopped across the cold lino floor and hurried back to her bedroom. Fiona had told her earlier that her fiancé was joining them for dinner this evening, but as he counted as family there was no need to dress up. Christina slipped on her tweed skirt and a pale-peach twinset before brushing out her ponytail and pinning up her hair.

She should start to earn her keep, Christina thought, and took her notebook from the dressing table. Sitting in the chair by the window, she began to jot down ideas on suitable images and angles for Alex to photograph.

She had listed a number of ideas and was about to go downstairs when there was a knock on the door. She jumped up and opened it, to find Fiona standing there.

'Come in,' said Christina, taking a step back.

'I'm not stopping,' said Fiona. 'I just came to ask if you have everything you need.'

'Yes, thank you, Fiona. You've been very kind.'

'Not at all. I'm pleased that my brother has someone to help him with his hobby. He needs a break from work sometimes.'

'He's made a good job of the photographs he's already taken,' said Christina. 'There are some excellent pictures of Helen.'

Fiona laughed. 'Yes, well, Helen's a professional model – catalogues, mainly. She was very keen to pose for Alex. She needed a few more portraits for her portfolio.'

Christina frowned. 'I thought agencies arranged that for their models?'

'I've no idea,' said Fiona. 'But Alex said it was easy to take those images, as she helped him tremendously, knowing how to pose and so on.'

Christina forced herself to smile warmly. 'Yes, I could see that.'

'But he really wants to specialise in outdoor work,' Fiona went on, 'which is where he hopes you will be able to help him. Anyway, see you downstairs in about five minutes?'

'Perfect. Thank you.'

When she'd gone, Christina clipped on tiny silver earrings and refreshed her lipstick. She drew in a deep breath and opened the bedroom door. She crossed the landing and saw in the hall below, Alex standing with Helen and a man Christina took to be Fiona's fiancé.

As she descended the stairs, the others looked up. She swallowed; she could do this.

Alex stepped forward. His eyes lingered on her face for a moment.

'Christina,' he said, 'this is Stewart, Fiona's fiancé, on leave from the Royal Navy. Stewart, allow me to introduce Christina, who is staying here to help me with some photographic work.'

'Pleased to meet you,' said Stewart with a friendly smile and holding out his hand. He was a tall, slim man, older than Fiona, with a feathering of grey in his temples.

Fiona appeared from the direction of the kitchen. 'We're all here. Let's go through to the dining room, shall we?'

The curtains had not been drawn this evening as it was still early and Christina saw the French windows that gave onto the terrace. That's where Vanessa brought the news about her father-in-law, Christina thought, which led to my being here.

There was no branch of candelabra on the table tonight, but a central arrangement of short-stemmed roses, the same apricot colour as the dress Helen wore.

Helen observed Christina looking at the flowers. 'I did the arrangement myself,' she said. 'It's just a little something I like to do. My way of saying thank you for inviting me.' She flashed a polished smile. 'I'll be coming back after my modelling assignment. London is so busy these days – simply *ghastly*, in fact – and I just love the peace and quiet here. It's heavenly, don't you think? And Alex is such an attentive man.'

'Yes,' Christina said, her voice sounding unsure in comparison to Helen's. She was so busy inwardly chastising herself, she didn't notice Stewart arrive beside her.

'So, Christina,' he said, drawing out a chair for her, 'I hear you're at Craiglogie to ensure Alex works hard.'

'I've been told he already works hard,' Christina said, smiling at him as she smoothed the back of her skirt and sat on the offered seat.

Stewart pulled out his own chair and sat next to Christina. He grinned across the table at Alex, who glanced up from where Helen was whispering to him.

'Who could possibly have said that?' asked Fiona, seating herself at the head of the table. 'That Alex works hard?'

Christina saw the same twinkle in Fiona's eye that she'd seen in Alex's once or twice. She hid a smile. 'Why, Alex MacDonald himself,' she said.

Laughter burst out around the table. 'Do you doubt the best authority there is on Alex MacDonald?' Alex said, with a broad smile.

Feeling ridiculously happy, she broke away from his gaze and said to Stewart, 'We'll be working on photography. The house, estate, anywhere that will produce a decent image.'

'Of course, Alex doesn't need any help with *portraits*,' put in Helen, smiling sweetly at Christina as she rested her hand on his forearm.

'He has taken some excellent photographs of you,' said Fiona, 'but let's not make my brother too conceited.'

'I mean it,' repeated Helen. 'Alex doesn't need any help.'

Christina picked up her soup spoon.

'For goodness' sake, Helen,' said Alex, the annoyance in his tone quite clear. 'There is still a lot I have to learn.'

As a hush descended over the table, Christina slowly lifted her eyes to his face and felt a rush of conflicting emotion. He was fond of Helen, she was sure, but he was trying to protect her from Helen's comments. The question that came to her mind was why?

Alex ran a hand through his hair. 'I'm sorry, Helen, I didn't mean it to come out like that.'

Christina watched Helen blink in surprise and then saw her lips curve into a half-smile.

'Goodness,' Helen said slowly. 'A man who apologises. Whatever next?'

Christina wasn't sorry when the meal was over. She was wondering how soon she could excuse herself when Alex pushed back his chair.

'I'm afraid that Helen and I must leave you now,' he said. 'She has to catch the sleeper to London and I've promised to take her to the station.'

'I only heard this morning about the modelling assignment,' Helen said. '*Such* a bore, when I was enjoying myself here tremendously.'

Alex rose. 'I may not be back until late, I'm afraid, as I have a visit to make to a friend in Aberdeen. It's a duty that's well over-due.' He helped Helen to her feet. The smile she gave was for him only.

'Old Mr Thompson was our gardener until he retired and moved to be close to his daughter in the city,' said Fiona to Christina. 'He likes to chat. So, Alex, I know you won't be home until late.'

Alex turned to the rest of the gathering. 'I'll wish you all good-night. And Christina, we'll start work at nine o'clock tomorrow morning.'

A small part of Christina couldn't help wondering if Helen really was taking the sleeper down to London. She watched them leave the room. Was it an excuse for the two of them to spend the night together? Christina knew it shouldn't matter to her, for they could do as they wished, but it surprised her to discover that it very much did.

Unsettled, Christina made her excuses to Fiona and Stewart, pleading a letter to write. She was ashamed to admit, even to herself, that the sparkle had gone out of the evening once Alex left.

Back in her room, she was restless, unable to settle to anything. A letter could be written to her mother, but she'd sent a picture postcard a few days ago, so there was no urgency. She picked up from the bedside table the novel she'd brought with her and read the title aloud. 'Jane Eyre.' Flipping through the well-thumbed pages, she said in a theatrical voice to the silent room, 'The story of an impressionable young woman who falls in love with the owner of the country estate where she goes to work.'

Christina flopped backwards onto the bed, kicked off her shoes and sighed. Why had she chosen to bring *Jane Eyre*, of all novels, on holiday?

Was she imagining it or did Alex perhaps like her? He'd asked her to stay at Craiglogie – but that was so she could help him with his hobby. It didn't matter; there was obviously something between him and Helen. Helen was at pains to let her know that.

She lay there a while, her eyes closed. Perhaps giving up her flat had been too hasty. She dreaded the thought of returning to live at her mother's house. No, she must make a success of this opportunity.

Christina slid from the bed, went over to the writing desk and sat down. She pulled her notepad towards her and turned over the used pages until she came to a fresh one. As she began to plan the sessions for the next few days, she felt clearer in her head. She'd been imagining Alex's interest in her. And that was perfectly fine.

She worked diligently, all thoughts of the mess her life seemed to have become pushed from her mind. Eventually, tired, she lifted the sash window to let in the cool night air, drew the curtains across, undressed and slipped between the sheets. The bed was soft and comfortable and she wriggled her toes with pleasure.

A thought struck her. How long was this room to be hers? They hadn't discussed the length of her employment, her working hours or pay. These things would have to be sorted out with Alex in the morning.

A little frisson of nerves and excitement flooded her chilled body and she snuggled further down under the bedcovers. She was looking forward to their sessions together and dreading them.

Outside the window an owl hooted and Christina, unable to sleep, turned onto her side. Alex might have left the house, but she was having difficulty making him leave her thoughts. Did he really want to learn how to take professional-looking photographs or was he simply being kind, knowing without his offer she would have to cut short her holiday? But if the latter, why would he care, given he hardly knew her?

She should count herself lucky. Whatever the reason, he had made it possible for her to stay here longer. She'd conduct herself as the consummate professional and when the time came to leave, she hoped her services would have impressed him enough to give her a good reference.

Christina rolled onto her back and thought about the other people she'd met. She liked Fiona very much, and Stewart and Fraser seemed nice. As to Helen – well, she'd made it clear from the beginning that Christina's presence was unwelcome.

Were Alex and Helen just good friends, as Alex seemed to indicate? Or was there something more, as Helen would have her believe?

For a while longer she lay in the darkened room. She blamed the owl for keeping her awake, but she knew the truth when she heard the chugging of the Land Rover's engine. She felt relief as the car door slammed and a single set of footsteps crunched across the gravel.

At last, she fell asleep.

A light rain was falling in the early dawn as Alex drew back his bedroom curtains. It was Monday, the first day of his instruction from Christina, and now they probably wouldn't be able to take photographs outdoors. He still couldn't quite believe that she was here, sleeping under his roof, and that very soon he would see her downstairs.

An image filled his head of her tousled hair framing that perfect face, her soft, warm body against him as his arms had encircled her to demonstrate how to hold a tennis racquet. He'd believed he could work with Christina without being distracted by her, but she had already lodged herself firmly in his waking thoughts.

Alex leaned his head against the cool glass of the window. What was he doing, longing for what was impossible? He knew it wasn't right; she deserved a better man than he, one who was strong and brave and not reduced to a wreck. Shell shock, combat stress, whatever name it was given, it was all the same – a feeling of helplessness and an inability to sleep without nightmares. He turned away from the window.

At least she seemed oblivious to the effect she was having on him, so he had better work to keep it that way.

As soon as he was dressed, he went down the stairs to the kitchen.

'Morning, Tess,' he said as the dog rose from her blanket by the warm Aga and padded over to him. He let her out of the back door and prepared her breakfast.

Within minutes she scampered back inside and he placed the bowl on the tiled floor. Standing by the sink, he drank a glass of water as she wolfed down her food. 'I'm off to feed the calves,' he said.

Tess wagged her tail in response and followed him to the porch. He pulled on his boots and went out into the gloom of the early morning.

≈

A grey-looking day had dawned by the time Christina made her way down to the kitchen, unsure what to expect. Tess was there to greet her, but there was no sign of Alex or Fiona.

'Are you all alone?' said Christina, gently rubbing the top of the Labrador's head as she cast her eyes around the room. The kettle and a teapot stood on the Aga's warming plate and she made herself a cup of tea. She found the cool pantry and lifted a jug of milk from the marble shelf before sitting down at the long oak table.

It had been set with a box of cereal, a loaf of bread with a knife on a board, the butter dish and a pot of home-made marmalade. A bowl, spoon and mug left upside down on the draining board suggested that someone had already eaten. Probably Fiona, as she'd said last night that she would leave early for her work at the local school.

Christina wrapped her hands around the steaming cup. The Aga kept the room wonderfully warm, but this simple act gave her comfort. She couldn't decide if she was relieved or disappointed that Alex wasn't there. Of course, she would be seeing him this morning, working with him, but until then she was happy to have more time to prepare herself.

Tess trotted over to the table, her tail wagging hopefully, and stood looking at Christina.

'Have you had breakfast?' she asked.

Tess sat and her tail thumped harder on the floor.

'Now, what does that mean? That you wouldn't say no to any breakfast that's going?' Christina laughed and stroked the dog's warm, solid flank. 'You don't feel like you're starving.'

'Labradors don't have an off switch when it comes to food.'

She spun round as Alex came through the door. He was dressed in a work shirt, blue crew-neck jumper and old jeans, his hair was damp and he smelled of fresh soap. The colour crept into her cheeks.

'I fed Tess earlier, before I went out to see to the cows,' he said. 'Don't let her tell you otherwise.' He raised an eyebrow. 'Porridge?'

Christina opened her mouth to ask for just a slice of toast, but instead found herself saying, 'Porridge would be lovely, thank you.'

'Good choice.' He turned and took two blue-and-white striped bowls from the dresser.

She followed him with her gaze as he moved about the kitchen with ease. He didn't look at her as he chatted on about the estate and that the rain had put paid to their plans for the morning.

Alex crossed to the Aga and slid a dish from the lower oven. She watched as he ladled porridge into the two bowls and placed them on the table. She studied the breadth of his shoulders.

He placed on the table a jug of cream, a bowl of sugar, the salt cellar, a jar of honey and a bottle of whisky. 'Help yourself – whichever you like.' He took a seat opposite her.

Christina stared with astonishment at the array of accompaniments. 'I've never had such a choice before with porridge. What do you recommend?'

'The cream and the whisky. Not too much of the latter. We need to work this morning.' His eyes crinkled with a smile. This was as relaxed as she had seen him so far. And it was very pleasant.

She did as he suggested, then tasted a spoonful. 'It's delicious! I shall have this every morning.' Her spoon stopped mid-air. 'Sorry, that sounded presumptuous.' She lowered the spoon. 'The truth is, I'm not sure how long you want me to work here.'

He ran a hand through his damp hair. 'Let's see how it goes. If you're all right with that?'

'Yes.' She felt embarrassed but had to ask him. 'What about the other terms of my employment – hours, salary and so on?'

'I'll pay you weekly.' He pulled an envelope from the pocket of his jeans and pushed it across the table. 'In advance. I hope that's acceptable?'

Christina took the envelope, opened the flap and looked inside. She frowned. 'This is too generous. I can't accept it.'

'I want you to,' he said. 'Your expertise is worth that much to me.'

She shook her head. 'You could find someone else to teach you for less than this.'

'But I'm asking you,' he said. 'I trust you.'

Trust, she thought. Christina held Alex's look, saw the flicker of uncertainty in his eyes, and her heart melted. He's not David, she told herself.

'Thank you.' She smiled at him, breaking the tension, and swallowed a spoonful of porridge. 'Is there anywhere in particular you would like to start?'

'You're the boss.'

She glanced out of the window. 'The rain has stopped, so the weather should be good for the rest of the day.'

Alex laughed. 'This is Scotland. You can experience all four seasons in one day.'

'Really? It's been sunny all the time I've been here.'

'You've been lucky to have experienced continuous sun for more than three days in a row.'

'It can't be that bad,' said Christina.

'If you believe that, I might have a few haggis wandering about the field that I'd be glad to sell to you.' He grinned and popped another spoonful of porridge into his mouth.

'Well, that aside,' she said with a smile, 'let's start by taking photographs close by, in the grounds, in case the rain comes back.'

He nodded and reached for his mug of tea.

'The thing is,' she said, 'photography is all about the quality of the light. Your studio work is impressive, I've seen that in the photographs in the library, but studio lights can be easily adjusted. Outdoor pictures are more challenging.'

He took a gulp of tea. 'Okay.'

'Shall we start by considering the types of photos that work best in various weather conditions?'

'Why not?' he said, spooning up more porridge.

'Are you taking this seriously?' Christina affected a schoolmarm voice.

'Yes, miss.' There was a twinkle in his eye.

'Very well.' She rose, poured herself another cup of tea from the pot on the Aga and returned to the table. 'Firstly, there's the morning blue hour.'

'I thought the blue hour was in the evening.'

'There's a morning one, too. It can last from half an hour to several hours before sunrise, depending on the time of year. Ironically, that's the best time to capture night photos, especially in a city.'

'That's interesting. But we're not in the city and it's too late for this morning's blue hour. What's the next one?'

'Dawn. Just before sunrise is a great time for nature landscapes. The light then tends to have a subtle, pastel feel.'

'Hmm, too late for that, too,' he said.

'The morning golden hour, just after sunrise, gives a warm tone to images.'

'It's damp this morning.' His eyes flickered to the window. 'There's a bit of a mist, too, so visibility is poor.' His voice faltered, as he kept his gaze ahead. 'Sorry, I'm beginning to sound like a killjoy.'

When he turned back to her, she caught her breath at the vulnerable look in his eyes. It lasted only a moment and then was gone.

Christina cleared her throat. 'Misty mornings can produce atmospheric pictures.'

'Just as well, since we get plenty of those.' He pushed away his empty bowl. 'But would it be better to wait for the sun?'

'Not necessarily.' She made her voice professional again. 'On sunny days, the midday light tends to be harsh. Wooded areas with high sun streaming through the trees work well in those conditions, though, and in wintertime with the long shadows.'

He swallowed a mouthful of tea and put the mug down. 'And overcast days? We get a few of those, too.'

'Portraits are good then, as it gives an even light on the subjects.' She thought of his collection of George Washington Wilson's black-and-white photos. Buildings and people, especially people. Unsmiling, ordinary Victorian men and women in front of tumbledown buildings or working in fields. 'Are you interested in outdoor portraits?'

'I'm interested in everything,' he said, 'but for the time being, buildings and landscapes are what I'm hoping to photograph.'

'The flat light of a cloudy day is ideal for wildlife photography. A herd of deer, perhaps?'

He nodded. 'Sounds good.'

'Then there's evening golden hour,' she continued, 'just before sunset, when the sunlight has a warm quality. Midsummer gives the longest hours, of course. In the depths of winter, evening golden hour may last only a few minutes.'

'When is your preferred time?' he asked, leaning back in his chair.

Christina thought for a few moments, as she spooned up the last of her porridge. 'I like dusk, just after the sun has set. That's the perfect time to photograph silhouettes. But I also like the evening blue hour – at least, for capturing city views. The sky is deep blue then. Once it's night, the sky is solid black and you lose the variety of textures in the buildings.'

'So we need an evening out in a city?'

She laughed. 'And rainy evenings are great for capturing the reflections of lights in the wet streets.'

'A rainy evening in Edinburgh, then?' He raised an eyebrow.

'Sounds wonderful.'

'Not many girls would think so.' He smiled and the dimple appeared in his left cheek.

A warmth spread through Christina. Concentrate; this is a business relationship, she reminded herself. 'We also need to discuss shutter speeds, angles, composition. And if you want to do your own developing and printing, you will need specialist equipment and a darkroom.'

Without warning, a coal exploded in the Aga firebox. Alex jumped, his arm jerked and his mug tipped over, making a little pool of liquid on the table.

'Goodness, that was some bang,' said Christina, grabbing the mug to stand it upright. 'Perhaps we can call in the haggis to lap up the tea,' she teased.

Alex seemed not to hear her. For a moment he sat as if frozen to the spot, a look of anguish on his face. The laughter stuck in her throat. He rose, his face averted, but not before she saw how pale he had become. He took a cloth from beside the sink and began to mop up the liquid, but his hands were shaking too much and the tea pooled across the surface of the table.

'Let me,' said Christina, taking the cloth from him.

She cleaned up the mess, rinsed the cloth in the sink and returned to the table.

'Yes,' he said after a moment, meeting her eyes again, and continuing as if the incident just now had never happened, 'we'll take a trip into Aberdeen one day to buy whatever is needed.'

'That sounds like a good idea,' she said. 'When were you thinking of going?'

'I'm not sure yet. I'm fairly busy at the moment. In fact, I think it best if at first we work together for only a couple of hours each morning.'

Christina nodded. 'Of course.' Just as she was beginning to think he was serious about the project, he seemed to be drawing back.

CHAPTER 7

The morning remained dull and grey clouds hung overhead. Christina discovered that Alex owned a Graflex Ciro, a good quality new camera – she'd expected no less. She showed him how to capture interesting angles of the house and gardens. By the time they were ready for lunch, she was sure he had some photographs he'd be pleased with.

'Thank you,' he said. 'You certainly know your work.'

'As soon as I left school, I got a job with a photographer. And my father was a war photographer, so I suppose you could say the work is in the blood.' She smiled, warming to her theme. 'One day I hope to have my own business and so I need a good portfolio of images. That's why I decided to take up your offer of work here.'

He shot her a glance, then looked away. 'It's good to have an ambition.' His voice was toneless as he checked his watch. 'I've got a meeting now with Fraser. Fiona should be back, so you can have lunch with her.'

She watched him walking from her with long strides and was concerned that she had upset him in some way.

As he strode away, Alex admired Christina's ambition, but he had been hurt by her admission it was the only reason she'd accepted the job. He forced himself to accept that he had no reason for expecting it to be otherwise. At least she seemed to find Craiglogie as special as he did and that pleased him.

For a moment in the kitchen earlier this morning, he had been afraid he'd made a mistake with the money and she would refuse the work.

He rounded the corner of the house and headed towards the Land Rover. The meeting with his factor was taking place in the upper field, where Fraser wanted to speak to him about the soil sample taken from there.

It was always better to be outdoors. Alex could manage indoors now, as long as the place wasn't too confined or too dark. He raised his hand and tentatively touched the ridge of scarred skin on his forehead. There was no longer much to show of the physical wounds he'd suffered in the explosion, and for that he was grateful. He disliked others staring at him, seeing the scar, turning away or, worse, asking questions.

The scarring was the least of his problems. It was the mental wound which still plagued him and it, thank goodness, was invisible. The explosion in the Aga had triggered the memory of his being buried under rubble – the burst of light, a smell of cordite, the sudden silence – but it had passed before Christina noticed. She knew nothing of his war experience and he wanted to keep it that way.

He'd allowed very few to know what had happened to him, first at Dunkirk and then in the gun emplacement. And, apart from Fiona, he'd allowed no one to get emotionally close. Helen had asked why after Dunkirk he'd not been sent to Singapore with the rest of his regiment, and why after the explosion he'd not returned to work at the coastal battery.

Alex had told her what had happened to him and his men, and that he was just about managing to function normally. Apart from the panic attacks and the nightmares, that is. The army doctor said these would last a few weeks, perhaps even a few months, but not that they might continue for years. Even though Fiona and Helen knew he still had these attacks, he couldn't talk to anyone about them and he didn't want to.

Christina made her way to the kitchen for lunch, her thoughts on Alex's response to the sudden eruption in the Aga. She'd teased him, then wished she hadn't. His violent jump and then freezing, the shaking hands and white face – what had caused such an extreme reaction?

She found Fiona removing baked potatoes from the oven.

'Alex said he'll be in later, after he's seen Fraser.' Fiona placed two of the potatoes on plates and returned the third one to the oven. 'I put these on this morning before I went to work. Jacket potatoes okay?'

Christina remembered Fiona's comment about the twins having their lunch with Mrs Morrison on Saturday. 'Perfect, thank you. But I'm sorry, I thought Vanessa said you had a cook. I could have come in earlier to prepare lunch.'

'Don't apologise,' said Fiona. 'Mrs Morrison comes in the afternoons during the week and other times when we have the occasional party, like dinner the other evening and lunch after tennis. She doesn't live in, but has one of the estate cottages. Her husband is our handyman-gardener. Besides, I enjoy cooking. If you can call it cooking to put potatoes in the Aga! You can clear up afterwards, though, if you like. Mrs Morrison is a bit of a tartar, so I take care not to get on the wrong side of her.' Fiona blushed at the admission, and she and Christina laughed.

'How was your morning?' Christina asked, as they sat down to lunch.

'Busy,' she said. 'Thank goodness I only teach part-time.'

'Vanessa told me that you'll be teaching her boys when they go to school.' Christina lifted a chunk of baked potato on her fork and saw a drop of melted butter slide down to land on her plate.

Fiona nodded. 'I know most of the children before they arrive at the village primary school.'

They ate and chatted, until Fiona laid her knife and fork on her empty plate and glanced at the clock. 'I have to get back to school shortly. What are your plans for this afternoon?'

'Nothing, really.' Apart from Fiona, Alex and Vanessa, there was no one she knew here. 'Is there anything I can do to help?'

'Mrs M will have it all under control. Why don't you go for a walk, explore, read a book, whatever you wish.'

If she didn't ask now, Christina thought, she might not have the courage later. 'Before you go, can I ask you something, Fiona?'

'Of course you can.' Fiona eyed her quizzically.

'It's about Alex…' Christina hesitated for a moment. 'When Alex and I were eating breakfast this morning, a coal exploded in the Aga. His reaction was – well, quite extreme. He jumped violently and seemed to freeze.'

The colour drained from Fiona's face.

'I'm so sorry.' Christina suddenly felt very uncomfortable. 'I shouldn't have brought it up.'

'No, it's okay. Since you're staying for a few weeks, you should know that he can seem a bit odd sometimes. But it's as a result of his experiences in the war.'

Fiona cupped her hands around her tea and stared into the brown liquid for a few moments, while Christina waited.

Then she looked up and met Christina's gaze. 'Alex joined up in early 1940, despite our parents trying their best to dissuade him. He was eighteen. The Gordon Highlanders were sent to

France as part of the British Expeditionary Force and before long he ended up in Dunkirk.'

'Oh,' Christina breathed.

Fiona nodded. 'With what was left of his company, he fought a rearguard action to keep the Germans back and for that was awarded the DSO.'

Christina nodded, unwilling to speak and break the moment.

'Back home he had a nervous breakdown, was diagnosed with shell shock and sent to work at the coastal battery in Aberdeen,' said Fiona. 'Alex was a good officer and the men liked him. He was doing all right, pulling himself together again, until towards the end of the war a German plane dropped a bomb next to their gun emplacement and he was buried under a mass of rubble.'

Fiona paused and continued. 'By the time they had dug him out, they thought he was dead.' Her voice wobbled. 'As it was, he was terribly lucky. A broken leg, but no life-threatening injuries. He was the only one of his artillery to get off so lightly.'

'Dear Lord,' Christina murmured.

'Alex remembered it all afterwards, of course; the discussion about what to do with his body and the need to notify his next of kin. He heard it all but couldn't respond. He was conscious, but too weak even to lift his eyelids.' Fiona's eyes glistened with tears.

A lump stuck in Christina's throat. To have heard such a conversation and not be able to tell them he was still alive. No wonder–

'They patched up his body,' said Fiona, pulling out a handkerchief and wiping her eyes, 'but he had shell shock all over again. He still gets these sudden attacks of memories and nightmares. Thankfully, he no longer sleepwalks.

'I do worry about him,' Fiona said. 'Stewart and I are getting married in the summer and then Alex will be at Craiglogie on his own.' She drew in a shaky breath. 'Most of the time he's fine, as he does his best to keep away from places that might trigger an attack.'

Christina heard the back door open and slam shut. She looked at Fiona.

'That's Mrs Morrison,' murmured Fiona.

'Alex will make it through, I'm sure,' Christina said, giving Fiona's hand a quick squeeze. 'He just needs time, that's all.'

Fiona pressed Christina's hand. 'It's such a relief to speak to someone about this. I hope you'll forgive me.' She tucked away her handkerchief and got to her feet.

Christina rose too. 'There's nothing to forgive. Thank you for taking me into your confidence.'

Fiona picked up her bag, kissed Christina on the cheek and went out of the door.

Christina heard her speak to Mrs Morrison in the hall, as she began to clear away the remains of lunch. She was desperately sorry for Alex. To be buried alive and, when finally pulled out of the rubble, deemed dead. Every loud explosion, each time he was in a dark place, he must be afraid that he would be buried again. How did anyone even begin to deal with that? The fear and the pain he experienced were beyond her, beyond anyone's, imagination.

She paused, dirty knife in hand. Did she want to get involved with Alex? Such a man would have problems she wasn't capable of dealing with at the moment.

The kitchen door opened and Christina started, almost dropping the knife.

'An' who micht you be?' A short, plump woman entered the room. Keeping her eyes on Christina, she dropped her large bag on the floor and unpinned her hat.

Christina didn't immediately answer as she struggled to translate in her head Mrs Morrison's words. She'd heard Doric spoken when in the village post office with Vanessa, but it took her a moment to work out what was being said.

'I'm Christina Camble,' she said, 'staying here for a little while.'

Mrs Morrison stared at her. 'The master said naething aboot a hoose guest.' She looked Christina up and down.

'It was a late decision, I'm afraid,' she said.

'Hmmm.' Mrs Morrison placed her hat on the peg behind the kitchen door and turned back to Christina. 'Be that as it may, the poor laird works verra hard, an' it canna be easy for him to hae extra bodies aroond needin' to be entertained.'

Christina wondered what reply to give. 'Well, I won't need him to entertain me. I'm really here as an employee and not as a guest that requires special attention.'

Mrs Morrison pulled a flowered overall out of her bag and put it on. 'Ach well, ye should hae said, for I canna be makkin' special dishes every dinner time.' She tightened the belt on her overall.

'I'm happy to eat whatever you normally cook.'

'Ach well, it's nae for me to tell the laird's guests what to eat, but tonicht we've got rabbit pie, so it's tak' it or leave it. My man aye enjoys my rabbit pie an' says I'm famous for it.' She pushed up the sleeves of her blouse.

Christina smiled. 'I've never had rabbit pie, but I'm sure it's delicious. I'd be happy to lend you a hand in the kitchen.'

Mrs Morrison bristled. 'Indeed ye will not! That's my job, an' I canna hae anybody that disna ken what they're doing makkin' a mess in my kitchen.'

Christina felt like she was back at school in front of the headmistress. She opened her mouth to assure Mrs Morrison that she had no intention of making a mess in that or any room, but the housekeeper-cook was in full flow.

'Although the Lord kens I hiv' enough to do anyway, an' noo with an extra body to feed, an' this kitchen is that auld-fashioned an' needs to be modernised. Ach well, I dinna ken how I'm going to manage, I'm sure. It wis all I could do to get roond a'thing afore you came an' noo–'

'I will do my best not to cause you extra work, Mrs Morrison,' Christina said.

Mrs Morrison eyed her coldly. 'Ach well, I dinna ken, I'm sure. I expect I should be grateful the other un's gone for a few days at least. She has gone, hasn't she?'

Christina guessed she meant Helen and nodded. Mrs Morrison turned on her heel and marched out of the room. Christina stood there, looking at the kitchen door after it had been slammed shut, uncertain what to do next.

The telephone in the hall sprang into life and she jumped. When it continued to ring and showed no sign of stopping, Christina walked to the door, opened it and looked down the hallway. When Mrs Morrison didn't reappear, she felt she should answer it.

She lifted the heavy black receiver. 'Hello?'

'Christina! Is Alex there?'

'Vanessa?' Christina frowned. 'Is everything all right?'

'Not really,' she said. 'George's train was due in at one. I was going in the car to collect him, but the twins are under the weather and I didn't want to take them out, so I arranged for the taxi man to meet him at Aberdeen. I had lunch ready for George when Mr Lowe rang from the station and said he wasn't on the train.'

'He must have missed it. He'll be on the next one,' Christina said, keeping her voice calm as she could hear how worried Vanessa sounded.

'Mr Lowe offered to meet the next train at two, so I've asked him to do that. But I can't believe that George would miss the train. He's been ill, as you know, and he's probably tired, but he has all his mental faculties.'

Christina could imagine the horrifying thoughts Vanessa must be having. He'd slipped on the platform before getting on the train at Dundee and been knocked unconscious, or he'd boarded the wrong train and now had no idea where he was, or–

'Try not to worry,' she said. 'It's almost two o'clock, so he should be at Aberdeen soon.'

'I expect you're right,' she said, still sounding tense. 'Can you tell Alex, though? He'll know what to do.'

'Of course, Van. I'll go and look for him now.' Christina put down the phone.

Alex would surely be in for lunch at any moment, but she didn't want to wait. She opened the back door and stepped out into the courtyard. To her relief, he was striding across the gravel on his way to the house.

He saw her face. 'Christina, what's wrong?' he said, hastening towards her.

'It's Vanessa's father-in-law,' she said. 'He hasn't arrived on the train he was supposed to have caught.'

He put out his hand. 'Come back indoors.'

They returned to the house and he dropped his jacket onto a peg in the porch. 'I expect he went to get some lunch and missed it.'

'But he told Vanessa he'd have lunch with her.'

'Perhaps he changed his mind about that. I'm sure he'll be on the next train.'

'That's what I said, but I don't know... She sounded really worried about him and the twins aren't well, either.'

'Would Vanessa like me to go to the station and meet him?' Alex reached for his jacket again.

'She said the taxi man is already there.'

The sound of the vacuum cleaner began upstairs. 'Come through into the small sitting room,' he said, 'where we'll be out of Mrs M's way.'

He led her into a cosy room lined with books. A coal fire burned in the small grate and Tess lay stretched out in front of it on the hearth rug. Christina hadn't seen this room before and she thought it must be where he and Fiona spent their evenings when not entertaining.

Alex gestured to an armchair and she took it. How comforting this man's physical presence was…

The telephone rang.

'Perhaps that's news from Mr Lowe,' Alex said and left the room.

Christina waited, listening to the rise and fall of his voice through the door of the sitting room. When he came back, his face was grim. Christina got to her feet, her heart pounding.

'Vanessa said he wasn't on that train, either. I'll ring up Dundee to see if they know anything.'

'Yes,' she said, feeling helpless.

Alex returned to the hall and she followed him. He spoke to the station master, listened for a moment, thanked the man and replaced the receiver. He turned to her. 'There's no gentleman of his description at the station.'

Her heart thumped painfully. 'What can we do to help?'

'I'll telephone the local police.' Alex picked up the receiver again and gave the number of the police office. 'Fred? It's Alex MacDonald. Yes, fine, thanks. Fred, could you see if you can track down a friend's elderly father who's gone missing in Dundee?'

Christina watched his face as he looked at her while he gave the police officer the details, and saw him blink and glance away.

'What did he say?' she asked, when Alex put down the phone.

'He'll contact the Dundee bobbies, but meanwhile he recommended I call the hospital down there.' Alex's voice was soft, kind.

Christina's stomach churned. 'This is dreadful. I must go to the cottage and sit with Vanessa,' she said, moving towards the door.

'Let me try the hospital first.'

She sank onto the bottom of the stairs and watched as he phoned the hospital in Dundee, shook his head at Christina's unspoken query, and then rang Vanessa to tell her what he'd done.

'Yes, I will,' he said, finishing the conversation. He turned to Christina. 'Vanessa said thank you but it isn't necessary. The boys have fallen asleep at last and it's better they're not disturbed any further. There's nothing else we can do at present. I'll make us a cup of tea.'

His calm authority was soothing. Christina rose from the stairs. 'I'll make it.' She wanted something to do, to try to distract her from the waiting.

She made tea, carried it through to the small sitting room and they sat in silence. There was a *Woman's Journal* lying on a side table and she picked it up and flicked through it, not seeing the pictures or reading the words. When she looked up, Alex was leaning back in his chair, watching her, and he gave a reassuring smile. She felt a desire to touch his face, feel the roughness of his cheek under her palm.

She caught herself and returned to the magazine, aware of his presence. A coal shifted softly in the grate, sending a little shower of sparks up the chimney.

At nearly three o'clock, the phone went again. Alex hastened into the hall to answer it and Christina followed close behind.

She watched his face, searching for clues, as he listened on the phone for a moment.

'That's good,' he said, meeting Christina's eyes. 'Yes, she's here.' He handed the receiver to her and smiled as he did so.

She hurriedly took the phone from him. 'Vanessa?' she said into the receiver.

'Christina, he's arrived.' The relief was clear in Vanessa's voice. 'On his way to the station, he met an old friend who was coming up to Aberdeen and the friend offered him a lift. They stopped at Arbroath for lunch and then the friend brought him here.'

Christina let out her breath. 'Thank goodness.'

'He's apologised no end and I haven't got the heart to scold him. Anyway, he seems to have enjoyed his journey. He's gone for a sleep now. He's worn out, poor thing. Thanks for listening to me when I was so worried and please pass my thanks to Alex for his help. I forgot to say that just now. Could you ask him to let the police know? I'll tell Mr Lowe when he rings again.'

Christina promised to take the boys out when they were feeling better and she put down the phone. She turned to Alex, waiting by her side, and told him what Vanessa had said.

'So all is well,' she concluded. 'Thank you.'

Alex raised an eyebrow. 'What for?'

How strange, she thought, that the puckering of his scar was so attractive. 'Offering to help,' she said. 'Being calm.'

'You were composed yourself.'

'I'm not sure that I really felt it.' She pushed the hair away from her eyes.

His gaze lingered on her for a moment and there was a gentle light in his eyes that she hadn't noticed before. 'I think you are a good person to have around in a crisis,' he said.

She smiled. 'Let's hope there are no more of them.'

He nodded.

Christina was stunned as the realisation hit her. She was in danger of falling in love with Alex MacDonald.

Alex was relieved to be outside again, proud to have been of use. Christina had looked to him for help and that made him feel good, better than he'd felt in a long time. There had been such trust in her eyes that he'd felt his heart lurch and had to look away for fear of what she might read in his gaze. She was playing havoc with his emotions, but somehow he felt more complete in her company than he could remember experiencing since he was a child.

The sun had come out. He kept walking, although he had no idea where he was going. Fiona would be back from school shortly, asking about his day. She was a wonderful sister, but he couldn't face her questions. They were always kindly meant, but probing, worrying if he'd managed to get through without the memory overwhelming him.

'Alex!'

He turned to see Christina. She was clutching her jacket, running along the path towards him. God, but she was beautiful. He waited, trying to read her expression as she drew near.

She slowed and stopped, her voice a little breathless from running. 'I'm so glad I caught you…!' Strands of hair curled at the side of her neck where they'd broken free from her ponytail and she tucked them behind her ears carelessly. 'I thought I'd go to the beach and take some photographs.' He saw that, as well as the jacket, she carried a camera in its case.

'It's a longer walk to the beach from Craiglogie than from Vanessa's,' she said. 'I wondered if there was a bicycle I could borrow?'

He saw a glimmer of uncertainty in her eyes. 'There's one that Fiona uses occasionally. It's old, but the tyres and brakes were fine when I last looked. I'll check them for you, to be certain they're safe.'

She looked grateful and he indicated she should follow him to the barn at the back of the house.

'I'm hoping to find some good compositions for my portfolio,' she said, slipping the camera strap over her shoulder as they walked.

'Of course.' Alex nodded. The sooner he could convince himself that photography was the only reason she'd agreed to stay, the easier it would be. 'What make is your camera?'

'A Rolleiflex. I've not had it long.'

They continued in silence to the barn, the only sound that of a tractor working in a distant field.

They reached the open doors of the building and she drew in a breath. 'This is amazing. So many things.'

Alex looked at the familiar equipment piled onto benches and stacked against the walls. Farming implements and garden tools, coils of rope and wooden chests filled with spare parts for the Land Rover, tins of paint and old flowerpots.

'I'd love to photograph this another day, if that's all right? Perhaps when the sun is at the correct angle to throw long shafts of light.'

'These are all necessary for work on the estate,' he said, staring around the place in surprise. 'They're not pieces of art.'

'Oh, but it is like an artwork! I mean, it looks so appealing.'

'But look at the mess.'

'Think of how Washington Wilson would see its potential. He'd want to photograph it with the light streaming through the skylights, I'm sure.'

Alex ran a hand through his hair. 'I'm sorry. Forgive me.'

'For what?' She turned her head to look at him.

He didn't know what to reply.

She smiled hesitantly. 'I've taken up enough of your time already. Could you just tell me where the bicycle is and I'll get out of your way.'

She could never be in his way.

He nodded, pulled the cycle from behind the lawnmower and wheeled it out to where she stood in the doorway. With his thumb and forefinger, he pressed each tyre in turn. 'They're firm.'

Holding the handlebars, he ran the cycle forwards, pressed both brakes and nodded his satisfaction when the pads met the rims of each wheel and the bicycle came to a sudden halt. The wicker basket mounted on the handlebars squeaked.

'And it has a basket,' she said. 'Somewhere to put my camera.' She laid the camera in the basket and tucked her jacket around it.

'You know where you're going?' he asked.

'Yes, thanks, it's a straight run.'

'I'll let you go, then.' Holding the handlebars out to her, he stepped back.

Christina sat on the saddle and slipped her right foot onto the pedal. He started to walk away.

'Wait!' she called.

The catch in her voice pulled him up short.

'Why don't you come with me? We could continue our lesson on the beach.' She gazed at him with expectant eyes.

Alex's pulse jerked. She had pushed up the sleeves of her jumper. He saw tiny goosebumps springing up on her smooth forearms and he had to resist the impulse to run his hands along them to warm her skin. She leaned towards him and then her hand was on his arm. He looked into her blue eyes and he knew it would be wrong to encourage her. He couldn't allow himself to be drawn in.

'No. I have work to do on the farm.'

'Of course…' She fell silent for a moment and removed her hand. 'I understand.'

No, you don't, he wanted to tell her. You don't know about the nightmares, the panic attacks, the memory of what happened. He couldn't tell her about any of those things. Not if he wanted her to see him as a man.

She shot him a curious glance.

Had he said that aloud?

'Well, then, I suppose we should each get on.' She pushed down on the pedal and moved off.

CHAPTER 8

Christina cycled along the drive and onto the road leading down to the sea. She wanted to visit the stretch of beach she'd been to a few days earlier, the one with the wreck of a boat. Putting all confusing thoughts of Alex from her head, she enjoyed the simple motion of the wheels spinning beneath her, the wind lifting the loose strands of her hair.

At the sound of a horn, she wobbled and almost fell. The Triumph swerved past her, overtaking at speed. It swept on, round a bend in the road and out of sight. Christina was left with her heart racing. She pedalled on, but the pleasure had gone out of the ride.

When she reached the grassy piece of ground which served as the car park, there stood the Triumph, parked with no driver in sight.

Fiona's bicycle had no parking stand, so Christina looked around for a suitable place to rest it. Down near the shoreline was a low building. As she pushed the cycle over the tussocky grass, she saw it was the lifeboat house. Leaning the bicycle against the back wall, she shrugged on her jacket and plucked her camera from the basket.

The tide was in and it almost completely surrounded the upturned wreck on the sand. She looked for the best angle, crouched down and framed the composition, placing the hull in the left-hand corner. A natural triangle. Perfect. Christina adjusted the speed setting and pressed the shutter button.

A short distance away, two young children and their mother strolled on the beach. One of the children held a small red bucket and the three of them looked like shell seekers. Another pleasing image. The mother called to the children to look and they turned towards the sea, Christina's gaze following. A seal, its head bobbing up out of the waves. Delighted, the little family stood and stared at the sleek, black creature with its puppy-dog face.

Christina wound the film on to the next frame and refocused. Keeping the adult out of this picture, she captured the small children, dressed in identical yellow coats, staring at the seal, this time creating an implied triangle.

Now she wanted to add a bit of tension in her images, to make the image dramatic and unsettling. She was keen to use the Dutch tilt, which placed the horizon at an angle. She'd seen *The Third Man* a few years earlier and admired Carol Reed's use of the technique in his film. But there were no tall buildings here, so what could she focus on? A fishing boat came into view, far out at sea, but it could work. She tilted her camera to one side so that the sea and the boat appeared to be listing, and captured the image.

Christina took a few more photographs. Pleased with her afternoon's work, she wandered back to the lifeboat house and bent to retrieve her bicycle.

'Well!'

The intonation in the voice was familiar, but Christina spun round to see a stranger. A tall, sturdy-looking woman, wearing a mackintosh down to her ankles and a brown crocheted hat perched on tightly-curled grey hair, glared at her. 'Don't you know it's dangerous to dawdle along country roads on a bicycle?'

'I beg your pardon?' Christina was still absorbed in the images she'd created and didn't immediately understand what the stranger was talking about.

'You know what I mean,' the woman continued. 'I passed you on the road a while ago.'

So this was the thoughtless driver. She must have walked in the opposite direction to Christina along the beach.

'I wasn't dawdling, merely cycling and enjoying the view,' she said. 'I might have fallen off from your pressing the horn so close behind me.'

'I like to make sure cyclists know I'm there. In case they decide to make a sudden move. *That* would have been dangerous.'

Christina bit her tongue. She was a guest of the laird and his sister, and didn't want to do or say anything that might cause trouble for them in the community. 'Christina Camble.' She stuck out her hand. 'Pleased to meet you,' she added insincerely.

There was a short pause, then the woman said, 'So you're the young person staying at the big house?' She looked Christina up and down. 'You *have* fallen on your feet there. The MacDonalds are such delightful people.'

'Yes.' Christina dropped her hand, but before she could finish what she was saying, the woman began again. 'The laird and his sister do so much locally. Fiona does more for the children than just teach, you know. She nursed Mrs West last winter after the poor old dear had taken a bad tumble on the ice. And the captain is so generous. He paid for all the estate cottages to have electricity installed a couple of years ago.'

'The captain?' said Christina.

'Oh yes,' she said. 'And he was awarded the Distinguished Service Order for exceptional bravery in the war. Didn't you know?'

Christina opened her mouth to speak, but the woman went on, 'The captain and his sister help to organise events, present prizes at the agricultural show, host a party at Craiglogie House every New Year for the ordinary people in the village – where he, the laird, actually waits on them. I do hope that you will be of some help to them during your stay there.'

'I will do my best,' said Christina when the woman paused for breath.

'*Splendid!* But I hope your stay doesn't tax them too much. They need their time and energy for their good works, don't you think?'

Christina couldn't think of a suitable response, so she just nodded. The woman frowned at her one last time and turned away. Christina watched her march to the car and drive off.

She pushed her bicycle onto the rough ground of the car park and climbed onto the saddle. Pedalling off more abruptly than she meant to, she skidded on the loose stones and chastised herself. She knew she shouldn't take any notice of the sour woman, whoever she was, but she found herself worrying about whether or not she should continue to stay with Alex and Fiona. Yet she knew there was still much she could teach the laird, and he could teach her.

'Wearing a long mac? And grumpy?' Fiona said over dinner that evening in the kitchen. 'That'll be Mary Telfer.'

Christina remembered the name. 'The woman you told me about earlier? The one on the dance committee?'

'And on just about every other committee,' said Fiona.

'To be fair, Fiona,' said Alex mildly, 'so are you.'

'Only on the village hall committee. And events related to the school. Oh, and the church…'

'Exactly.' Alex grinned at his sister. 'And I believe you've formed a committee to host a tea party in celebration of the Queen's coronation next month.'

'But every time Mary opens her mouth something unpleasant always manages to come out.'

'And you're all sweetness and light?' There was a glimmer of mischief in Alex's eye.

Fiona laughed and put down her knife and fork. 'Okay, you win, Alex.'

'Naturally,' he said, sending a wink and a smile in Christina's direction, making her pulse jump.

'I know it's not Mary Telfer's fault.' Fiona sounded contrite. 'She's had a hard time. Her husband was killed in the war. They had no children, so she's pretty much on her own now. All she has is her niece, our friend Helen.'

'They're related?' Christina couldn't stop herself. She blushed. 'I thought there was something familiar about the woman's voice.'

'I know *just* what you mean.' Fiona gave a wicked grin.

Christina was confused. 'So Helen lives with her aunt? From the way she spoke, I thought she spent most of her time in London.'

'She lives in London with her father,' said Fiona. 'During the war, when the bombing was really bad down there, he sent Helen to her aunt's house. He felt that she would be safer here, away from the Blitz. She came up in 1940, when she was fourteen. Being the same age as me, she was put in my class and we got on well.'

'Then you've known each other for quite a long time?'

Fiona laughed. 'Not to put too fine a point on it. Yes, thirteen years.'

Christina coloured a little and smiled. 'Sorry. I didn't mean that to sound cheeky.'

Fiona lifted her glass and sipped the water. 'It is a long time, though.'

'And do you see her often?'

'Fairly often,' said Alex. 'She stays with Mary Telfer, but spends a lot of time here.'

Before Christina could decide if Alex was pleased with the situation or not, Fiona caught sight of the mantel clock and rose.

'Goodness, is that the time? Will you excuse me? I have some preparation to do for school tomorrow. Alex, would you be a dear and clear the dishes for me? I'll wash them before I go to bed.'

'I know how to wash dishes without your being there to supervise me,' he said as she laughed and left the room.

'And so do I,' Christina added. 'It's the least I can do.'

'We'll do them together, then.' Alex took a gulp of his tea. 'And if you're keen to muck in, we have eight calves, between two and three weeks old, and a baby bull of two months. Would you like to help with the feeding tomorrow?'

'I'd love to!' she said, setting down her cup.

'Glad to hear that.' He smiled. 'There's a great deal of milk to be handled this month, so an extra pair of hands would be welcome.'

'You want me to milk the cows?' she said, her eyes widening in alarm.

He laughed. 'No. That takes a bit of practice. I was just giving you an idea of the work involved on a dairy farm and I thought it might be something you'd want to photograph one morning. It looks a lot more interesting to me than the storage barn.'

'We'll see about that.' Christina liked the way his spirits seemed lighter when talking about his life on the land. 'But tell me more.'

He threw her a glance. 'Are you sure you want to hear more?'

She smiled. 'Definitely.'

'Okay then,' he said. 'In the mornings, there's the milking to be done and the churns to be filled, labelled and ready for the lorry which collects them at seven. Then there are the dry cows, the two bulls and the yearlings to be fed and watered. And the evening routine is the same.'

'It sounds a lot of work,' she said. 'How many people do you employ on the farm?'

'Ten at present. There's a dairyman and an orra-loon, a tractor man and his orra-loon, and six women who work solely in the dairy.'

'Orra-loons?' She wrinkled her brow. 'What are they?'

'Orra is the Doric for other and loon for boy or man. Joe, my dairyman, and Bert, the tractor man, each have a fellow who works with them as a sort of assistant. The orra-loons can turn their hands to most general farm work. We're a mixed farm – arable as well as dairy.'

Alex leaned back in his chair and stretched out his long legs. 'There's also a gamekeeper, who's employed by us and the tenanted farms. He catches rabbits for the table and disposes of vermin, although the farm cat does a good job with the mice. Of course, there were more farmhands before the war, when my father ran the farm.' He sighed. 'Fewer men are available for the work now.'

'You must miss your father,' she said gently.

'Yes.' He shrugged in a casual way, but she saw a look of pain cross his face. 'He knew it was vitally important to produce food, but he felt bad about not being allowed to fight. It seems ironic somehow that he died of a heart attack in the last few months of the war.'

'I'm sorry.'

'At least he died at home, on his own soil which he loved,' Alex said abruptly. 'And not trying to fathom what he was doing with his leg blown off or his guts hanging out.'

Christina drew in a silent breath. She pictured Alex trying to staunch the bleeding of the men he described. How helpless he must have felt as blood pumped out of them. She tried to imagine the effect that would have on a young man.

She reached out her hand, put it on his and squeezed it gently. His lids flickered, his eyes met hers and in them she saw a host of raw emotion – hurt, guilt, gratitude.

All at once she realised she should, and could, be strong for Alex. What had happened between her and David was nothing compared to what Alex had experienced. Her pride had been damaged, that was all. Whereas Alex's suffering was deep-seated, long-lasting.

Tess nudged her head onto Alex's knee and her large brown eyes looked sorrowfully up at him.

'Ah, Tess, what would I do without you?' said Alex. He ruffled the fur on her head.

'Come on,' Christina said to Alex, 'these dishes won't wash themselves.'

She rose and helped him carry the empty things to the deep sink.

'Tell me more about Home Farm,' she said as he ran the hot water tap. She loved the timbre of his voice when he talked of something he really cared about, the way a lock of dark hair would fall over his forehead.

'What would you like to know?' He swished a glass in the soapy water and set it on the wooden draining board.

She lifted a warm tea towel from the rail at the front of the Aga. 'Well, anything, really. You said you are a mixed farm. What crops do you grow?' She picked up the glass and dried it. She couldn't stop looking at his tanned profile, wondering how his strong arms would feel around her, while she listened to his assured voice as he spoke of the farm.

'Just oats at present.' He submerged another glass in the water. 'And now that winter is over, the snow gone and the ground drying, we need to get the seeds planted. We use land-levellers to make the seedbed, then the combination drill so manure is put on with the seed. The fields are rolled to press the loose soil round the seeds – and that's it until harvest in mid-August.'

'That doesn't sound too onerous–'

It was the work of a moment and she didn't realise what he was doing until a dollop of bubbles landed on her nose. She squealed.

He laughed.

'Mr MacDonald,' she said, wiping the bubbles off her nose, 'I suspect you did that on purpose!'

She was laughing and it suddenly occurred to Alex that he was having fun. She looked sweet with suds on the tip of her nose. He wanted to dab them off tenderly, but before he could do so, she'd brushed the bubbles away with the back of her hand. As she'd protested, he'd caught a glimpse of mischief in her eye.

'I meant that's it concerning the oats,' he said, making his voice stern.

She was gazing at him. Had he suddenly lost the ability to speak coherently? He didn't think so. But he wasn't sure if what was happening between them was real or just his imagination. The laughter they were sharing was making him giddily happy.

He forced himself back into speaking instead of gazing at the angel in front of him.

'There's a lot more work to do on the rest of the farm. It never really stops. In early June, for instance, we start the silage; that's fodder for cattle over the winter. And, of course, all year round there are the animals.'

She nodded. 'Sorry, I didn't mean to be so dismissive, but what can I say in my defence? I'm a city girl.'

'In Surrey?'

'Well, maybe not,' she said. 'But I did move to the city last year to gain more experience as a photographer.'

'So, in fact, being a city girl is a bit of a new thing for you.'

'You've caught me out!'

He could hear the teasing in her voice as he laid a plate on the draining board.

'Is it usual for calves to be born in May?' she said. 'It seems late, from what I remember of them in the fields at home.'

He liked her voice. He'd thought that when he'd found her wandering in the corridor outside the library. Or had it been right from the start, when she'd chastised him for letting Tess wander off?

'This is the north-east of Scotland. Our summer is shorter. I favour late spring calving, from the middle or end of April until the end of July. It makes best use of the grass-growing period.'

'How long do the calves stay with their mothers?' She picked up the plate.

Alex paused and turned to her. 'Are you really interested in all of this?'

'Yes,' she said. 'It's new to me and it's interesting.'

He smiled. 'Milk feed is reduced from ten weeks of age, so the calves are fully weaned aged twelve weeks. But before then, we leave the youngsters with their dams until the fourth day when the calf goes on the bucket.' He put the last soapy dish on the draining board, looked at her and a smile split his face. 'That's the job I have lined up for you tomorrow. Be up and ready to start work early in the morning.'

As she stacked the clean plates on the dresser, he added, 'Oh, and Christina.'

She met his gaze squarely. 'Yes?'

'Dress in the oldest clothes you have. It's a messy job.'

It was barely dawn when Christina wound her hair up in a scarf and crept down the stairs.

'Good morning,' said Alex when she entered the kitchen. He wore a thick, dark jumper, a pair of worn corduroy trousers and a flat cap. There was no sign of the wealthy, tennis-playing member of the landed gentry; he looked every inch the farmer. He smiled at her and she felt a sudden pleasure in being alone with him while others slept.

'You must eat before we work,' he said.

'I'm not sure that I'm hungry yet.'

'You will be, so let's have something.'

He poured out two mugs of tea from the pot on the table, then cut two thick slices of bread and spread them with butter and marmalade. Putting one slice on a plate, he passed it to her. She took a bite and found she was suddenly hungry after all.

'Good.' He nodded, before polishing off his own bread and marmalade.

They went outside, their breath foggy in the cold air. 'You can borrow a pair of Fiona's overalls,' he said as they walked to the feeding shed.

Light flooded out from the shed's open door. Inside, she was greeted by the sweet fragrance of fresh straw and the earthy smell of warm cows.

Alex reached down a pair of blue overalls from a peg. 'Here we are.'

She took them from him and, self-conscious as he watched her, slipped her feet into each leg in turn and pulled the overalls up, shrugging her arms into the sleeves as she did so.

He grinned. 'I think they are a little too long for you.'

Christina looked down at the arms and legs, and smiled. 'I think you're right.' She did up the buttons down the front, then rolled up the long sleeves and legs until they fitted her.

'Next, the socks,' he said.

'I'm already wearing socks.'

'But these are thick ones and you will need them.' He lifted a pair of balled-up chunky-looking socks from a box on the floor. 'Take a seat.' He pointed to a low bale of straw.

She climbed up to perch on the bale.

'Allow me, madam.' He got down on one knee. For an absurd moment, Christina felt like Cinderella. But instead of sliding a glass slipper onto a bare, dainty foot, he pulled the thick woollen socks over the pair she wore.

'Hmm, Fiona has longer feet than you.' He smoothed the socks on, then reached for a pair of Wellington boots and eased her feet into them.

He looked up at her from under his lashes. They were remarkably long for a man, she thought, but really rather nice. His lips were distracting, too.

At once she wanted him to kiss her. Her eyes lingered on his lips.

And suddenly it was not just his mouth she was thinking about, but his whole body, in a rumpled bed. Her heart raced.

'Ready?' he said.

If he knew she'd pictured him naked in bed…

She swallowed and nodded, and forced her thoughts and her gaze onto the various buckets, sacks and containers stored along one wall. There was what looked like a kitchenette in one corner. A kettle had already been filled and it was whistling softly on the gas ring in the corner.

'Let me show you what needs to be done,' said Alex. 'First, you boil the water and mix the milk powder. It has to be presented to the calf exactly right – without lumps, neither too hot nor too cold, and with a proportion of its mother's own milk.'

She watched as Alex rolled up his sleeves, exposing his tanned and muscled forearms, giving her a jolt of pleasure. Taking a silent breath to control the beat of her heart, she turned her concentration to the bucket and saw how he made up a portion of perfectly mixed gruel. They stepped over to the individual pens, where a calf bellowed as they arrived.

'Her first day in the calf pen,' said Alex.

'She's a little beauty. What is she?'

'A Friesian. I've got a herd of twenty-five cows, plus an old bull that services several herds in the area. Angus is getting on a bit, so I've got a baby bull, too.'

Christina gestured to the calf in front of them. 'She looks like a toy cow with her black-and-white-spotted markings.'

'Even small calves are very strong, so take care.' He opened the gate for Christina. 'And you don't want the bucket tipped over, so remember to put it down in a safe place.'

Alex showed her how to manoeuvre the calf into a corner of the pen. 'Hold her gently between your knees. Good. Now dip two fingers into the milk and put them against her lips.'

The calf smelled the milk and sucked Christina's fingers eagerly. 'This is easy,' she said with a proud smile.

He smiled, but said only, 'Do it again.'

She repeated the process.

'Now, carefully lift the bucket with one hand and gently but firmly push the calf's head down into it with the other.'

Christina did so – and the calf plunged her whole face into the milk and came up spluttering. 'Oh, poor thing,' Christina said with dismay.

'Wet your fingers again and as she sucks them draw her head down into the milk.'

This time the calf became so excited that she blew bubbles and splashed, then butted the side of the bucket with her hard little head and upset half the gruel.

Alex looked at Christina and the calf and tried not to laugh. 'You are both in a mess.'

The calf's face was wet and slimy and Christina's borrowed gumboots, knees and arms were soaking. 'It's not funny,' she muttered.

'No,' he agreed. 'Check the milk left in the bucket. What's the temperature like?'

Her heart sank. 'It's almost cold.'

'Have one more attempt,' Alex said, his voice more gentle. 'Second time lucky, for both of you.'

Christina wiped the calf dry with the towel he handed to her and went back to the feeding shed. She mixed up a fresh lot of feed, returned and tried again.

This time it was very different. After a few tries, the calf suddenly got the right idea. Instead of spilling most of the food, she went on sucking at the milk when Christina took her fingers away. In less than a minute, she had drunk the lot. Excited by her success, she stamped her small feet in the straw, shook her tail and banged about in the bottom of the bucket for the last few drops.

Christina was soaking wet, but she had a huge sense of satisfaction.

'Well done,' said Alex, with a slow smile, the dimple appearing in his cheek.

Christina smiled back. He was letting his guard down by degrees and a few degrees could change everything. But was it a good idea, what she felt happening? Fantasising about him was harmless, but she couldn't let herself really like him, couldn't allow herself to get too close. She'd been hurt before and she wouldn't let it happen again. Yet the laughter in his eyes as he watched her made her legs go weak.

'Is this work you normally do?' she said, trying to make her voice sound businesslike. 'I'd imagined that you had little to do with feeding the animals and that one of the men did that work.'

'Why would I not do what I can? It's Eddie's day off – he's one of the orra-loons – so feeding the babies reduces the workload on the others.'

'You know exactly what to do.' She didn't mean to sound surprised.

'I like to think that I am good at my job, Christina.'

Chastened, she bit her lip. 'Yes, I'm sure you are.'

'Really?' He raised an eyebrow. 'Sometimes you've given the impression you believe I am merely privileged.'

'I'm sorry. I can see you are far more than that.'

What was she doing here? This needed to stop. She must get back to what he was hiring her to do. Teach him photography. And she was supposed to be building up a portfolio of work. There could be no space left for anything else, especially this romantic nonsense that was building in her head.

He was staring at her, a puzzled expression on his face.

'I did enjoy feeding the calf,' she said hastily, 'although I'm afraid I wasn't very good at it.'

They left the pen and Alex closed the gate behind her.

'You will find it easier this evening,' he said.

He saw the look on her face and laughed, slid his arm around her shoulders and pulled her in for a hug. Then he swiftly bent and kissed the tip of her nose.

As Christina got ready for dinner in the evening, she thought again about what had happened that morning. It had taken everything she had to listen to his instructions on feeding the calf and not to stare at his sensuous lips. And she'd been very aware of the raw masculinity of his presence.

She'd wanted him to kiss her. Not just a kiss on the nose, but properly. What would it be like to be kissed by Alex?

She'd pictured him in bed with the sheets rumpled and her heart thudded again. There was a strange sensation under her ribs.

Good heavens, what was wrong with her? She was employed to teach Alex photography and that's what she was meant to be doing.

She took a deep breath, trying to clear her mind. How was she going to respond to him when they next met? After all, she couldn't avoid him. The kiss he'd given her was just a friendly one. If he knew what she'd been thinking, she would never be able to look him in the face again.

Christina was no longer sure that she didn't want to get involved with him, but his romantic interest was with the exotic Helen and not with her.

~

Alex was right about the calf-feeding, Christina discovered after dinner. It was a lot easier when she came to do it again in the evening.

'Can I help with the older calves, too?' she asked when the babies had been fed and were sleeping peacefully in the straw.

'Of course,' he said, looking pleased.

He took her over to the group pen and showed her how to hold the bucket over the low door. Even in the dim lighting, she could see his smile. 'Hold tight to the bucket. An extra eager bump could knock it out of your hand.'

Her own lips curved into a smile. 'How could I forget?'

Each youngster in turn swallowed its drink in a very short time. Christina wiped their faces and, following Alex's instructions, gave them a little dish of crushed oats and a small bundle of sweet hay to nibble on.

When she finally finished and lifted her eyes, she was surprised to find him staring at her. Immediately she felt a little breathless and moistened her lips. His eyes rested on her mouth. Her heart pounded against her ribcage. Was he going to kiss her? She couldn't take her eyes from his lips. She had never before anticipated a kiss with such heightened senses. David's kisses had been... disappointing, but she'd assumed it would be better, more exciting, once they were married.

She swallowed, and met Alex's eyes again. Perhaps she was wrong about his interest in Helen.

He kept his serious, dark eyes on her. 'Today has been very pleasant, working with you.'

'I've enjoyed it too.'

'Let me show you the rest of the barn.'

He put his hand on the small of her back and guided her round, standing so close when he stopped to explain something that she was aware of the heat of his body and her legs felt strangely languid.

The tour at an end, they stood at the rail looking at the calves again.

'You have been so careful and patient with the little ones,' he said.

She met his gaze, her face growing warm with pleasure, despite the coolness of the evening.

'I love the way you blush,' he murmured.

She gasped softly as she felt his gentle fingers lift her chin, turn her face towards his and brush a soft kiss on to her lips.

CHAPTER 9

*A*lex didn't know why he'd laid himself bare like that, but all evening he'd been seeing a glimmer in her eyes that felt like an invitation. He was sure of it. When he'd turned her face up to look at him, she'd gasped softly. Then he couldn't stop himself.

Slowly, he lowered his mouth to hers, and as their lips touched, he felt hers soften and rise to meet him. She wanted him, too. A flame burst within him as, gently, he pressed his mouth against hers. And felt her tender response.

He hadn't meant it to happen. He'd allowed himself a taste of that eternal longing and he knew that he could lose himself at any moment. The urge to touch her was overwhelming.

He pulled away, saw her eyes hazy with desire. The sight took his breath away. What was he doing? He had no right to draw this ravishing girl into his troubled life.

Alex straightened and stepped back from her. She looked at him in confusion.

'What's wrong?' she asked, her voice barely above a whisper.

'I never meant to kiss you, but somehow it happened.' He felt the catch in his breath. 'I'm sorry.' He turned away.

He left her there, at the rail, the calves lowing softly, as he strode towards the open door of the barn and out into the darkness beyond.

Christina went down to breakfast, unsure what to expect after last night. How could she carry on working for Alex? She'd come to Scotland to recover from David, but there was no peace for her here, not now, not after… after what happened.

Why had she even responded to his tentative kiss? She had no answer, except that when his eyes locked on hers it made her head spin. The kiss was a surprise, but his walking away was an even bigger surprise.

She entered the kitchen and found Fiona finishing her breakfast. Christina couldn't stop herself glancing at Alex's empty chair.

Fiona saw the look on her face and answered the unspoken question. 'Alex has gone into Aberdeen to pick up Helen from the station,' she said. 'The sleeper was due in shortly after seven.'

Christina helped herself to porridge from the pan on the Aga, keeping her back to Fiona to hide her mixed emotions. She could still feel the way his mouth had caressed hers… see a look of pain in his eyes when he'd stepped away.

'He didn't mention that yesterday, about going into Aberdeen,' she said, managing to sound casual. 'I thought he and I were working in the mornings.' She moved to the table and took a seat.

'He said to say sorry that he'll miss this morning's lesson, but perhaps you could work this afternoon instead.' Fiona pushed aside her empty cereal bowl.

It was the oldest story in the book. The boss behaves as he wishes with his employee. He'd kissed her, then decided he didn't want her. And now, to make it worse, he simply expected her to fit in with any changes to the working day that suited him.

That wasn't fair, she thought. She'd agreed with him her hours would be flexible and it wasn't as if she had something planned for this afternoon. Maybe she should cycle over to Vanessa's. Surely her friend could give her some advice? No, Christina knew she would have to sort matters out on her own.

She ate a spoonful of porridge without tasting it, as her thoughts returned to his kiss and what it meant. The way he'd looked at her, the way his lips had brushed hers, she'd thought she'd felt something real. She would get through this – lose herself in the photographic work and forget everything else.

'Is there anything I can do to help this morning?' she asked Fiona.

'Would you mind doing the washing-up?' said Fiona, glancing at the clock and getting to her feet. 'I'm afraid I'm running late.' She paused, clearly wondering whether or not to speak further, and added, 'I'm afraid Alex had one of his nightmares last night. It woke me up. I hope he didn't disturb you.'

'I didn't hear anything,' she said, 'but my room is quite far from his. I'm sorry–'

Fiona nodded. 'They mainly seem to come when he's stressed.'

Christina frowned. Had the nightmare been brought on by his feeling of guilt in kissing her the night before Helen came back?

She forced a smile onto her face. 'Yes, of course I'll do the dishes.'

'Thanks, Christina.' Fiona headed towards the door. 'Oh, Alex thought you might enjoy a walk in the woods this morning, since you're free. There's a path from the back of the house that will take you there. Must go. See you later.'

'Bye.'

As Fiona went out through the kitchen door, Tess wandered in. She made her way over to where Christina sat and nudged her leg.

Christina laughed. 'You must have heard the magic word. So you'd like to go for a walk?' The dog fixed her deep-brown eyes on Christina and wagged her tail furiously. 'How can I resist such a plea?' she said, fondling the dog's ears.

She walked to the window. The day looked to be fine. Perhaps a walk would help in dealing with her confusion.

She'd finishing cleaning and tidying in the kitchen when the phone rang, and she went into the hall.

'Hello, Christina,' came Vanessa's cheerful voice down the line. 'The twins are so much better. Can you hear them?'

'Yes.' Christina laughed at the sound of boisterous play in the background. 'How is George settling in?'

'Really well, thanks, considering. His illness and the business of the travel here knocked him for six.'

'I'm sure it did. Can I take the boys out soon?'

'It would certainly give me a bit of breathing space. At the moment, though, I think George actually likes having them around. And they're delighted to have him here. I'm sure the novelty will wear off, though! Perhaps you could have the boys when it does?'

The children were darlings, but lively and noisy as three-year-olds tend to be. 'Of course,' said Christina. 'Just let me know when.'

As she ended the call, Tess sighed and Christina looked down to see the dog sitting at her feet, watching her closely. 'You have been very patient,' she said. 'All right, let me get my jacket and camera, then we'll go.'

There was a pale sun but a chill in the air, so she pulled on her jacket and set off at a smart pace to keep warm. Taking the footpath behind the house, she found it soon joined a track leading into the woods. Tess ran ahead, following a scent, hoping to sniff out a rabbit or a squirrel. Beech and silver birch were coming into leaf, mixed with the fir and pine.

As Christina breathed in the soft air, she felt the tension slide from her shoulders. She walked on, enjoying the rhythm of her easy stride. A bird sang sweetly and she tried to remember what it was. A chaffinch? Bright primroses grew in clumps along the side of the path. She could see why Alex loved it here.

Yet he wasn't happy. A sadness for him ran through her. How could he figure so much in her thoughts, this man she'd known for less than a week?

A shaft of hazy sunlight slanted through the trees. She lifted her camera before the light could change. The picture composed to her satisfaction and the shutter pressed, she felt the glow that followed after she captured a shot. Christina wandered further into the woods, absorbed in looking for the next glorious image.

By the time she felt ready to return to Craiglogie, the fine morning had clouded over and she felt chilly. As she hung the camera strap across her shoulder, she looked around. Where exactly was she? She wasn't sure whether to go on in the hope it was a circular walk or to turn back.

A little way ahead the track came to a rough crossroad. Tess turned to the right. Clearly this was a walk she knew well and it probably led back to the house. Sure enough, after another half an hour or so following Tess, Craiglogie House was visible in the distance.

By now the sky was grey and the temperature had dropped. 'Oh dear, Tess, it looks like rain.'

The dog paused to glance at Christina and to wag her tail. Christina smiled, as she remembered that Labradors love getting wet.

At last they joined a path which she recognised as the one they'd taken from the house. She'd walked further than intended and felt tired.

Tess cocked an ear. Then Christina heard it, too – the clip-clop of a horse's hooves.

'Tess, heel,' she called sharply. She should have lifted the lead from its hook in the back porch. It would be dangerous for a dog to go near a horse's hooves. Relief washed over Christina as Tess trotted back to her and sat by her feet.

Christina waited. Round the corner, wearing a dark jumper and a pair of light-coloured jodhpurs, came Alex mounted on a glossy bay.

At the sight of him she felt a familiar thrill in her veins.

'Hello,' he said, as he brought the animal to a halt where she stood.

For a moment Christina's eyes flickered on his thigh as it strained against the fabric of his jodhpurs. She tore her gaze up to his face.

He looked down at her from what seemed a great height. 'I was wondering where you'd got to, so I saddled up and came out to look, just in case you'd twisted an ankle or something.' He smiled down at her, all trace gone of the awkwardness over his leaving her in the barn last night. 'Can I give you a lift back?'

Was he joking? Could two people really sit on a horse or was that just in films? 'Should I sit in front or behind?' she said lightly.

'Whichever you prefer, but you might be more comfortable behind me.'

Oh, he wasn't joking. Christina shook her head. 'Our combined weights might be too much for your horse.' She wasn't heavy, but Alex had such a large, strong body that she feared for the horse. Perhaps, too, she didn't want to sit so close to him...

'I could get down and walk with you,' he said, 'but I can assure you that Autumn will easily manage both of us for the distance to the house.'

A few drops of rain fell on Christina's head.

He glanced at the sky. 'I don't much like the look of those dark clouds.'

More drops splattered and she made up her mind. 'All right, thank you.'

'Put your left foot on mine in the stirrup, use both your hands to clasp my forearm and I'll pull you up.' He reached out his hand. 'Come.'

She curled her fingers around his arm. Even through the

thick sweater, she was aware of his hard muscles. He leaned down and with his other hand gripped her elbow. In a moment he had swung her up and into the saddle behind him. Side-saddle.

'The ground looks a long way down,' she said, clutching the leather seat. 'I don't feel very safe.'

'Put your arms around my waist,' he instructed.

'Surely my legs should be straddled across the horse like yours? I thought side-saddle was for when the passenger was seated in front of the rider.' She knew she was talking to put off the inevitable.

'You've been watching too many films,' he said.

She slid her arms around his body. 'I can't reach all the way around you,' she said.

'It's enough. Now hang on.'

Alex clicked his tongue, turned the horse round and at the sudden movement she clutched his waist more tightly. His body felt warm through her thin woollen jacket.

'Tess,' he called, and they set off back to the house, the dog trotting beside the horse.

'Comfortable?' he asked, over his shoulder.

'No, but thank you for asking.'

The movement of Alex's body on his horse was playing havoc with her senses. She had an urge to hold him even tighter, to snuggle into his broad back…

She cleared her throat. 'I imagine that you ride well.'

I imagine that you ride well. What a ridiculous thing to say. She knew nothing of horses and no doubt he'd been riding for years. 'Did you learn when you were young?'

'Yes. I learned without stirrups or reins. My father wanted to ensure I had a good seat and hands which would not lean on the pony's mouth for support. Is this the first time you've been on a horse?'

'A donkey or two at Brighton,' she said, 'but no, it's not something my parents would have encouraged, even if I'd thought about it. It would have been an expensive hobby.'

Alex's back tensed and immediately Christina wished she hadn't said that. Had he thought she meant to remind him he'd been a fortunate – perhaps even spoiled – little boy?

Searching for another topic, she could only come up with Helen, so reluctantly she said, 'Did Helen have a good journey?'

'Yes. She's tired after the assignment and the travelling, so I took her straight home to her aunt's to rest. She'll join us for tea this afternoon.'

The thought filled Christina with dismay and she knew Helen would be looking forward to it as much she was.

The brief shower of rain had stopped by the time they came out of the trees. As Tess scampered ahead towards the house, Christina lifted her cheek from where it had been resting against Alex's back.

'Slide down here, onto the mounting block,' Alex said, indicating a slab of granite in front of the house. 'I'll take Autumn round to the stables and see to her before I join you.'

Christina slid inelegantly off the horse, stepped down from the block and onto the gravel. As she watched Alex ride elegantly away, she acknowledged that stylish Helen had much more in common than she did with the Laird of Craiglogie.

'Since, after all, no work can be done outside this afternoon,' said Alex, 'I'll show you the studio.'

The rain had returned during lunch, falling so heavily that the lights needed to be switched on indoors.

He led her along a passageway to a small room on the ground floor.

'It's nothing special, but it does the job.' He threw open the door and flicked the switch. 'As you see, big window, lights on stands, large white sheet as a backcloth, stool for sitters and a side table,' he said, standing back for her to enter. 'The floor was already dark and I've painted the walls light grey.'

'It's perfect for portraits,' she said, 'and well-equipped.'

'I told you I was keen.' He smiled. 'Now I must show you how I work in here.'

'I think I can guess. I'm used to portrait photography in a studio as well as taking images outdoors.'

'I mean,' he said, holding her gaze, finding it harder to say than he thought he would, 'I'd like to take your portrait.'

'Oh.' Her eyes flickered with an emotion he couldn't read. 'But first show me some of the portraits you've taken,' she said. 'I've seen those of Helen in the library, but are there any others?'

He let out a silent breath. She hadn't refused. 'Come over here and look.' He crossed to the side table and opened a folder of black-and-white prints.

Alex watched as she turned over each photograph, inspecting his work. She'd pushed up the sleeves of her red sweater and the light caught the sheen of fine blonde hairs on her forearms.

'Here's Fiona,' she said, 'smiling happily into the camera.' She flipped the print over to reveal the next one. 'And Fraser, looking solemn and businesslike in his three-piece suit. Oh, and Mrs Morrison, staring glumly into the lens, dressed in a Sunday-best hat with a fancy pin.' She looked up at him with a smile in her blue eyes and he felt a sudden dryness in his mouth.

With difficulty, he swallowed. 'What do you think of them?'

'Not bad at all.' She turned more pages. 'I don't recognise any of the men, but they have interesting weather-beaten faces, so I guess they are farmhands.' She looked at him. 'You have captured something of the character of each of your sitters. You do have talent, Alex.'

'But I think you'll agree I need more practice.'

'Well, yes.'

'So…?' He quirked an eyebrow.

She laughed. 'All right, show me how you work.'

Alex grinned and pulled the wooden stool from under the side table and placed it in front of the draped white sheet. 'Sit here.'

His camera was already mounted on a tripod. He moved around the room, turning on a couple of the floor lamps and adjusting the angles until he was satisfied.

'It's unnerving,' she said, 'sitting here like this. I'm used to being on the other side of the lens.'

'Then enjoy the experience.' He stood in front of Christina, examining her face. She flushed and looked away.

'No,' he said, 'keep that position. I like that look.'

He moved round to his camera and peered through the lens. 'Can you turn your head slightly to the left? A little more?' He straightened up and a frown creased his brow. 'There's something not quite right.'

'What?'

He pretended to consider her question. 'I know,' he said suddenly. 'It's your hair.'

'My hair?' Involuntarily, her hand went up to her ponytail.

'Yes. Could you let it down?'

The look in her eyes showed that she suspected he'd arranged this.

'No, I don't think I could,' she said, meeting his gaze. 'You will just have to do your best with me as I am.'

'Oh, but that's not the portrait I'm after. Don't you know that it's the artist's job to draw out the character of his sitter?'

She smoothed down her skirt. 'You don't need to tell me my job.'

'Well, then. Humour me. I need the practice, remember?' He gave a slow, mischievous smile and saw a gleam in her eyes.

'I warn you,' she said, 'I shall look very serious.'

Reaching up, she loosened the ivory clip. He watched, hardly daring to breathe, as she shook out her hair and it fell about her shoulders in a delightful tangle.

'I must look a mess.' She went to slip from the stool. 'Let me tidy myself in the bathroom.'

'No,' he said, his voice husky. 'It's perfect. Exactly the look I had been hoping for.'

Christina scowled.

'What is that face about?' He smiled.

She pressed her lips together and he was sure it was to hide a smile of her own. 'I told you,' she said. 'If you want to photograph me, I will look very serious.'

'Did you hear the one about–'

'That's not going to work.' The corners of her lovely mouth twitched.

'Then what if I persuaded Mrs M to lend you her hat?'

She burst into laughter.

'That's it!' He dashed back to the camera and took a quick shot.

'It will be out of focus,' she said, getting her breath back. 'And that will serve you right. What a mean trick.'

'Let's see, shall we?' he said, with a satisfied smile. 'I will take a couple more and let you look as solemn as you wish.'

She assumed a dignified expression. Alex studied her from behind the lens as he worked. His heart surged. She was not like Helen, pushing herself forward, possessive, flirtatious. Christina had a natural charm, an instinctive elegance, and she was kind. She was also gorgeous. It wasn't just her wide blue eyes, or her fair hair and slim figure. It was... She was perfect. His body tightened.

He straightened up behind the camera. 'I'm satisfied with the portraits,' he said. 'Tell me what I need in order to develop and print my own film.'

Christina played with the hair clip in her hand. She thought for a moment, before reeling off a list. 'A large table to work on, a processing tank, chemical solutions for development, stopping and fixing, jugs and scoops to mix the chemicals, a timer. For the printing: photographic paper, clamps for handling the paper, three trays to soak the paper in the various stages of development, enlarger, scissors. A spirit thermometer and an old film to practise on. Oh, and a short line and two clothes pegs. Do you have running water in the darkroom?' She stopped. 'Do you have a darkroom?'

'Not yet, but there's the old pantry which is no longer used, and it has a stone sink with a tap.'

'That should work well. It can easily be converted into a darkroom,' she said. 'We'll have to tape off every possible sliver of daylight that might come in through windows, vents, floorboards and under or around the door, to achieve total blackout.'

He turned his back to her and began to remove the camera from its tripod, pushing away the rising panic in his chest. Just thinking about a pitch-black place, one with absolutely no light… His pulse raced and he forced himself to take a breath to slow it down.

'It's a basement room, so it has no windows and the floor is made of flagstones,' he said after a few moments and was relieved to discover his voice sounded normal. 'There's a vent but it's small and can easily be covered. A curtain across the door could work as a light excluder.'

'Good. You'll need a portiere rod that rises as the door opens. And, of course, a red lamp so that we can see. Photographic papers are sensitive to blue, and blue and green light, but a red-coloured light can be safely used.'

'That's quite a lot.' He shook his head. 'But I do have some of the things on the list.'

'What are they?'

The camera came free of the tripod and, holding it, he looked at her and smiled. 'Clothes pegs and scissors.'

She laughed. 'We can cross those off then.' She slid from the

LINDA TYLER

stool. 'What about the other items – can we buy them in Aberdeen?'

'There's a shop in Bridge Street that I'm sure will have them.'

'What have you been doing for developing and printing so far?'

'I take my films into Lizars, the shop I've just mentioned.' He hesitated, then said, his voice soft, 'Christina?'

She was in the act of clipping up her hair and she paused. 'Yes?'

'Thank you for your help.' He studied her for a moment. 'It means more to me than you know.'

'That's what I'm here for,' she said, tucking up the rest of her hair. 'To help you with your photography.'

She'd misunderstood his meaning, but how could it be otherwise? Thank you for being here, for helping me to forget the unbearable memories, he wanted to say.

Instead, he nodded. 'Tomorrow, I'm going to Perthshire on business. I'll be away for a couple of days, but when I arrive back we'll go into the city for the things I need.'

She frowned. 'I won't be working then? I'll pay for my bed and board while you're away.'

'There's no need,' he said. 'Think of it as a retainer.'

'I can't do that.' She looked upset. 'It doesn't sound like the basis for a professional relationship.'

A professional relationship? Surely she could see it was more than that, thought Alex. It was to him.

She took a step back from him.

'Please,' he said quickly, 'stay as my guest. If it makes you happier, I won't pay you a salary for those two days.'

She nodded and turned away. He squeezed his eyes shut and cursed himself for a fool.

CHAPTER 10

*C*hristina could not stay angry with Alex for long. He had not meant the suggestion of a retainer to be insulting. And she had no right to feel upset that he was going away for a few days.

They were back in the drawing room, the formal room used for entertaining guests. He and Fiona must consider Helen a guest and that thought made Christina's heart lift a little. She had sat with him in the small sitting room, where he felt most at home.

'What have you been up to while I've been away, Alex?' Helen said, breaking off from a detailed account of her modelling work in London. Smiling at him, she curled her long legs under her on the sofa.

'Christina has been teaching me how to take better photographs,' Alex said. 'I believe I've got some good images, but I won't know until the film is developed and printed.'

He turned to Christina and there was the ghost of a smile about his mouth. 'Do you think I'm improving?'

'Yes, but you've got a way to go yet.'

She saw Helen glance from her to Alex with a small frown. Before Helen could pass any comment, Christina stood up.

'Shall I make the tea?'

'Thanks, Christina,' said Fiona. 'Would you like a hand?'

'No, that's fine. I know where everything is now.' Turning to leave the room, Christina caught the glimpse of a scowl on Helen's face.

Relieved to be out of the room, she filled the kettle, set it on the stove and stared out of the window. The rain had stopped and there were puddles in the courtyard. The hens appeared, shaking their feathers and scratching in the gravel.

Christina heard the kitchen door open and she turned.

'Sorry about Helen,' said Alex. 'She can be a bit overpowering at times.'

'This is your house and she is your friend.' Christina shrugged and crossed over to the Aga, took up the silver teapot Fiona had left out and poured a little hot water into it from the kettle. She swished the liquid around in the pot, feeling its warmth on her hands before tipping it out. 'I'm here as an employee.'

'Christina, you know our relationship is more than that.' He pushed his hands into his trouser pockets and looked awkward.

'I don't know what you mean. I'm here to work and I'm happy to do so.'

Had he been flirting with her just now in front of Helen? Surely he had been earlier, in the studio? But she hadn't forgotten what had happened the previous evening in the barn.

'Excuse me, the kettle is coming to the boil.'

He stepped to one side.

'You shouldn't stay here too long,' she said, 'or Helen will wonder what you are doing.'

He frowned. 'What do you mean?'

Christina spooned tea leaves into the warmed pot. Not meeting his gaze, she said, 'You must know that Helen is in love with you.'

'She is not. It's just a front she puts on. We're simply old friends.'

Christina sighed and looked at him. 'I think you'll find Helen takes it more seriously than that. I'm sure she expects one day to marry you.'

He stared down at her. 'Whatever gave you that idea?'

'Let's just say female intuition.'

Alex ran his fingers through his hair. 'She's told me of the various suitors chasing after her in London. I don't know why she spends so much time here, when everything she really wants is down there.'

Christina poured boiling water over the tea, replaced the lid on the pot and took china cups and saucers from the dresser. 'Could you put milk on the tray, please?'

She had to give him something to do, other than stare at her with his dark brows drawn together. It was unnerving. She took the lid off the box of biscuits and arranged a few on a plate.

He picked up the laden tray and carried it along the hallway. She followed him, saw how rigidly he held himself and felt a wave of guilt at upsetting him. Perhaps he really hadn't seen that in Helen.

They entered the drawing room. He set down the tray on the coffee table and began to place cups on saucers.

'Alex, you are quite domesticated!' cried Helen. 'Who would have thought it? Shame on you, Christina,' she added, 'expecting an intelligent, educated man to do the work of a woman.'

Too surprised to say anything, Christina felt herself flush.

'The war has changed many things,' said Alex. 'There's less of a divide now between men and women's work. Look at the jobs women did during the war. They were plumbers and engineers, they drove fire engines and worked behind enemy lines in the resistance.'

Christina shot him a grateful look, but Helen hadn't finished. 'Well, I think a woman's place is in the home.'

'But you have a job, Helen,' said Fiona, pouring the tea.

'I meant *married* women,' said Helen, taking the offered cup from Fiona. 'I won't work once I'm married. I intend to devote myself to my husband.'

She sent a sidelong glance at Alex as he took a seat.

'I'm going to carry on teaching when Stewart and I are married,' said Fiona.

'But not once you have children, surely?' said Helen.

'Well, no…' admitted Fiona.

'There!'

'But once they are at school, I can go back to work.' Fiona sounded a little defensive.

'Women have a much greater choice now,' said Alex, sending a glance of displeasure in Helen's direction.

'What would *you* like your wife to do, Alex?' Helen asked.

'Whatever she chooses to do,' he said flatly.

'Of course, your wife will be lucky in that respect, as she won't *need* to work.'

The room fell silent. The atmosphere was tighter than Christina could stand. She opened her mouth.

'Biscuit, anyone?'

The following morning Christina rose early to take pictures of the rhododendrons' blooms sparkling in the dew. To her dismay she felt restless, unable to concentrate on the photos she took. Sighing, she blew a strand of hair off her face. The sound of Tess barking and a tractor humming in a distant field was distracting. The everyday life of Craiglogie continued, yet it wasn't the same with Alex away.

Why was she thinking about him? She had to stop this sometime, so let it be now, while he was in Perthshire. When he returned, she would be able to face him simply as his employee and nothing more.

A sense of melancholy stole over her as she went back into the house, hoping to find something to do, to occupy her thoughts.

As she pushed open the door, she saw a scrawled note lying by the telephone on the hall table. It was addressed to her in Fiona's handwriting and she snatched it up.

Vanessa rang, she read. *Callum is back home and she hopes that you and she can do something together. Please ring her when you get this. Fiona.*

Christina felt a sense of relief. Now she would be able to talk to Vanessa about the confusion she felt and perhaps her friend could tell her what she should do.

Lifting the receiver, she gave the operator Vanessa's number.

'Christina!' came Vanessa's voice. 'It's lovely to hear you again. Callum got back yesterday, so I thought we could go into Aberdeen today and do some shopping. I invited you for a holiday, but you've been hardly anywhere.'

'I'm free and I'd love to do that.'

'Thank goodness! I need a break from the house and it will be good for Callum to have time to himself with his dad and the twins. All boys together – nightmare! I'll pick you up in about ten minutes.'

The arrangement made, Christina replaced the receiver. She was on her way up the stairs to collect her things when the telephone rang. She ran back down.

'Christina?' said a man's voice at the other end of the line.

'Yes,' she said, unable to keep the surprise out of her reply. She didn't know any men here, apart from Alex, and it didn't sound like him.

'It's Fraser.' He sounded tentative.

'Hello, Fraser.' Christina smiled down the phone. 'I'm afraid that Alex isn't here at present.'

'Yes, I know.' He cleared his throat. 'I was wondering, since you have some free time with Alex away, if you would like to come hillwalking tomorrow afternoon. Nothing too strenuous. Only if you would like to, that is.'

'That's very thoughtful of you. I would like to, yes.'

She heard the smile in his voice as he let her know the arrangements.

She just had time to gather up her kid gloves and bag, and pull on her jacket and beret, when Vanessa drove up in the Morris.

'This is a treat, Van,' said Christina, as she climbed in beside her. 'Much as I love Craiglogie, I'm interested to see the city.'

'Is Alex all right with your having time off?' Vanessa asked.

'He's away on business for a couple of days, so I don't have any work to do.'

'Good,' said Vanessa. She put the car into gear and pulled away from the house. 'Since fuel rationing ended, it's such a treat to be able to drive again.'

Christina settled into the seat. 'Was there much damage done to Aberdeen during the war?'

'Callum says that although London was the most heavily bombed city in Britain, Aberdeen was the most frequently bombed.'

'I didn't know. Why was that?'

'It's close to Norway, which was under German occupation. Aberdeen was the first urban area the Luftwaffe saw when flying in from the North Sea.' She glanced at Christina and smiled. 'But enough of that. We're going to have a super day out. Where would you like to go?'

The only shop Christina had heard of was Lizars, which she would soon be visiting with Alex. What sort of a day would that be? Vanessa was much easier company. Christina didn't have to wonder what her friend was thinking or feel disconcerted under her gaze. 'I don't know the city at all,' she said, 'so you choose.'

'Let's go to Isaac Benzie's. It's a huge department store. I need jumpers for the twins and we can have lunch there.'

A thought struck Christina. 'I'd like to buy a little thank-you present for Fiona, for being so kind to me.'

'Isn't Alex kind to you, too?' Vanessa glanced at her and laughed.

'Of course he is! But you know what I mean. It's Fiona who is doing the most work in looking after me.'

'A woman's work, eh?'

'Don't remind me.' She told Vanessa about yesterday's conversation with Helen.

'You are an ass, darling,' said Vanessa. 'Don't let that ghastly woman upset you. You ought instead to be laughing at her.'

'I do try to,' she said, 'but she's got the knack of saying unpleasant things.'

'Then ignore her.'

Christina laughed. 'You make it sound so easy.'

'It is. The poor thing is after Alex and knows he's not interested, which is making her desperate.'

Christina thought of the provocative poses in Helen's portraits. 'I think Alex might be interested in Helen.'

Vanessa frowned, her eyes on the road ahead. 'What makes you say that?'

'Her portraits in the library. Don't you think for a person to gaze at the photographer like that, there must be some reciprocal attraction?'

'No, I don't,' said Vanessa, her voice firm. 'Look at all those famous film stars. Do they have affairs with the men who take their pictures?'

'I suppose not…'

'I think it's Helen who is doing the chasing,' said Vanessa.

'I'm not so sure. Alex can be very personable sometimes, you know.'

Vanessa gave her a shrewd look. 'Didn't I tell you that?'

Christina felt her face grow warm. This was her opportunity to tell Vanessa of her confused emotions about Alex. She took a breath, her heart thudded – but instead she turned her head as if to look out of the window. What she saw, though, were images of Alex. He'd made her laugh and he could be kind. And there was that kiss, so tender. What was she to make of that?

Her head was in a whirl. She couldn't tell Vanessa, after all. She had to be strong and sort things out for herself.

Vanessa chatted away, about the boys, Callum and her father-in-law, and the time passed quickly.

'Just coming into the city now,' she said.

Christina saw the remains of a bombed-out house, its patterned wallpaper flapping in the breeze. A pigeon flew out of the ruin and into the morning sunlight.

'It's ten years since Aberdeen experienced its worst air raid,' said Vanessa, noticing Christina's gaze. 'In less than an hour, over one hundred bombs fell, killing almost the same number of people. The harbour, hospital, school and homes, more than twelve thousand homes were damaged or destroyed that night.'

Christina shook her head. 'I had no idea.'

'Because of laws that were introduced at the time to protect morale, newspapers weren't able to mention the city by name. And now the war is over, people want to forget.' Vanessa sighed. 'I suppose it's only natural.'

She turned the car into George Street. 'Here we are. I love this department store. I dream of spending whole days here with no children in tow and lots of money.'

Christina smiled. 'I don't think I will ever tire of seeing so many wonderful things available – even if we can't afford them!'

Vanessa parked the car in the street, the doorman ushered them into the building and Christina stared round in awe. The shop was crammed with all sorts of colourful goods, piled up on counters and hanging from the ceiling. They made their way through the departments, as models sashayed around wearing divine frocks for sale.

'Bliss,' said Vanessa, after she'd stopped every model, felt the fabric of their garments and asked questions. 'But back to real life – children's wear.'

The sales assistant was unpacking boxes as they strolled towards her counter. The girl swiftly moved the packaging to one side. 'Can I help?' she asked.

'I'd like to see sweaters for three-year-old boys, please,' said Vanessa.

'These have just come in, madam.' The assistant slid one of the boxes back across the counter and from layers of tissue paper removed little Fair Isle jumpers.

'They're perfect,' said Vanessa. 'I can barely knit and certainly not such intricate patterns.'

'I know what you mean.' The assistant smiled. 'A scarf is about my limit.'

Vanessa discarded each sweater in turn. 'The colours are too pale,' she said. 'They'd be grubby in no time.'

'There are some nice blue ones in the other box,' said the salesgirl, motioning towards the second box she'd been unpacking.

Vanessa nodded. 'I'd like to see those.'

The girl laid them out on the counter.

'Perfect,' said Vanessa, as she examined them. 'I'll take one in blue and one in green if you have it. I need to be sure I can distinguish between the twins,' she added with a chuckle.

'I have younger twin sisters,' said the assistant, 'and my mother always says having twins is a blessing because they entertain each other.'

'Lead each other on to mischief, more like,' said Vanessa, rolling her eyes.

They took their time in the jewellery department. Vanessa lost herself in the diamond section, while Christina made her way to the costume jewellery counter and looked at earrings for Fiona. She bought a pair with tiny stones that almost could have been black opals. They would match Fiona's dark eyes. Eyes as dark as her brother's.

The assistant was counting out Christina's change into the palm of her hand when Vanessa appeared at her side.

'Lunch,' said Vanessa firmly, pulling her towards the lift. 'Restaurant, please,' she said to the attendant when the door slid open and they stepped inside.

On the restaurant floor, the door opened to the sound of 'Stardust' being played on a grand piano by a smartly-dressed young man.

'This is delightful,' Christina said as they were shown to their seats. She and Vanessa removed their hats and gloves, and gave their order to a waitress in a black dress, white frilly apron and matching headpiece.

'I love this one,' Vanessa said with a sigh as the pianist started to play a different tune. '"Tell Me Why". And Eddie is dreamy. I'm such a romantic at heart.' She closed her eyes, sung the opening lines softly and swayed gently in time to the music.

Christina bit her lip. The words of Eddie Fisher's song squeezed her heart. She'd tried to forget, but she still thought of David. He had known he wasn't free from the moment he'd introduced himself, so why had he pursued her so intently? Even going through the farce of giving her an engagement ring. How could she have been so naïve? She sipped from her glass of water self-consciously.

The pianist moved on to 'No Other Love' and Vanessa opened her eyes. 'Christina,' she said, suddenly serious, 'I hope you find true love one day.'

'I'd be very lucky to find a man as good as Callum.'

'You know what I mean!'

'I meant it,' said Christina. 'Callum is a good man.'

'Yes, he is, bless him.' Vanessa smiled. 'And there must be such a man somewhere out there for you.'

Christina laughed. 'Goodness, Van, don't make it sound as if he's quite so far away.'

'Perhaps he's a lot closer than you think,' Vanessa said, giving Christina a sly look. 'What is your type?'

'Oh, I don't know…' Christina looked down at the table setting and repositioned her cutlery a little.

She was saved from having to say more by the arrival of the waitress with their ham salads and boiled potatoes, and a pot of tea for two. As they ate, Christina was relieved that the subject of her love life was forgotten, despite the flow of romantic melodies from the pianist.

'If you don't mind,' said Vanessa as they finished their lunch, 'I should be getting back. It's not fair to leave Callum for too long – good man though he is –with a pair of boisterous three-year-olds and an elderly father. Although George is so much better now, thank goodness. I think the poor fellow just needed a bit of pampering and some company.'

'I've had a wonderful time, Vanessa. Thank you so much.'

'You said Alex is away for a couple of days,' said Vanessa, gathering up her gloves and bag. 'What plans do you have for tomorrow?'

'Fraser rang this morning. He wanted to know if I would like to go hillwalking with him tomorrow.'

Vanessa raised her eyebrows. 'Did he indeed?'

'There's no need to say it like that!' Christina pulled on her beret. 'He's just making sure I'm not bored in Alex's absence.'

'Oh yes.' Vanessa shot an amused look at Christina. 'I'm sure that's what it is.'

CHAPTER 11

*T*he view from the top of Bennachie was spectacular. A patchwork of sun-dappled fields, with tiny farmhouses dotted about and a single car like a child's toy travelling along a distant ribbon of road.

'This view is certainly worth the climb,' said Christina, a little breathless. 'The first part was easy, the track winding through the trees, but then that steep, stony path… and finally having to clamber up large rocks to reach the top…' She blew strands of hair from her face. 'It makes me feel like quite the intrepid climber!'

'I'm glad you're enjoying it, but this is just a hill.' Fraser smiled. 'Only about one and a half thousand feet high. I heard on the wireless that the expedition climbing Everest has reached Camp VI. That's at twenty-three thousand feet. I really hope they make the summit. If you want truly spectacular scenery, Christina, you need to climb a mountain.'

Christina laughed. 'I'll bear that in mind. Have you climbed many?'

'I've bagged some Munros – mountains over three thousand

feet. But as there are two hundred and eighty-two Munros in Scotland, I've got a few to go yet.'

'Which will be your next one?'

'Shall we sit?' Fraser gestured to a slab of rock and she made herself comfortable on the smooth, warm stone.

'I'm hoping to do the Aonach Eagach ridge walk,' he said. 'It's the narrowest ridge walk in the UK and links two Munros. The ridge falls away sharply on both sides to cliffs below, so I won't be doing it on a windy day.'

He gave her a boyish grin and Christina thought again how much she liked him. He was sweet, effortless company.

'The area is filled with raw rocky beauty and tragic history,' he added.

'Tragic history?' She tucked a strand of hair which had come loose from her ponytail in the breeze.

'Yes, at the end of the walk you scramble down into Glencoe.'

Glencoe. She knew the story. To her surprise, he began to sing. He had a good voice, but the song told the tale of the cruel foe that murdered the MacDonalds.

She glanced at Fraser and knew what he was going to say next.

'The Campbells. Your surname is Camble, isn't it? I suppose that must be a derivation of Campbell.'

She sighed. 'I suppose it must be.'

'Some Campbells and MacDonalds still believe in the feud.'

'And is Alex one of those people?' She made her voice sound casual.

Fraser laughed. 'I doubt it. Although he might like to pretend he is.'

Christina felt strangely relieved at Fraser's reply. Turning her attention back to the view, she said, 'He told me the story of the massacre and how the Campbells had betrayed the MacDonalds.'

'It's true that the MacDonalds were massacred by the Campbells, but it wasn't simply a case of betrayal. Would you like to hear the whole story?'

So Alex had told her only part of it? That didn't surprise her. 'Yes,' she said. 'I'd like to know.'

He sent her a pleased look and cleared his throat. 'Well, we have to go back over two hundred and fifty years.'

Christina nodded.

'To the end of 1691 when King William offered a pardon to the Scottish clans whose chiefs would swear the oath of allegiance before the first day of January. As soon as the chief of the MacDonalds received the news, he set out from their lands in Glencoe to ride to Fort William. That's only about sixteen miles,' Fraser added, 'roughly half an hour in a car on today's roads, but you have to imagine what it would have been like for him, a seventy-year-old man, on horseback across wild terrain, heading further north in the depths of winter.'

She drew her arms around herself, sensing the cold of that long-ago journey.

'He arrived on the last day of December. The military governor refused to administer the oath, saying it had to be taken before the civil magistrate in Inverary. MacDonald journeyed on again, a further sixty or so miles, in bitter conditions. There he had to wait three days for the return of the magistrate. By this time, of course, the deadline had passed, but MacDonald swore the oath of allegiance anyway.'

Christina watched Fraser as he talked, his face so intense that he might have been there, in that frozen landscape, all those years ago.

'Four weeks later,' he continued, 'one hundred and twenty men arrived in Glencoe. The Protestant Captain Campbell and his men were offered hospitality by the Catholic MacDonalds and stayed for over a week. Unknown to the MacDonalds, Campbell had orders to put them all to "fire and sword" because the oath had not been sworn before the deadline.

'Without warning, in the middle of the night, Campbell and his troops – very few of whom were Campbells, by the way – fell upon the MacDonalds, burning all the houses and massacring the people. Thirty-eight men, women and children, including the chief himself, were killed. Others fled from the village, but snow was falling heavily and icy winds swept over the mountains, so yet more died from cold and starvation.'

Christina turned to stare across the landscape. Instead of the peaceful fields and cottages far below, bathed in the spring sunshine, she conjured up the picture of a family – more than that, a group of families, a clan – asleep in their own homes, believing they were safe; places of sanctuary and shelter in the harsh winter. Then screaming as the people woke to face their attackers and, as they desperately tried to escape, bloodshed in the houses, outside on the white snow…

Fraser's voice jolted her back to the moment. 'So you see,' he said, 'the two clans may have been religious enemies of old, but Campbell was acting under the orders of the king. As a soldier, he had no choice but to obey.'

Christina frowned. 'Which means that Alex told me only the bits that reflected well on the MacDonalds and badly on the Campbells?'

'It looks like it.' Fraser saw the look on her face and laughed. 'He was teasing you.'

'And I fell for it.' Christina made a rueful face. 'I must admit that finding he is someone who likes to tease has been a surprise to me.'

'The war changed a lot of people.' A glimmer of discomfort coloured Fraser's face, as if he'd said too much. He rose and held out his hand to help Christina to her feet. 'We should probably get back now.'

As the sun's rays sank lower, they made their way back down the hill, not talking but concentrating on their steps. At the bottom, when they reached his Land Rover, he held the door open for her and said, 'Would you like some dinner on the way home? There's a little public house a mile or so along the road.'

'I'd love to, but will they let us in? I'm not dressed for eating out.' She gestured to her pale-peach sweater, woollen slacks and ankle boots.

'Och, they will. And you look very nice,' he said with a smile.

'Then thank you, Fraser. That's very kind of you.'

He beamed as he walked round the front of the vehicle and jumped into the driver's seat. As he drove them along the winding road, Christina thought how much simpler it would be if she had feelings for Fraser, rather than for Alex.

Alex felt the evening sunlight warm his face as the train crossed the vast Montrose Basin. A flock of greylag geese took off from the water, their large grey-and-white bodies rising majestically. Leaning his head back against the seat, he closed his eyes. Every mile that he travelled took him closer to Craiglogie and to Christina.

He'd never meant to kiss her, that night in the barn, but somehow it happened and it had shaken him. It had taken a huge effort of will for him to walk away, but staying had not been possible. It wasn't the right time. It might never be the right time. He couldn't find the words to tell her that he was a mess. That he felt on edge most of the time, not knowing when the next panic attack would grab him, leaving him shaking with fear, his heart thudding. How could he explain to her that he barely slept and when he did, he had the same nightmare?

Then the day after that kiss, he'd behaved like a weak fool. Why had he gone to look for her in the woods? For what? To feel her soft, warm body against his as they rode on his horse? It had been nothing but a torment. And later, when they'd been in his studio, he'd wanted to bury his lips in her hair, feel her face nuzzling into his neck.

Enough of this secrecy, he thought. Tonight he would tell Christina why his mood seemed erratic sometimes. It wasn't – his desire for her was consistent – but she didn't know that.

Tonight he would take her out to dinner. It couldn't be just the two of them, as he'd already made the invitation to his sister and Helen, so he must stand by that.

At the thought of Helen, his brow creased. Did she really believe they would marry? He'd given her no reason to think that. They were simply friends.

As soon as they were back at the house after dinner this evening, when Helen had returned to her aunt's and Fiona had gone to bed, he would tell Christina about his past.

His war experience had tested him to the limit, but he was still standing. He had to be honest and tell her about his panic attacks and the nightmares, before she became aware of them for herself. At least to give her the chance to walk away before anything really started between them. He needed her, he was sure of that, but did she need him? In his mind's eye, Alex saw her lips curl into a smile and her eyes fill with a soft light. He felt a surge of happiness he knew he had no right to feel.

Fraser pulled up outside a pub, its windows already cheerfully lit in the approaching dusk.

'I've eaten here a few times and the food is good,' said Fraser as he helped Christina down from his car. He walked ahead of her, guiding her towards the entrance, and stepped aside to let her go through the door first.

Inside, it was warm and welcoming, with a fire blazing in the hearth. Several people were sitting at the wooden tables and the air smelled of beer and cooking. This wasn't a date, Christina knew, but she hadn't eaten out with a man since David and it felt strange.

Fraser led her to a corner table and pulled out a chair for her. 'What would you like to drink?'

'A lager and lime, please.'

He nodded. 'I won't be a moment.'

Christina looked around the room and saw to her relief that everyone was dressed in casual clothes. She began to relax. This definitely wasn't where a man would bring a date.

'Here we go,' said Fraser, putting two glasses on the table and taking a seat.

The waiter appeared almost immediately. 'Baked ham for two?'

'Is there anything else available?' said Fraser.

The waiter shook his head. 'Just the baked ham tonight.'

Fraser looked at Christina. 'I hope you like baked ham.'

'I do,' she said.

'Then that's what we'll have.'

When the waiter had gone, Fraser caught her eye and laughed. 'I said only that the food was good.'

Christina smiled, thankful for his easy humour.

He settled back in his chair and took a gulp of lager. 'How are you getting on at Craiglogie?'

'Fine, I think,' she said. 'Alex certainly isn't working me too hard.'

'He's like that, is Alex. This is my first job. He's taught me a lot and been patient with it, too,' Fraser said, with a rueful face. 'Once, I ordered seven sacks of layers' pellets for the hens, but the mill read my number seven on the order form as a number one and delivered one sack. Alex gave me a ticking-off and a lesson about the need to write clearly, but he laughed about it afterwards.'

It was interesting to hear about Alex from someone who knew him. Fiona loved him, Christina could see that when the two of them were together, but Fiona was his sister and naturally biased. Fraser was different though. He worked for – and with – the man.

Their food arrived and the evening passed in pleasant conversation. By the time they were coasting down the hill back to Craiglogie, it was late. The porch light was on, but the rest of the house seemed to be in darkness. Fraser stopped the car and pulled on the handbrake.

'I see Helen is here,' he said, nodding at her little red sports car parked close by. 'She must be staying the night.' He gave a small sigh. 'Alex would be lucky to catch a woman like her for his bride.'

Christina's heart sank. Whatever Alex may have said to her a couple of days ago in the kitchen, it was clear others thought of them as a couple.

'You sound fond of Helen, Fraser,' she said hesitantly.

'She's way out of my league.'

Is Alex out of mine? she wondered.

'Thank you for a lovely afternoon and evening,' Christina said, turning to him.

Fraser leaned forward and gave her a peck on the cheek. 'It was my pleasure.' Even in the semi-darkness, she could see his blush.

'Goodnight,' she said and climbed out of the car.

He lifted his hand in a wave and drove away. The main door had been left on the latch and Christina let herself into the house. Not wishing to disturb anyone, she crept towards the kitchen to make a cup of tea.

There was a chink of light under the door. Surprised, she opened it and went in. Helen was seated at the table. She lowered her glass of wine and looked at Christina.

'*There* you are,' she said. 'You missed the most wonderful evening.'

Christina's brows drew together in puzzlement.

'Had you forgotten that Alex was taking me, Fiona and you out to dinner tonight?' said Helen.

Christina's mouth fell open. Alex was to take them out to dinner? She gazed at Helen's silky evening clothes and her make-up even more perfect than usual, and she felt a fool.

'I didn't know.'

Helen wrinkled her brow. 'Really? Are you *sure* Alex didn't tell you?'

'Of course I'm sure.' Christina's voice came out abruptly and a small smile flitted across Helen's face.

'I expect he forgot,' Christina said quickly, feeling the colour rise in her cheeks. All of a sudden she didn't want a cup of tea any longer.

'And now you're upset.' Helen put her head on one side and eyed Christina carefully. 'Nothing wrong between you and Alex, I hope?'

'Of course not. It's just that if I'd known about the dinner engagement, I wouldn't have eaten out with Fraser. Where are Alex and Fiona?' Christina glanced round the kitchen, as if they could be somewhere in the room. 'I'd like to apologise to them.'

'They've gone to their beds. Alex was tired after his journey back from Perthshire and Fiona's not feeling too well. I offered to stay here until you arrived home, just to make sure all was well. Don't worry,' she added soothingly, 'I told them you had probably been having such a splendid time with Fraser that the dinner had slipped your mind.'

'That wasn't the case at all,' Christina blurted out. 'I did have a pleasant evening with Fraser, but I didn't know about the dinner and I wouldn't have hurt Alex's feelings for the world.'

Too late Christina remembered Vanessa's advice not to let Helen upset her. She took a deep, calming breath as Helen looked her up and down.

'That's all right then.' Helen shaped her lips into a smile before draining her glass.

Christina fled from the kitchen and up the stairs, her own words ringing in her head. *I wouldn't have hurt Alex's feelings for the world.*

She was startled by the passion of her reply.

Christina was up early and in the kitchen the next morning, her hands around a cup of tea, waiting for Alex and Fiona to come down to breakfast. She needed to apologise for what must have seemed her shockingly bad manners last night.

Eventually Fiona appeared, bleary-eyed and muffled up in her dressing gown. She yawned and put a hand over her mouth. 'Sorry, Christina. I'm a bit groggy. I think I've got a cold coming.'

'I'm the one who needs to apologise,' said Christina. 'About last night. I honestly didn't know Alex had planned a meal out.' She got to her feet. 'But you poor thing. Sit down and I'll make a fresh pot of tea.'

Fiona sank into a chair while Christina emptied out and refilled the pot.

Fiona sneezed into her handkerchief. 'That's all right, Christina. I know you wouldn't have deliberately stayed away. Alex and I were worried about you. We were almost dead on our feet by the end of the evening, though, so Alex asked Helen if she wouldn't mind staying here a little longer and to bang on his door immediately to wake him if something had happened to you.' She sneezed again. 'Did you have a nice time with Fraser?'

Christina set the pot back on the table and sat down. 'I did.' She looked at Fiona and frowned. 'But I feel so bad about what happened.'

'I don't know what went wrong,' said Fiona. 'Alex phoned here yesterday morning before I left for work. He was looking forward to coming home and wanted to give us a treat. He asked me to let you and Helen know. I rang Helen and told her, and said I'd leave a note on the kitchen table for you.' She blew her nose. 'Anyway, Helen told me she'd pop round later and let you know, and as I was in a rush to leave for school, I'm afraid I left it to her. It's my fault; I should have written the note. She must have forgotten to tell you.'

'Yes.' Christina smiled reassuringly at her. 'You're probably right.' She poured out a cup of tea and slid it across the table. 'Drink this. It should make you feel a bit better.'

'Thanks.' Fiona sipped the hot drink. 'I'm so glad it's Saturday and there's no work today. I think I'll take this back to bed, if you don't mind.'

'Of course I don't mind. Have a rest and I'll bring you up some lunch later.'

'Thanks, Christina.' She gave a watery smile and shuffled out of the kitchen.

Christina pushed up her sleeves and washed her breakfast things, splashing crossly. There was no doubt in her mind that Helen had deliberately cut her out of the evening.

As Alex came down the stairs to breakfast, he reminded himself that he needed to focus on his work and keep his thoughts tightly leashed. It was the only way he could get through the day. He had lain awake last night for some time, before sleeping fitfully, his dark and suffocating nightmare overlaid by the image of her warm eyes and smile.

He should never have allowed himself even to think of caring for her. Although he'd included Fiona and Helen in the dinner invitation, he'd thought only of Christina. He'd believed she had feelings for him, but she had chosen to go for a meal with Fraser instead.

Not that he blamed her. Fraser was a good man, a steady man. She'd already been let down by someone – he had seen that in her eyes – and he couldn't allow that to happen to her again. She needed a strong man to restore her faith, not someone like him.

He took a deep breath and pushed open the kitchen door. She was already there.

'Good morning,' he said.

'Oh, good morning.' Christina turned and stood with the washing-up brush in her hand.

He nodded, took a seat at the table and helped himself to cereal. Finding his lips pressed into a straight line, he tried to relax them.

'Um, about last night,' she said.

'You had a better offer, I believe.' His throat was dry.

'No.' She dropped the brush into the sink. 'I did have dinner with Fraser yesterday evening, but I didn't get your message.'

He shrugged. 'I asked Fiona to let you and Helen know, and Helen certainly received my message.' Good Lord, his voice was surly. He hadn't meant it to come out like that.

Christina chewed her lip. She seemed to be struggling how to reply. He stared at her for a moment, then she broke his gaze and her flush deepened.

'I see,' he said slowly.

'I don't think you do…' Her voice trailed away.

Alex ate his bowl of cereal in silence, watching her tense back as she finished the washing-up.

He pushed away the bowl and poured tea. 'What are your plans for today?' he asked, keeping his tone level.

She put a plate on the draining board. 'I've not done any work for you for the last couple of days and I need to earn my keep.'

His long fingers curled around the mug. She was here only because he was paying her, he knew that, not because she wanted to be. He had no claim on her, so why did that sentence of hers drive a knife into his heart?

'Would you like to take photographs or start setting up your darkroom to develop those you've already taken?' she said, over her shoulder.

'I'd prefer to develop the images I've taken, but we haven't bought the necessary equipment yet.'

'Perhaps that's what we should do this morning, then?'

'That's–' Before he could say anything further, the telephone rang. He put down his mug and went out into the hall. Lifting the receiver, he heard Helen's voice.

'Hello, Helen,' he said.

'Are you free today?' she asked.

'I was planning to go into Aberdeen with Christina to buy a few things I need for the darkroom.'

'A darkroom, Alex?' Her voice was sharp. 'Do you really need one of those?'

'If I want to develop and print my own photographs, apparently I do.'

'Well, can I come with you? I need to do some shopping.'

He knew it was best not to be alone with Christina, so he said with some relief, 'Of course you can come.'

'*Wonderful.* I'll be with you shortly.'

Alex put the phone back on its cradle and returned to the kitchen. Christina had washed the rest of the dishes, emptied the water and was drying her hands. She turned to look at him.

'That was Helen. She's driving over now to come into Aberdeen with us for some shopping.'

Christina nodded. 'I won't be a moment,' she said, stepping towards the door. 'I just need to run upstairs and collect my things.'

As Christina ran a brush through her hair, her emotions stirred. This was the first time she would be out with Alex and she felt a fluttering of butterflies in her stomach. Except that Helen would be with them, for part of the time, anyway. Did Helen really want to go shopping or was that simply an excuse to stick close to Alex?

But they were already close, Christina reminded herself. Helen had made her look bad last night and Christina couldn't say anything against her. She was an old friend of the family. It was natural that Alex would have believed Helen over her.

There was more. Alex had not closed the door when he went into the hall to answer the telephone and she'd heard the relief in his voice when he told Helen that of course she could come with them.

How mistaken she had been to look forward to Alex's return from Perthshire. For she had been looking forward to seeing him again, whatever she'd tried to tell herself. But what had she thought would happen? She dropped her hairbrush onto the dressing table. She'd hurt him last night, and annoyed him this morning with her evasive response, but she couldn't explain and he hadn't really given her a chance to do so.

She snatched up her lipstick and applied a touch of pink to her mouth.

Helen was standing in the hall, looking glamorous in a fur jacket and matching hat, her back to Christina as she made her way downstairs.

'Goodness,' she was saying to Alex with a breathless little laugh, 'you don't give a girl much notice.'

'I'm sorry,' he said. 'It was a spur-of-the-moment decision.'

He looked up as he saw Christina descend the stairs. 'Christina, I'd like to go to Footdee and Old Aberdeen first, and take some photographs there.'

'Those places are a bit far from the shops,' said Helen, her tone petulant.

'General shopping isn't our purpose in going, Helen,' Alex said mildly, 'but I'll be happy to drop you off on Union Street first. I'll start the car,' he said, picking up his keys from the hall table as Christina reached the bottom of the stairs.

As soon as he had gone, Helen turned to Christina. '*So* sorry about that little mix-up yesterday. I could have sworn Fiona said she would leave you a note about the restaurant. We will have to make sure it doesn't happen again, won't we?'

'We will,' said Christina, walking outside.

Leaving the Land Rover's engine idling, Alex climbed out and opened the front passenger door. Helen immediately slipped into the seat. Alex said nothing, but Christina saw a muscle jerk in his cheek. He moved to the rear passenger door and held it open while she slid inside.

She turned to look out of the window and left Helen to chat to Alex. Sunshine bathed the fields of grazing cows and the North Sea glistened in the distance. Soon Helen's voice became nothing but a low murmur, barely heard under the hum of the car, while Christina wondered what the woman would do next.

CHAPTER 12

*W*ith some relief, Alex saw ahead the bridge over the river. A sea fog had sprung up, and it was making visibility poor and Helen's chatter difficult to deal with. 'We're just about to cross the Don, Helen. Would you like me to take you on to Union Street?'

'No, I'll come with you but I'll stay in the car,' said Helen, peering out the window and wrapping her fur jacket around her, 'then I'll go shopping while you buy your equipment.'

'Surely that won't give you long enough?'

'There's nothing I *particularly* need. I'm happy simply to have a quick browse.'

'Isn't quick and browse something of a contradiction?' Alex laughed. 'Never mind, we'll all go to Footdee.'

He glanced at the rear-view mirror. Christina's gaze met his and he looked quickly away, back towards the road. The Land Rover crossed the narrow bridge and turned left onto the broad avenue which ran parallel to the now grey sea.

Christina stared at the pall of fog hanging over the water. 'What a pity a mist has come down.'

'Not so much come down,' said Alex, 'as come in. It's the haar, a sea fog, caused when warm air passes over the cold North Sea. We'll have to be quick. It'll spread to the land soon.'

'It's horrid.' Helen shivered. 'And it's worse when you know that a few miles inland people are basking in sunshine.'

'It's not entirely bad news for a photographer though,' Christina said. 'Depending on what we find when we get to Footdee, the mist should give an opportunity to capture some atmospheric images.'

Alex felt his heart lift a little. He liked Christina's positive attitude.

A cloak of cool air, which smelled of sea and mist, hung over them when they climbed out of the car. Close by, the sea roared.

'The village is this way,' said Alex, his voice low, unwilling to break the strange magic of the setting.

'I will come with you,' said Helen, opening the passenger door. 'It'll be better than just sitting here.'

He was pleased to find the haar was not too dense. A black cat jumped from a low garden wall and stalked across the communal green. Clustered round the grass were tiny, brightly-painted cottages. Marigolds and poppies filled the neat little gardens.

'It's utterly delightful,' said Christina.

'I can see its attraction, I suppose,' said Helen, 'as it must make an interesting picture. But as for living here' – she wrinkled her nose – 'the houses are rather poky.'

'Those,' said Alex, indicating the tiny wooden cottages to Christina, 'were the sheds where fishing nets were once hung to dry. The granite houses behind them are also small, but they would have been luxurious once. The village was laid out in the early 1800s, to rehouse the local fishing community. It was truly forward-thinking. There was a one-house, one-family rule – very different from the overcrowding of fishing families in less prosperous areas.'

Helen wrapped her mink more tightly around herself. 'Hurry up and take your photos, so we can go somewhere nice for lunch.'

'Do you remember the different types of light?' Christina asked Alex. 'Sorry, Helen,' she said, glancing at her, 'but we are here to do a job.'

Alex frowned in mock concentration. 'Morning blue hour, dawn, morning golden hour, evening golden hour, dusk, evening blue hour, night.'

'Very good.' She smiled. 'And the different weather conditions relevant to photography?'

'I believe I do, Miss.' He felt his mouth curve into a smile. 'Misty, sunny, overcast and rain.'

'Full marks.'

She laughed and his heart gave a small flip.

'We're too late for the first three types of light and too early for the last four,' she said, 'but we have mist. Look around and see if anything appeals to you.'

He did so and almost immediately said, 'The end of the village with the lighthouse in the distance.'

She nodded. 'Yes, that's what I would have chosen. The houses in the foreground are well defined with plenty of contrast, while the lighthouse in the background will seem faded by the mist in the air. It will help to create a sense of depth. If you take it from this angle,' she added, 'the parallel lines of the estuary will give the impression that they meet at a watery infinity, the North Sea.'

Under Christina's guidance, Alex took a few photographs, including the fronts of some of the pretty little cottages, while Helen sighed loudly.

'Right,' he said eventually, 'let's move on to Old Aberdeen.'

'Drop me as close as you can to the city centre,' said Helen in a miserable voice. 'I've had enough.'

They returned to the car, left the fishing village behind and drove past a busy shipyard, timber yard and railway goods depot.

'These would all make good images for photographs,' Christina said and Alex smiled at the enthusiasm in her voice.

'Not now!' cried Helen.

'I meant for another day,' Christina said.

The Land Rover emerged onto the road leading into the city centre. 'Here okay?' said Alex to Helen, slowing down.

'Look, there's a taxi dropping someone off. Catch him for me,' she said. Alex pulled over and jumped out. 'Tell him Esslemont and Macintosh!' she called after him.

Alex gave the instruction to the driver and handed money through the open window. He returned to help Helen out of the car and she gave him a charming smile. 'I'll see you in the Athenaeum for lunch at one o'clock.'

Alex offered his arm to Christina as they walked through Old Aberdeen. It was a simple courtesy, nothing more, she told herself. She felt the hard strength of his muscles as her fingers closed around his arm.

Perhaps he'd heard the catch in her breath, or maybe she'd inadvertently squeezed his biceps, because he caught her in an enquiring gaze. She smiled quickly and looked down, pretending to be watching her feet on the cobbles of the High Street, as the stones glistened in the damp air.

They strolled along the Chanonry to the kirkyard of St Machar's Cathedral, deserted except for the two of them. A watery sun penetrated the mist to sparkle on the grey head-stones. Alex took photographs of King's College with mist wreathing round the trees, as small groups of students moved from one lecture to another, their sounds muted in the haar.

'We should move on,' said Alex, looking at her softly, a flicker of something in his eyes.

Maybe he could sense it too, the strangeness, she thought.

'Yes, it can't be far off one o'clock.' She smiled. 'It's been an interesting morning. Thank you.'

He stood looking at her. For a long moment he made no move

to go anywhere and neither did she, until they heard the old clock chime the hour.

The damp pervaded Union Street as Christina and Alex hurried along arm in arm, with their coats tight round them and their hats lowered. Lights shone in the restaurant through the steamed-up window. As they entered, Helen looked up from the table with barely-concealed impatience.

'Sorry we're a little late,' said Alex, bending to kiss her cheek.

'Did you enjoy your shopping?' Christina asked, determined to be civil, as she took a seat opposite. Alex waved over a waiter.

'Rather a waste of time,' Helen said. 'There wasn't really anything that took my fancy.'

Christina let the pause lie between them, before asking, 'You're not interested in photography at all?'

'Not unless the pictures have been taken by Alex. He's actually rather good. I don't know why he felt the need for instruction from you. You should see the portraits he's taken of me.' Helen smirked and sipped her gin and tonic.

'I have,' said Christina.

'Oh.' She put down her glass. 'Where did you see them?'

'In the library.'

She frowned. 'You've been in there? Alex, I thought that room was private. Alex!'

He turned from conferring with the waiter, raised his brows in enquiry and Helen repeated her question.

'Fiona suggested that Christina look at the collection, which was fine with me.' He turned back to the waiter.

When they had placed their orders, Helen said, 'Alex, how did those photographs turn out, the ones you took when we were in Perthshire?'

Christina was stunned. Helen had been there with Alex?

'The film hasn't been processed yet,' he said. 'I have it with me to take into Lizars. They'll post the prints back to me in about a week. After this film, though, I'm looking forward to Christina showing me how to do the developing and printing myself.'

She was relieved when their omelettes arrived and for a while conversation could be dispensed with. But Alex was quiet over coffee and eventually Helen stopped talking. What a desultory little group we are, thought Christina as they made their way to the photographic supplies shop. What had happened to the happiness she'd felt, and was sure Alex had shared, not so long ago?

Christina looked up as Alex entered the kitchen. 'Good morning.'

'Good morning.' He poured himself tea from the pot on the table. 'Fiona is only a little better this morning, so she's going to stay in bed.'

'I'm sorry to hear that,' said Christina, getting to her feet. 'Shall I take her up a cup of tea?'

'I have already, thanks.' His eyes searched her face and then he seemed to make up his mind. 'Would you like to come to church with me this morning? Only if you want to, that is. The laird is expected to attend, but you need not.'

She smiled warmly. 'No, I'd like to.' His eyes softened and she fought the urge to reach out and touch his hand.

He nodded. 'We can walk there, if you're happy with that?'

Christina looked out the window. The sun shone in a pearly-blue sky. 'Yes,' she said. 'It's a lovely day.'

When they met again at the agreed time, Alex was dressed in the dark suit he had worn on the evening of the dinner party. Her pulse beat a little faster. He looked as handsome now as he had then. She had put on her pale-yellow cotton dress and hoped she looked presentable. Alex seemed to think so, judging by the look he gave her.

They strolled through the kirkyard as the ten-minute bell began to toll. Alex exchanged brief greetings with others in front of the church and Christina saw their curious glances at her. Some minutes before the clock struck the hour, he slid his hand under her elbow and they passed under the porch, through the entrance where the heavy oak door stood ajar and into the church.

Inside, the little building shone with polished wood, gleaming brass and a large arrangement of pink astrantia. At the organ, a woman wearing a black beret was swaying back and forwards, hands and feet in action on the keys and pedals.

Alex led Christina to a pew at the front of the church and discreetly gestured to a brass plaque engraved with his family name.

'This is the MacDonald's,' he murmured, ushering her in.

'You have your own pew?' she whispered, sliding onto the wooden bench.

'It's a tradition.' He sat next to her.

Christina leaned towards him. 'Is that Mrs Telfer on the organ?'

'Yes.' He smiled. 'She's very good.'

The minister entered, Mrs Telfer stopped playing and the congregation rose noisily to its feet.

'We will begin the service today,' said the minister, 'with the hymn, "Father, hear the prayer we offer".'

Alex's voice was a pleasing baritone and Christina sang happily beside him. The voices of the congregation and the small choir soared to the vaulted roof of the church. From somewhere behind her she heard the sweet, high voices of Vanessa's twins.

Out of the corner of her eye, she noticed Helen in a pew on the other side of the nave. When the hymn came to an end, Christina glanced over. Helen turned her head and, although

Helen wore a black toque with a spotted veil which covered her eyes, Christina knew she was being scowled at.

The minister cleared his throat to lead them in prayer and she turned back towards the altar. She concentrated on the service, refusing to let Helen distract or dismay her.

After the service they made their way out of the church. Alex introduced her to Reverend Greig, who was standing by the door and shaking hands as the congregation filed out.

'This is my house guest, Miss Camble,' Alex said, taking her arm and smiling down at her.

'Pleased to meet you, Miss Camble. It's good to meet a friend of Alex's.'

Alex led her outside and onto the path, where he bid others good morning. He introduced her and she watched him shaking hands and chatting easily, and could see he was liked by everyone they met. As they moved on, Christina's eye caught Helen standing alone, dressed in her mink jacket and wearing the little hat with its veil.

'There's Helen,' she said.

Alex looked up. Helen waved and strolled over.

'Hello, Alex.' She smiled at him. 'Christina.' She turned back to Alex. 'Do you like my new hat? I bought it when I was in London – in Lock's, St James's Street. It cost the earth, but I think it was worth it.'

'Very smart,' said Alex.

Christina saw Vanessa and her family talking to some friends a little distance away.

'Aunty Chrissie, Uncle Alex!' The twins spotted them and came skipping over, their sandy-coloured hair unnaturally tidy.

Helen smiled at Alex and drifted away.

'Hello, boys.' Christina crouched down to them. 'How are you both today?'

'Very well, thank you,' they chanted.

'Do you know our favourite hymn?' asked Nicholas.

'No, what is it?'

'It's the one about the otter.'

'Otter?' She couldn't think what he meant.

'You know.' Nicholas frowned at her.

'*Father, hear the prairie otter,*' sang William, his voice high and innocent.

Christina glanced up at Alex and his face twitched with laughter. She rose and managed to subdue him with a glare, made the more ferocious because she was on the verge of giggles herself. The twins ran back down the path and she turned to him.

'Oh dear,' she said.

'I remember when we were little, my sister and I thought the second verse of "Away in a Manger" began with, *The kettle is boiling.*'

They were still laughing when Vanessa wandered over. 'What's so funny?'

'Your boys,' said Christina, and told her.

'I need to have a word with them.' Vanessa smiled.

'Please don't!' said Alex. 'They're the best comedians around here.'

Christina remembered her earlier offer. 'Would you like me to take them out, Van – perhaps tomorrow afternoon?' She glanced at Alex. 'That's if you don't need me then?'

'Would you mind if I came, too?' he said.

Vanessa stared at him. 'Really? Are you sure about that?'

'Why not? I'm very fond of them.'

'I know you are. And they are fond of you. But they can be hard work.' She smiled, barely able to keep a look of hope from her face. 'Although with the two of you it should be easier. They rarely have a nap after lunch these days, so perhaps you could pick them up about two o'clock?'

When Christina and Alex returned to the house, he told her he wanted to check on a heifer that was due to calve.

'Joe, my dairyman, doesn't need me. In fact, he'd probably be happier if I played the haughty laird and stayed away, but I want to see her progress for myself.' He excused himself and went away to change his clothes.

He hadn't appeared by midday, so Christina took Fiona's lunch up to her in bed. Fiona was propped against the pillow and she looked up from the previous day's *Press and Journal* as Christina entered the room.

'I'm pleased to see you looking a lot better,' said Christina.

'I feel it.' Fiona smiled, setting aside the newspaper. She took the tray from Christina and settled it on her lap. 'Stay and talk to me for a while.'

Christina perched on the edge of the bed. 'What would you like to talk about?'

'Anything! I'm not very good without company.'

'Well, then…' Helen came at once to her mind. 'Tell me about Helen,' she said.

'Helen?' Fiona looked up from cutting into the beans on toast. 'Why?'

Christina coloured a little. 'Only that you mentioned her father and her aunt earlier, but said nothing about her mother.' Her hand flew to her mouth. 'I'm sorry, it's none of my business.'

'Oh, don't worry,' said Fiona. 'It's common knowledge around here and old history. Helen's mother left her husband and the young Helen years ago. Went off with another man. Rather a sad story.' She swallowed a mouthful of beans on toast.

'Helen seems to like spending time here,' she said carefully.

'I did think once that she and Alex might become engaged, but…' Fiona sighed. 'Poor Helen. She seems to have a couple of men friends in London, but nothing has come of them. And for all her talk, her modelling jobs are drying up.' Fiona lifted the mug from the tray and sipped her tea. 'Anyway, I don't believe she loves Alex or that he loves her.'

Fiona placed the mug on her bedside cabinet. 'Your being here is good for him,' she said with a smile. 'I can see Alex is happier since you came.'

Flustered, Christina rose. 'I'll let you finish your lunch.'

She went down the stairs and slipped outside, telling herself it was purely to see how the heifer was getting on and not to escape Fiona's observant eye.

Alex is happier since you came. Fiona's words echoed in her head as she crossed the yard and entered the shed.

Alex smiled as she walked towards him. 'She's had her baby. It was an easy birth, but you'd better not come inside the box. As it's her first, she may be a bit wild.'

Christina leaned over the half-door and watched as the heifer continued to lick her wet staggering baby with her long, rough tongue. Then, at last, with her nose she pushed the calf towards her udders.

'Good girl!' said Alex, as the little calf began to suck. 'I'll give mum a bran mash in about half an hour.'

'I'll make it now, so it will be cool enough,' said Christina.

As she turned towards the feeding shed, she heard Alex say again, 'Good girl.' She glanced back to see him looking at her and he winked.

Christina spent the afternoon carrying hot drinks up to Fiona, chatting with her when she wanted company and preparing the evening meal when she slept.

About half past five, Alex appeared in the kitchen. 'Joe wasn't feeling well, so I sent him home and helped Eddie with the rest of the jobs,' he said.

Christina closed the door of the Aga and straightened up. 'The rest of the jobs?'

'Yes, washing down the concrete floor of the shed and the dairy. Feeding and watering the old bull and the young one, and the calves and the new mum. Giving new bedding where it was needed.'

He looked pleased with jobs well done, but she could also see he was very tired. She lifted the kettle from the hob and poured boiling water over the leaves in the warmed pot. 'I've lit the fire in the little sitting room, so we can have tea there.'

'Thank you, Christina.' Alex looked about the kitchen, at the saucepans simmering on the Aga. He sighed and ran a hand through his hair. 'Not just for the tea, but for all of this.'

'Go and sit down,' said Christina. 'I'll be through in a minute.'

When she entered the little sitting room, tea tray in her hands, he was slumped in the large armchair, his long legs stretched out in front of him. He'd switched on the side lamps and Tess had already taken up her favourite position in front of the fire. Alex's face was flushed with heat and exhaustion, and his hair clung to his temples.

She poured out a cup of tea and handed it to him. 'You should have asked me to help you. I can do more than just take photographs, you know.'

Alex smiled. 'I know.'

She took the chair opposite him in front of the fire. As she looked at him in the light of the flickering flames, she realised how much her feelings for him had grown.

For the first time she saw him looking exhausted and vulnerable. She remembered how he had told her, that night of the dinner party, he liked to keep himself busy on the farm. How it had made him sound as if he treated the place as a hobby, something to occupy his otherwise empty time. But that wasn't the situation at all. Alex was more than simply a disinterested landowner. He was a man who cared deeply about his estate and the farm.

'Actually,' Christina said in a teasing voice, 'you were lucky to get me. Not only have you got a tutor in photography, but also a willing pair of hands on the farm...'

'I'd be a fortunate man indeed if I truly had you.' Alex smiled at her, leaned forward and held out his hand.

She caught her breath and, in that moment, saw that his words and action seem to have taken him by surprise too, for a flush crossed his cheeks. She wanted to go to him; against her better judgement, she wanted to go to him. Before she was even aware of what she was doing, she knelt by his chair, took his hand and pressed it lightly against her cheek.

The door opened and Fiona appeared, dressed and smiling.

'Fiona.' Christina started up. 'You're looking much better, but are you sure you should be up?'

'Yes, honestly, I am feeling better.' She dropped onto a footstool by the fire. 'Just one of those forty-eight-hour things.'

'Have my seat,' Christina said to her. 'I need to check on the dinner. I've made shepherd's pie. It's not exactly a Sunday roast, but I hope it's okay.'

'It's more than okay,' said Fiona, brightening even more. 'I'm very glad I don't have to cook this evening. And by tomorrow I'll be right as rain.' She looked at the two of them. 'Am I interrupting anything?'

'Yes,' said Alex with a smile.

CHAPTER 13

*A*lex folded his arms and looked round his new darkroom. It was Monday morning and everything Christina had recommended was now in place.

He had just removed the film from his camera when a knock on the door brought a familiar tingling in his body. He moved towards it, but she'd opened the door and was standing there. At the sight of her, he felt a rush of heat.

'You've done a good job,' Christina said, her gaze travelling across the equipment they'd bought in Aberdeen and Alex's modifications to the room.

He took a step towards her and motioned to the table. 'I've taken the film from the camera.'

She smiled. 'Good.' She came into the room.

Alex returned the smile. 'I'm keen to get started.' He glanced in the direction of the table, so she wouldn't see the uncertainty in his eyes.

'First we need to practise with the old film.'

'It's here,' he said, lifting it from the table. He felt the warmth of her fingers and she took it from him.

'First we need to take the film from its container and wind it onto the spool.' She crossed the room and picked up the spool. 'It sounds easy, but it has to be done in complete darkness, which makes it the most difficult part of the process. I'll talk you through it in the light first and then you can have a go.'

Alex nodded.

'We have to slide the film from its container,' she said. 'Now, taking care to hold the film only by its edges, it has to be fed onto the spool.'

She stopped speaking as she got the film into position and wound it round the spool. 'This holds the film in a spiral shape, with a space between each loop so the chemicals can flow across the film's surface.' He watched her small, capable hands as she moved through the actions. She tore off the plastic spindle taped to the film.

'Now we place the spool in the small processing tank and close the lid.' She turned to him. 'That's it. Your turn.'

He followed the procedure Christina had shown him, while she observed his movements closely. As he loaded the film in the spiral position, he fumbled a little.

'Take care,' she said, her hand briefly touching his. 'If that's not done properly, the film will stick together and the chemicals won't be able to reach those parts.'

He finished the work with a sigh of relief and looked at her. 'Was that okay?'

'Do it once more.'

Again she watched him and this time he completed the procedure smoothly.

'Much better,' she said. 'Are you ready to try it with the real film in the dark?'

Alex nodded. He wanted to develop his own photographs and he needed to overcome his fear. This small, dark space was perfectly safe. It couldn't harm him.

Christina switched on the floor-standing lamp by the table and asked him to turn off the overhead light.

As they stood side by side, she held his gaze. 'Ready?'

He took a steadying breath. 'Yes.'

She switched off the remaining light.

They were in total darkness. A wave of panic, of nausea, flooded over him. His breath came in shallow, silent gasps. *Slow your breathing*, he repeated to himself. *In through the nose, out through the mouth*. Concentrate.

His hands were wet with perspiration. White sparks danced wildly in his vision. There flashed in his mind the vivid memory of bullets flying past his head, shrapnel exploding about him, the dark quiet of the grave…

Alex wrenched himself out of his thoughts. *Pull yourself together, man*. He clenched his hands, grateful she couldn't see his reaction, although his body shook a little as he forced his thoughts to the present. He became aware of how close she was to him. It gave him comfort that he was not alone in the darkness.

'Okay?' came her voice, soft in the black void.

He cleared his throat. 'Yes.'

There was a pause. 'We'll do it together,' he heard her say through the dark mist swirling in front of his eyes. 'Put your hand lightly on mine; feel what I am doing.'

He did so and felt her slide the film from its container.

'Now we have to carefully feed it onto the spool.'

He sensed her movements as, purely by touch, she wound it round the spool.

'Give me your hand,' she said.

He wiped his sweating hands on his trousers, before her hand took his and guided his fingers onto the spool, so he could feel what she had done. 'All right?'

The warmth of her fingers on his skin seeped into him.

'Don't worry,' she said, 'it will be easier next time.'

His pulse raced in the darkness, but he heard the smile in her voice and found himself saying, 'Like feeding calves?'

'Yes.' She gave a soft laugh. 'We place the spool in the tank and close the lid.' Again, she guided his hand. 'Now it's safe to turn on the light.'

Alex felt for the switch on the floor lamp and a pool of light flicked over them. He could still sense the warmth of her fingers on his. With difficulty, he swallowed.

'It's easier now we can see,' Christina said. She sent him a gentle smile. 'The rest is often a case of trial and error, but we'll use the procedure I favour.' She picked up the first solution. 'You mixed the developer as I said, with one part chemical, one part warm water to keep the mixture at sixty-eight degrees?'

'Yes.' He felt the colour returning to his face.

She nodded. 'It's a mild alkaline. Now we pour it into the funnel in the lid of the processing tank and then agitate. We don't want to risk any air bubbles forming on the surface of the film.'

She tipped the little stainless steel tank backwards and forwards. 'Can you set the timer, please? This has to be done for ten seconds every minute for six minutes. Different temperatures and different makes of film require different timings, so we'll see how it goes. Here,' she said, handing him the tank. 'You have a go.'

His pulse had returned to normal. He raised his eyebrows and grinned. 'Luckily, I'm good at playing the maracas,' he said.

She laughed. 'Take care not to shake the tank vigorously. When the time is up, remove the lid, tip out the solution and pour in the next one. You need to agitate that for ten seconds.'

Alex did as she instructed. There was a faint vinegar-like smell as he poured in the stop solution.

He glanced at her sideways. She tucked a stray lock of hair behind her ear as she concentrated on watching the time.

'Now pour out the stop and add the fix,' she said. 'This one needs to be agitated occasionally for five minutes.' She reset the timer. 'The stop and the fix can be reused, but take care to pour them back into the same jugs.'

Alex studied her for a moment. He loved seeing her so

immersed in something she cared about. 'What made you interested in photography? Was it your father?'

'To an extent, yes,' she said. 'It was a job he'd loved, although less so during the war.' She took a breath. 'It was ironic that he was killed not while working, but when he was in London and a bomb fell in Victoria Street. It gouged a wide crater and brought down shops.'

Almost without his knowing, his hand touched her arm. 'I'm sorry.'

Christina took a breath. 'Thank you. It was more than my dad's influence though. I think it was seeing the posters outside the Odeon when I was young. The stars looked so glamorous. I knew that I couldn't possibly look like those women, but I thought that perhaps I could produce dazzling portraits of people. As I grew older, I also wanted to recreate the wonderful images, landscapes and so on, I saw on the screen.'

Alex thought she was wrong. She was as stunning as the film stars she'd seen on the posters. Perhaps she knew what he was thinking, because she stepped back.

'Don't forget to agitate,' she said with a frown.

He returned to his task. Neither spoke again until the timer sounded.

'Now you need to lift the spool from the processing tank and agitate it occasionally in slowly running water for at least ten minutes.'

'So much agitation.' He sighed in a melodramatic way and saw a smile form on Christina's lips. He needed to get his thoughts and feelings into perspective. They had a good working relationship, which was what he wanted.

He crossed the room to the deep sink in the corner and turned on the single tap.

'While you are doing that,' she said, picking up the piece of cord and the clothes pegs from the table, 'I'll erect the line we will need to hang the film.'

'You can use the large hooks embedded in the ceiling,' he said, gesturing to them. 'This was the game pantry, where birds and rabbits used to be hung to develop the meat's flavour. The game-keeper deals with all that now.'

'Have you any stepladders?' she asked.

'Yes, in the cupboard in the basement hall.' He glanced up from the running water. 'I'll get them when I've finished this.'

'It's all right, I'll do it.' She let herself out of the room and he heard her open the door to the cupboard and a clattering as she hauled out the wooden ladders.

'Found them?' said Alex as she returned.

'Amongst a lot of other things,' she said with a laugh.

He smiled. 'That's one of the problems – and pleasures – of large, old houses. Nothing is ever thrown away.'

'Definitely pleasures. When my father died, my mother had to sell the house and we moved into the small flat in Kingston. So many treasured objects had to be discarded.'

She pulled the stepladders into position under one of the hooks and climbed up. Tying a loop in one end of the line, she slipped it over the hook, then moved the steps to repeat the process with the next hook, making sure the line would hang low enough that she could reach it from the floor.

'Leave the ladders. I'll put them back in the cupboard later,' said Alex, as she climbed down. The timer sounded again. He silenced it and turned off the tap.

'We've almost finished,' she said. 'We need to remove the film from the spool by pulling gently on the free end. The whole length of the film will run out of the spool as it rotates. Like so.' She held up the wet roll of film. 'Now we have the negatives. I just need to give the reel a shake and it can be hung up to dry.'

Alex watched as she took one of the wooden clothes pegs from the table, clipped the top end of the film to the line and clipped another peg at the bottom to ensure it hung straight. 'You should put a tray on the floor underneath to catch drips,' she added. 'Then all you have to do is wash and dry the equipment. I can show you how to print the negatives when you are ready.'

'Thank you, Christina. I appreciate all you've done.'

'Well, we still need to see how they've turned out. It depends on the water temperature, timings and agitation.' She smiled. 'I've enjoyed the session.'

He studied her for a moment. 'I want to thank you properly for all your help. I'd like to take you to Edinburgh for the day. It would involve an early start, but we should be able to capture some interesting images and we can have dinner on the train coming home.'

'Edinburgh? I've never been. I'd love to see it.'

'Shall we say in a couple of days' time – on Wednesday?'

'That would be fine with me. After all, I work for you.'

He frowned. There it was again, her reminder that theirs was nothing other than a work relationship. But that was what he wanted, of course. And that was why he'd invited her to Edinburgh, to add to the collection he was building up. Yet he felt a small jolt of pleasure at the thought of the trip – and he was sure it had nothing to do with taking photographs.

As Christina left him washing the equipment after the morning's session, she couldn't push from her memory how pale and strained Alex had looked when he'd switched back on the floor light. He'd trembled, too, when she guided his hand to prepare the film. And when his hand touched her arm, she felt how he shook. She'd willed him to confide in her, to tell her what she now knew from Fiona, but he'd dropped his hand.

She chided herself. It wasn't any of her business.

Christina reached her room and sank onto the edge of the bed. Why had she agreed to the trip to Edinburgh? Was it really because she'd never been, or because she wanted to spend a whole day alone in his company? She fingered the eiderdown. The reason for her decision didn't matter. Alex had employed her to teach him and that was what she was doing. First, though, there was this afternoon's outing they'd promised Vanessa's boys.

Christina smiled at the excitement of the twins, as they bounced about in the back of Alex's Land Rover with Tess.

'We won't go far,' called Alex from the driver's seat to Vanessa standing on her doorstep to wave goodbye. 'Just to the woods for a picnic. We'll have them back in time for dinner!' He tooted the horn and they were off, down the short drive, onto the road and heading inland.

The boys delighted in making sheep and cow noises when they passed the animals in a field and soon Christina and Alex were joining in. By the time Alex parked the car and they all tumbled out, Christina was in the same high spirits as everyone else.

Alex took a plaid blanket and the wicker basket from the back of the Land Rover and slammed the door shut.

'Catch me!' shrieked Nicholas, running off, William close behind.

'Here I come,' said Alex with a grin and, blanket and picnic basket still in hand, he set off after the boys.

Christina watched and laughed as Alex did his best to run slowly and not catch them. She joined in the chase, weaving in and out of the trees, until the children were breathless with running and giggling.

'That's enough for me,' said Alex, coming to a halt and putting down the basket in a clearing. 'Shall we have our picnic now?'

'Yes, picnic!' the boys chorused.

Alex spread the blanket on the ground and Christina unpacked the basket.

'Can I have a fish paste sandwich?' said Nicholas, throwing himself to his knees.

'Let's see if we have any,' said Alex. He made a play of searching through the greaseproof packages. 'Yes, what luck! Fish paste sandwiches.'

'Everyone sit properly,' said Christina as she opened the wrapping and passed it round.

'Is there any fudge?' asked William, sitting very straight.

'I believe there is fudge for those who eat their sandwiches,' said Alex.

Christina's eyes widened in enquiry.

'I asked Vanessa what were their favourite foods,' he whispered in reply.

William was trying to push an entire sandwich into his mouth in his haste to get to the promised fudge.

'Easy,' said Christina. 'Eat it slowly.'

Christina looked about her, at the sun glinting through the trees. At this moment, in this place, with these people, she was content. Tess lapped water from the nearby burn and William fed her his crusts of bread when he thought Christina wasn't looking. Alex caught her eye and grinned.

Once the sandwiches and fudge had been eaten, and the bottles of orange juice drunk, Alex said to the boys, 'Shall we look for mini-beasts?'

The boys were up and off in a trice.

'I'll stay here and clear away,' Christina said.

Alex nodded and joined the twins in the hunt for insects. Christina remained sitting under the tree and breathed in the scent of the warm pines. She watched Alex and the boys crouching down, carefully turning over leaves and lifting twigs, and could hear the three male voices, two high and one deep.

After a while she began to pack away the remains of the picnic and had almost finished when Alex dropped down beside her on the blanket.

'Don't go any further,' he called to the boys, still busy in their search.

'If you can't see us, then we can't see you,' Christina added.

'That's a good one,' said Alex. 'Where did you learn it?'

'From Vanessa. She says it's her constant refrain when they are out together.'

He leaned back, supporting himself on his elbows. The neck of his shirt was open and Christina gazed at his tanned throat with its masculine Adam's apple. Hastily, she glanced away and plucked a blade of grass. She felt him watch her in silence.

He suddenly said, 'Are you happy here?'

'Yes.' It was true. She didn't need to think about her answer.

'Do you know what you will do when you leave?'

She studied him, surprised by his question, but he was no longer looking at her and she could read nothing from his profile. 'I plan to return to London, find another bedsit and look for a job.'

Alex turned to her, and she thought he saw the flare of sadness she felt at a bleak future. He frowned. 'Do you want that?'

She threw away the blade of grass. 'Yes.'

'And yet you are happy here?'

'Of course,' she said, striving to sound light when inside she felt like weeping. She forced a smile and gestured to the view around them. 'Look at all this beauty.'

'I am looking at it,' he said, not taking his eyes off her.

Her face grew warm, as his smile grew. The silence stretched between them and she felt no desire to break it.

A breeze tugged at a lock of her hair, so that it escaped its twist and flew across her face. Before she could move, Alex reached out a hand. 'Let me–'

'Hello!'

Christina heard the twins call a greeting and she looked up to see them pause in their search as a middle-aged woman came into sight.

'Well, hello to you, too.' The woman stopped and smiled at Christina and Alex. 'What bonnie wee children you have.'

'Oh,' she said, 'they're not–'

'Like this all the time,' finished Alex with a mischievous smile.

The woman laughed and strode on.

'Why did you let her think they were ours?' Christina asked when she had gone.

He shrugged. 'Just a fancy I had.'

He held her eyes and his gaze grew intimate, significant.

As she wondered what to say, a few raindrops fell on the remains of their picnic.

'Uncle Alex,' shouted Nicholas, running over to them. 'It's raining.'

Christina lifted her gaze above the trees. 'The clouds are looking ominous.' She uncrossed her legs and rose to her knees.

'We should get back,' Alex said, getting to his feet. 'Okay, boys, let's finish clearing up here. Put the rest of the picnic things back in the basket – carefully! – and Chrissie and I will fold up the blanket.'

He'd called her Chrissie. It had tripped off his tongue so naturally. Had he noticed what he'd said? The afternoon had been so pleasant for her. It must have been for him too and tricked his brain. But, of course, the boys knew her as Aunty Chrissie, so was it just for their sake he'd been so familiar?

Christina had picked a few pansies in rich yellows and blues in the garden, arranged them in an egg cup from the dresser and now they looked bright and cheerful on the kitchen table at Craiglogie.

'What a lovely idea, Christina,' said Fiona, spearing a piece of carrot. 'I hope you don't mind our eating dinner in the kitchen again, but it's warmer and more cosy than the dining room, which is rather formal.'

'Of course I don't mind.'

'Anyway, you're like one of the family,' said Alex with a smile in his eyes, over the top of his glass of water.

'I'm flattered,' said Christina. But was she? *You're like one of the family* could mean she was someone he'd become used to, in the way a person gets used to a piece of furniture. But no, that couldn't be it, she thought, remembering the way he had looked at her, spoken to her, only a short time ago. She felt her cheeks grow pink and turned her attention onto the portion of steak and kidney pie in front of her.

Alex regaled Fiona with the boys' enjoyment of their afternoon, and Christina added to the story. Finally, he set down his cutlery on the empty plate and said, 'Helen and I are out this evening. A concert I bought tickets for some months ago.'

Christina's head jerked up. She looked at him and forced a smile on her face. She felt he'd added that last sentence deliberately – but he didn't have to explain his movements to her, for this evening or any evening.

'Have an enjoyable time,' she said, her voice bright. She lowered her lashes to hide the disappointment in her eyes. The kitchen no longer felt cosy and secure.

After he'd left the room, Fiona chatted on about her day. Christina forced herself to concentrate and not wonder where Alex was now or what he was doing.

Eventually she said, 'I'll do the dishes, Fiona, then I'll go upstairs and read until bedtime, if you don't mind.'

'Not at all. I'd like an early night anyway,' said Fiona, stifling a yawn. 'Would you like to borrow a book from the library?'

The library. Christina hadn't been in there since her first evening in the house, when she'd seen Alex's collection of photographs.

'I've got a novel with me, but perhaps I could have a look anyway?'

'No need to ask,' said Fiona, taking the napkin from her knee and placing it on the table. She pushed back her chair and stood. 'Help yourself any time.'

Christina dealt with the dishes and made her way to the library. Even though there was no one to see her, she wandered along the rows of books as if looking for a particular volume. At the portraits she stopped.

Her heart sank. Helen was beautiful and classy. A suitable wife for a laird. What was the expression? Cut from the same cloth. Christina knew it was from among their own circle of friends that such young women found husbands. She should leave Craiglogie and let Alex and Helen take the path that everyone expected them to take.

She returned to the bookshelves and plucked a book at random. Adam Smith. Christina slid it back onto the shelf. She wanted fiction this evening, not a political treatise. Moving further along the row, she found the novels. *Treasure Island*, *The Hound of the Baskervilles*, *The Thirty-Nine Steps*. All Scottish authors and books she was familiar with. Here was a small collection of P.G. Wodehouse novels. She smiled, as she recollected Alex quoting the author about dogs who show off.

Christina stopped at a volume with the title *The Monarch of the Glen*. This one she didn't know. She took it down and opened it. On the front page was written, in an elegant script, *To Alex, with love, Helen*.

She felt as if her fingers had been burned and almost dropped the book. After staring at the handwriting for a minute or two, she recovered herself. It's just a book from one friend to another, she told herself, nothing more. But she wanted to read this story, so she took it to her room.

Climbing onto the bed and leaning back against the pillows, she opened the book again, turned firmly past the dedication and on to chapter one. The Laird of Glenbogle, fiercely protective of the MacDonald clan, might be fictitious, she thought, but Craiglogie and its MacDonald laird were very real.

She read and dozed, half-listening for Alex's Land Rover to come chugging up the drive. After a while, the sun having gone down and leaving her chilled, she undressed and got quickly into bed.

It was after midnight when she was startled awake by the sound of footsteps at the top of the stairs. They stopped and she heard the murmur of low voices. Helen must have returned with Alex from the concert.

Christina held her breath. One set of footsteps passed her bedroom, the other went along the landing in the opposite direction. The floorboards creaked and then fell silent as two bedroom doors were softly closed.

She released her breath and sighed at herself. She kept resolving to put her feelings for Alex behind her, but each time she was aware of him, all her emotions were stirred up again.

CHAPTER 14

*C*hristina looked up as Alex strolled into the kitchen the next morning. He was dressed in dark corduroys and an open-necked work shirt. His hair was damp and tousled and he hadn't yet shaved. Their eyes met and her pulse quickened.

'How was the concert?' Fiona asked, closing one exercise book and reaching for another from the small pile.

'What?' He dropped into a chair. 'Oh yes, it was very good.'

Helen wandered in, wearing a dogtooth print frock with a belt at the waist, her cropped hair in shining waves.

Conscious of wearing a simple woollen jumper and slacks, Christina looked down at her plate and buttered a piece of toast.

'Did you enjoy last night, Helen?' said Fiona.

'Oh, it was *delightful*,' Helen purred.

Christina looked up in time to see Helen flash a smile at Alex.

He poured out two cups of tea and slid Helen's across the table, to where she'd taken a seat. 'Thanks for driving last night,' he said.

'*Well*' – she gave a short laugh – 'I didn't think it would look terribly good if we arrived at the Cowdray Hall in your wreck of a Land Rover.'

The conversation was shattered by a loud bang.

'What was that?' Alex was up and out of the kitchen in an instant. The three women glanced at each other and ran to catch up with him.

In the yard, an old bull was playfully rocking Helen's MGB with his horns. The car swayed on its springs.

'Damn!' Alex said, coming to a sudden halt.

Helen screamed as the bull put his head down and lifted one side of the car completely off the ground. She rushed over to Alex and grabbed hold of him. 'Do something!' she yelled.

Alex's face was incredulous as he glanced from Helen to the bull and back again.

'Go indoors,' he shouted at Helen, prising her hands from him. 'Fiona, run down to Joe's cottage and tell him what's happened.'

'I'll go. I know where he lives,' Christina said quickly. 'Fiona can take your friend back to the kitchen. I'm sure she can be of more comfort than I can.'

Fiona looked at Alex for confirmation. He nodded and returned his attention to the bull. Fiona led the shaking and sobbing Helen away, as Christina, her heart thudding, dashed round the back of the steading and down the track to Joe's cottage. She knocked on the door, but the wireless in the dairy-man's kitchen was blaring and there was no response.

'Joe!' she shouted, banging desperately on the door. 'It's urgent!'

At last he heard her. Joe wrenched open the door.

'You must come at once,' she said. 'The old bull has escaped and is in the courtyard.'

His face white, he nodded, pulled on his boots and took from the porch a bull stick and halter.

'Take care, lass,' he said. 'We dinna ken where old Angus is now. He might still be there, but he might not. Stay close to me.'

They advanced cautiously towards the yard. Alex waited

there. Helen's car was lying on its side and there was no sign of the bull.

Alex nodded grimly at Joe. 'Angus is now in the storage shed.'

'Aye, he loves apples,' said Joe, 'and that's where they're stored.'

Alex turned to Christina. 'Go indoors now, Christina. It's not safe here.'

'I might be of some help,' she said, her eyes locking on his.

'No. Bulls are nervous animals and very powerful. I don't want to be responsible for anything happening to you.'

Her heart thudded with fear, but she found herself saying, 'I can take responsibility for myself.'

Surprise flashed in Alex's eyes. 'I haven't got time to argue. Whatever happens, keep your wits about you.' He took a step towards the shed.

Helen appeared at the back door, screaming again. 'He's in the house! I can hear him.' She ran out and flung herself into Alex's arms.

'He's not in the house,' Alex said firmly, holding her by her shoulders.

'He is,' she gasped. 'I heard him from the kitchen.'

Fiona ran out of the house and over to them. 'Angus is in the storage shed.'

Alex nodded. 'I saw him go in.'

'That door should have been shut,' said Joe, pushing back his cap.

'It must have been left unlatched,' said Alex. 'Angus walked in and accidentally pushed the door to with his behind.'

Christina saw Fiona standing with her arm around Helen's shoulders, before she turned back to the store attached to the house. With Alex and Joe, they walked towards the building. She stood on her toes and peered through the small, cobwebby window standing ajar.

In the gloom, she could just make out Angus munching apples from the straw-lined shelves. She stepped back down.

'How do we remove him?' she said. 'He fills the whole place.'

'The door opens inwards so it won't budge, but we'll have to get him out or he'll give himself colic,' said Alex.

'That's easier said than done,' said Joe. 'We can't break down the door. If we start battering at it close to his rump, he'll go mad.'

'The window is always left open for the cat,' said Alex. 'I'll climb in.'

'Dinna do it, Alex,' said Joe. 'I'll get one of the lads.'

With relief, Christina saw the other farmhands had joined them.

'No,' said Alex. 'I refuse to stand by and let one of the men do something so dangerous.'

He shot Christina a reassuring look, but her heart almost stilled at what he was about to do. Without another word, he heaved himself up, pushed open the window and squeezed through the gap.

'Don't,' Christina whispered, but it was too late. He had dropped down inside the storeroom.

Her pulse throbbing, she returned to the window and saw Alex slide onto an empty upper shelf. Lying on his stomach and using his elbows, he pulled himself along the wooden ledge. Angus went on chewing, but his eyes were watchful as Alex inched closer.

'What is Alex doing?' she whispered.

'He's going to unlatch the door and try to turn the bull round, I reckon,' said Joe.

Alex's stomach knotted up and he came to a halt. There was a dull ringing in his ears and he felt dizzy, unable to breathe. His heart pounded, the blood surged in his temples. The narrow shelf he was on had another shelf close overhead. It was like being in a coffin.

Through the beat of his blood, he heard Christina's soft voice calling through the tiny window.

'Alex, you must move.'

He wanted to, but he couldn't. It was as if his limbs were paralysed. A mist seemed to surround him like a blank wall and he was gripped by a wave of nausea.

'Alex!' He heard her voice again.

He shuddered and slowly turned his face towards the open window. His vision seemed to clear. Christina was there. He forced himself to breathe, to focus on her face, to make his arms and legs drag him along the wooden shelf.

'Keep going, Alex,' came Christina's low, encouraging voice. 'You're almost there.'

He hesitated again and could taste the cordite in his mouth. He had to do this, to prove to her that he could. Using all his willpower, he crawled forward.

Angus stopped chewing and fixed his eyes on Alex, as he reached the bull's head.

His mouth was unbearably dry. 'Come on, my lad,' he said. Hooking his finger in the bull's nose ring, he pulled Angus gently away from the apples and, sliding from the shelf, turned the animal to face the door. Alex reached forward and lifted the latch, pulling open the door enough to allow the latch to drop down and the door to stay open.

Joe carefully pushed the door wider and tried to ease in. 'I can't do it,' he breathed. 'Angus is too close to the door and it won't open any further.'

'Let me,' said Christina.

'It's not safe,' said Alex, his voice low.

She slipped through the doorway and his heart thudded at the risk she was taking. Quickly, she clipped the staff into Angus's ring and turned to look at Alex.

'Are you all right?' she mouthed.

He nodded his head, not daring to speak. He persuaded the old bull, now content, to back up enough that Christina could open the door. As soon as she had done so, Angus strolled forward and out into the sunshine.

'Well, I'll be damned,' Alex heard Joe say. 'Lucky you're just a slip of a lass or you'd never have got in.'

Alex emerged from the apple store and wiped his perspiring forehead with his sleeve. What a foolhardy but brave thing Christina had done. Thank the Lord she had not come to harm.

Helen pulled away from Fiona and ran to him. 'You're all right,' she said, throwing her arms around him.

'Yes.' He prised her arms off him.

'It's bad enough that my car is ruined,' said Helen, frowning, 'without you ending up the same way. You should have just left the stupid beast in there. And anyway, what were you thinking of, going into such a cramped space? You were lucky you didn't freeze up and have a fit.'

'Shut up, Helen,' said Fiona, sending her a dark look.

'I'm fine,' Alex said, his voice growing strong again, 'and so is Christina. I'm not sure what I would have done without her.'

And he had achieved something today. Not much, but it was something. His heart swelled. No one, and most importantly Christina, would see him now as a broken man.

Christina had noticed the furious, tear-stained glance Helen sent her as Alex and Joe led the bull back to his box, but she pushed it away. She'd seen Alex freeze in the tiny store, the sheen of cold sweat on his forehead and the raw ache in his eyes when he stepped out. He'd had a panic attack in there, in the same way he had in the darkroom. If she was to help him, and she knew she wanted to, then he must speak to her about it.

Yet when Alex strode into the kitchen at lunchtime, he grinned at Christina and dropped into a chair. 'What a morning,' he said, sounding almost buoyant.

'Fiona has taken Helen home.' Christina slid a mug of tea towards him and took a dish of macaroni cheese from the Aga. 'How did Angus get out in the first place?'

'I've had the whole story from Eddie, and Meg in the dairy. One of the cows came bulling. Eddie led Angus into the empty yard – it's securely enclosed – and let Angus loose to serve her. When the cow was ready to leave, Eddie led her away. The usual practice then is to give the bull some food, slip the stick into his ring and take him back to his own place.'

Alex forked up the cheesy macaroni and swallowed it. 'Mmm, this meal is delicious, thank you. Cheese off rationing can't come soon enough.' He gulped a mouthful of tea.

'Anyway, this morning for some reason, Angus didn't want his food and, as it was warm and sunny in the yard, Eddie decided to let him stay there until after lunch. Angus must have been asleep and almost hidden in the straw in the corner. On her way back from the dairy, Meg had no idea he was there and she took a short cut across the yard.' He ate the macaroni like a starving man.

'Knowing that Joe would shortly be bringing the heifers in from the fields, she opened the gate and fastened it back to save him the trouble. It seems that sometime later Angus woke up and decided to take a stroll.'

'I'm just thankful that all is well,' Christina said.

'Apart from Helen's car.' Alex made a rueful face. 'The damage should be covered by my insurance, but if not I will have to buy her a new MGB.'

He met Christina's gaze. 'You were a real help this morning. We might have been trying to get Angus out of the apple store for a lot longer if it weren't for you.'

She smiled. 'I suppose being *a slip of a lass* helped.'

'Who said that?' He drained his mug.

'Joe.'

Alex's eyes crinkled at the corners. 'I wouldn't describe you in those terms.'

The way he was looking at her made her bold. 'Then how would you describe me?'

'Slender, strong, fearless.' Alex's smile broadened.

Christina tried to ignore the tiny throb of longing she felt in her veins. To Alex she was another farmhand, but she wanted him to see her as beautiful, elegant, desirable.

There was a knock at the door. 'That must be the garage to collect Helen's car,' he said. 'Excuse me.' He got up and left the room.

Christina heard men's voices in the porch, then a female voice, and the sound of the back door closing.

Fiona walked into the kitchen. 'I see Mr Lowe's men have arrived. I hope Helen's car isn't too badly damaged.' She sank into the chair. 'It's a pity that Helen stayed over last night, but she told Alex she was too tired after the concert to drive on to her aunt's.'

Christina felt a wave of relief. Staying the night at Craiglogie had been Helen's idea, not Alex's. 'Sit down. I'll get your lunch.' She pulled from the oven the dish containing the remainder of the macaroni cheese and set it on the table. 'Tea?'

'Please.' Fiona sank into the chair. 'I'm starving after all the excitement.' She helped herself from the dish, heaping the food onto her plate. 'It took me a while to get Helen calmed down, but I think she's all right now. She was worried about Alex and her car, although I'm not sure in what order.' Fiona gave a half-smile.

Christina joined her at the table. 'Was her aunt there to take care of her?'

Fiona nodded as she ate her lunch.

'Fiona,' said Christina, her voice soft, 'Alex had a panic attack in the storage shed this morning.'

'Oh,' Fiona said, gripping her knife and fork. 'It's happened again.' She took a breath. 'I shouldn't be surprised. The shed is a dark, confined place.'

It wasn't just the storage shed, thought Christina. There was the incident in the darkroom too. When they were there yesterday morning, he must have been on the verge of another attack. Why had he wanted a darkroom, knowing what would happen to him?

She could guess the answer. Alex had been attempting to overcome his fear, the shell shock. What it must have cost him then, and this morning when he climbed in through the shed's tiny window. Was he attempting to prove something not just to himself, but to others? Her heart went out to him. Alex was a brave man.

Christina glanced up to see Fiona giving her an openly curious look. 'You care about Alex, don't you?' she said.

Christina caught her breath. Was it obvious?

'And I've seen the way Alex looks at you,' said Fiona.

Christina felt her chest tighten. 'You must be imagining–'

'No, I'm not. He's my brother.' Fiona sighed. 'More than anything, I want him to be happy again. I hope you don't mind my saying so, Christina, but I don't think you should let this go any further if it's something you can't cope with.'

Christina flushed. There was no 'this'. But she gave a slight nod, reached forward and squeezed Fiona's hand. 'I'm sure Alex will be fine. He has not just physical strength, but strength of character too.'

'I'm so glad you're here, Christina,' said Fiona, her face clearing. 'And I'm certain that Alex is.'

'Thank you for driving me to Vanessa's,' said Christina, glancing at Alex in the driver's seat.

He turned quickly to smile at her. 'My pleasure.'

There was a new confidence about him, she thought, studying his profile. As if… as if his experience this morning had shown him he could overcome his fears.

He turned to glance at her again. 'Are you okay, after this morning?'

'Yes. Now it's over, I see it as a bit of an adventure.'

He laughed and that deep sound set her stomach fluttering. Certain that he wasn't looking at her, she sank back in her seat and allowed her gaze to remain for a few moments on his muscled thighs. It was almost as if she could feel the heat from them.

'How is Helen's car?' she asked, pulling her gaze away.

'We managed to get it upright again using the tractor and the damage wasn't as bad as it first looked,' he said. 'Albert Lowe's hopeful he'll get it like new again. It's a case of some panel work and replacement windows.'

'Thank goodness.'

'Yes. Helen loves that car,' he said wryly. 'I need to see her this afternoon to let her know, but I can pick you up from Vanessa's in a couple of hours if that suits you?'

She smiled. 'Yes, please, if you don't mind.'

At the cottage, he jumped out of the Land Rover and came round to open the car door for her. 'See you later,' he said, holding her gaze and sliding his strong hands tenderly down her arms.

More than anything she wanted him to take her in his arms, to feel his muscles tighten around her, to breathe in his masculine scent. But she politely thanked him again for the lift, opened the little garden gate and walked up the path, trying to keep her legs steady.

Alex leaned back against the car seat and closed his eyes as Christina disappeared into the cottage. He should have said something about this morning, explain what had happened when he couldn't move, but the right words wouldn't come and he didn't want to see pity in her eyes. Sighing, he put the Land Rover into gear and eased it back onto the road.

Her scent lingered in the air, so that he couldn't immediately remember what he had to do next. He headed for the beach.

Alex walked across the sand, the cool breeze coming off the sea helping to clear his head. At the water's edge, he crouched to pick up a flat stone and skimmed it deftly across the calm, grey sea. He thought of when he had done this as a child, the simple pleasure it had given him, and he felt a yearning for simpler days. Before the horrors of the war. When he knew how to flirt with a girl. But they had been gone for some time.

He'd only known Christina for a short while, but she was making him feel things he wasn't equipped to deal with. He couldn't allow himself to feel this... What was it – love? He ran his fingers through his hair. Would she listen if he tried to explain about his terrifying flashbacks?

He'd tried to tell Helen once, years ago, but she brushed his attempt aside. *It doesn't do to dwell on such things, Alex*, she'd said. And though he'd thought her advice had helped him at the time, it only made him appear normal. It hadn't really changed a thing.

'Helen!' he said, stopping in his tracks. 'Damn, that's where I'm supposed to be.' He turned and jogged back to his car.

CHAPTER 15

*A*t the end of the two hours, it wasn't Alex who came to collect Christina, but Joe. As Christina climbed into Home Farm's old van, she felt ridiculously disappointed. Alex had stayed at Helen's and not come to pick her up as he said he would.

They rattled along the lanes in silence, while Christina's thoughts returned to her leaving Craiglogie and going back to the south. She'd said as much to Vanessa over tea, but how was she going to leave after that conversation at lunchtime with Fiona? It was clear, though, that Alex had feelings for Helen. Fiona and Vanessa were wrong – he had no real interest in her.

As they turned through the granite pillars, Joe said, 'The laird sends his apologies. Eddie got his hand caught in the new-fangled tractor and the laird's taken him to hospital.'

Christina chastised herself for being such a self-centred fool. 'Is Eddie okay?' she said.

'Dinna know yet, as the laird's not back.' Joe brought the van to a juddering stop at the front of the house.

'Thank you, Joe,' she said. 'I do hope Eddie's injury isn't serious.'

'Me too, lassie.' He nodded to her.

She climbed out and closed the door. He turned the van round and drove off in the direction of his cottage.

Christina entered the house. Everything was quiet, very different to that morning. She entered the kitchen.

'The mistress is nae here,' said Mrs Morrison. She paused in sweeping the floor. 'She's gone to see Eddie's mam. The poor wifie was in a bit o' a state aboot her loon.'

'Is there anything I can do to help?' Christina asked.

'In the hoose or at the loon's?'

'Either.'

'Nae, neither.' She picked up the broom and left the kitchen.

Christina stood in the centre of the room, unsure what to do next. It was a reminder again that she was a guest in the house and had no real purpose here.

The kitchen door nosed open and Tess, muddy and tired, slumped in.

'Look at the state of you,' Christina said with a smile. 'Where on earth have you been?'

The dog wagged her tail and flopped down on her blanket in front of the Aga. Christina tried to fix her with a stern gaze. 'I don't think you should be in here looking like that, you know.'

Tess stretched out and closed her eyes. Her tail thumped on the rug but she didn't move.

Christina rubbed the dog dry as best she could with the old towel kept on a hook in the back porch. Tess opened one eye briefly, and within minutes she was snoring.

Even Tess doesn't need me, Christina thought with a rueful smile.

She heard the Land Rover chugging up the drive and ran out to meet it.

'How is Eddie?' she said, as soon as Alex and Fiona climbed out.

'He'll be fine,' said Alex. 'He's been to the hospital and now I've taken him home.'

'What happened?'

'He was doing a repair job on the tractor and managed to cut his left hand between the forefinger and thumb. He's been stitched up and will be off work for a few days. It could have been a lot worse.'

'What a day it's been,' Christina said.

'Welcome to life on the farm.' He put one arm round Christina's shoulders, the other round his sister's, and walked them indoors.

❧

Christina brushed her hair until it shone, slipped on her blue tweed suit and matching beret, and ran lightly down the stairs and slid into the car beside Alex.

She glanced over at him and he turned, met her eyes and smiled. Her heart flipped. He looked so handsome in a well-cut wool suit and waistcoat.

'Okay?'

She nodded. More than okay. Happy beyond what she had ever expected.

The morning sunlight played across her face as he drove to the station and she tried to subdue the butterflies in her stomach. She was spending the day with Alex. And for once Helen wasn't with them.

The 8.50 pulled into Aberdeen with a loud hiss, pumping clouds of steam as the screeching brakes were applied. Alex ushered her towards the front of the train, his hand firmly placed on the middle of her back. His touch felt both natural and thrilling.

A guard stepped forward to open the heavy door.

'First class?' Christina's eyes widened and she looked at Alex in surprise.

'Of course.' He grinned at her expression.

'I've never travelled first class before,' she said as she mounted the step into the empty compartment. Sinking into the deeply-upholstered seat, she smiled at him. 'This is such a luxury.'

'The journey is about four hours, so we may as well be comfortable.' He dropped his trilby into the overhead luggage rack and took a seat facing Christina as the guard slammed the door shut. A minute or two later, they heard his whistle and, with a whoosh of steam, the train pulled away from the station.

'When we get there, where would you like to visit?' Alex said.

The carriage rattled gently as it picked up speed.

She smoothed her skirt over her knees. 'I don't know enough about Edinburgh to say. I've heard of the castle, of course, and Holyroodhouse – oh, and Greyfriars Bobby.'

'Hmm, yes. I wonder if Tess would be as faithful as Bobby?'

Christina knew the story of the little Skye terrier, who in the nineteenth century had guarded his master's grave in Greyfriars Kirkyard. 'How long did Bobby stay at the graveside?'

'Fourteen years, until his own death.'

'So long! And he never left it once?'

'Apparently, local people built a shelter for him. He was fed, too. When each day the One o'Clock Gun was fired from the castle, he'd leave his post and run to the eating house he used to visit with his owner. Then he returned to Auld Jock's grave. The news of Bobby's loyalty spread, and people travelled from far and wide to see him. Crowds would gather for the firing of the gun, to see him run for his midday meal.'

'That's some story.'

'Edinburghers like it.' Alex smiled. 'Greyfriars Kirk, Bobby's statue and the castle are at one end of the Royal Mile, and the Palace of Holyrood is at the other end. We could visit all four, but you might prefer to take your time in the castle or the palace.' He caught her eye. 'Perhaps visit one part of the city this time and one next time?'

Next time. Did that mean he wanted to take her to Edinburgh again one day? She fingered the catch on her bag and then told herself not to fidget. 'Can you tell me something about each of the places, so I can make up my mind?'

'Certainly. The castle is the city's most famous attraction. It stands on the peak of an extinct volcano and dominates the skyline, so you can't miss seeing it. It's been home to Scottish royalty for 900 years.'

Christina glanced at him, saw the animation in his face and the love for his country's history. 'And the palace?' she asked, keen to know as much as possible.

'That's the Queen's official residence when she's in Scotland. It's more comfortable than the castle. Visitors can see the apartments of Mary, where Rizzio was murdered by her husband Lord Darnley and his friends.'

Christina knew this story and shuddered. She pictured Mary Queen of Scots' chamber door bursting open and the frightened, pregnant Queen being held at gunpoint, while her secretary was stabbed to death in front of her eyes. Her lips felt dry with the horror.

'Shall I make a suggestion?' he asked.

She brought her gaze back to him. 'Yes, please.'

'We'll have lunch at the North British Hotel, then we can stroll through Princes Street Gardens to the castle, and back along Princes Street to the station. That will probably be enough for one day.'

She smiled and moistened her dry lips. 'It sounds perfect.'

Watching her lips, Alex felt a knot tighten in his stomach. He looked out of the window at the fields rolling by. He couldn't carry on like this.

After the war he'd immersed himself in the estate and Home Farm, hoping the work would absorb him. It had for a while, but only for a while. The hollow ache of loneliness in his heart wouldn't be suppressed and had grown stronger.

He'd tried to love Helen – he knew that had been expected of him – but he couldn't. And he felt sure she loved his position, and his money, more than she cared for him.

Alex had to admit that Christina had changed his life, and he wanted more, much more. He loved her sweet smile, the way she frowned when she concentrated, the scent of her hair. He couldn't think of anything he didn't like about her, so why was he reluctant to tell her how he felt?

The panic attack in the darkroom two days ago, and in the apple store yesterday… she must have been aware of his shaky reaction.

At once he knew he had to speak to her, to explain. He didn't know exactly what he'd say, but he must talk to her openly and honestly. His heart thudding painfully, he opened his mouth.

The compartment door slid open and his mouth snapped shut. From the corridor a woman in a black dress and white apron entered, carrying a tray of cups and saucers. 'Would you like something to drink?' she asked.

Alex quirked an eyebrow at Christina.

'Yes, please,' she said.

The waitress set two cups and saucers on the little table under the window and left. Two waiters in white jackets entered, the first carrying a jug in each hand. 'Tea or coffee, miss?'

'Coffee, please.'

He poured out a cup of hot dark liquid, as Alex breathed in the wonderful aroma to try to regain his composure. 'And for you, sir?'

'The same, thank you,' said Alex.

He waited impatiently as the second waiter poured milk into

the cups and the two men returned to the corridor to move on to the next compartment.

'Going back to travelling third class will be hard after this,' said Christina. 'You are spoiling me.'

'It's my pleasure,' he said. The moment to talk to her had passed. It would sound unnatural now, forced.

She smiled at him. 'From what you have told me, it sounds as though you know the city quite well.'

'I should. I was at boarding school there, Fettes, from the age of eight.'

'Eight! So young.'

'Yes, it was hard to start with, but you get used to it.' He shrugged. 'I came home for holidays.'

'But still…'

Silence fell between them and they sipped their coffees.

'This is a treat,' Christina said, after a while.

'For me, too.' He smiled.

'It's so different from my usual life.'

He put down his cup. 'Tell me about your usual life.'

Christina stared at him. 'You want to know why I have no job or place to live, don't you?'

'Forgive me,' he said, shifting his gaze to out of the window. 'It's none of my business.'

'I met someone, we became engaged, and he died.'

Alex turned sharply back to her. 'That's… that's… I'm sorry, Chrissie.'

Christina swallowed. She didn't want to talk about her past, but perhaps she owed Alex this much. The kindness in his voice almost brought tears to her eyes. She'd tried to keep her memories locked in her heart, to be taken out only in small stages and when she allowed. Now that she'd started, she wanted him to know.

'I had my own small flat, a good job with a photographic studio – but someone else's husband. It turned out my fiancé was already married.'

'I see,' he murmured.

She flushed with shame and anger. He was wrong; he couldn't possibly see. 'I only found out when he died that David had a wife and a young child.'

Alex sat in silence. She managed a smile. 'At least his wife never knew about me, so I'm glad she has good memories of her husband.'

He frowned. 'But sad memories for you.'

She took a sip of coffee from her cup. 'I carried on in London for the remaining three months of my tenancy. I was about to move back in with my mother when Vanessa invited me to stay with her for a few weeks.'

She sighed. 'It was painful; David's death and the discovery that he had never really loved me. I gave up my work and my bedsit because I wanted a clean break. Vanessa thought coming up here for a holiday would help while I decided what to do next. So I came.'

He gave a wry smile. 'And almost the first person you met was me, telling you not to throw sticks for my dog. And not long afterwards putting you to work.'

'You weren't to know. And you gave me accommodation and employment when I needed it. I'm grateful for that, and for being distracted from my thoughts.'

'What are your thoughts now?' he asked.

Alex was looking at her in such a way that she felt a dizzy awareness of him. She was confused by the question. Not wishing to appear any more foolish than she must already seem, she said nothing.

'What will you do when you leave Craiglogie?'

Leave Craiglogie… It was what she planned to do and now he was talking about it as if it had already been decided between them. Perhaps this outing was his way of saying goodbye, thanking her for what she had taught him.

'I've thought about it a lot, of course,' she said. 'I'll live with my mother in her flat and look for a job down there.'

As she finished her coffee, she couldn't meet his eyes. She should never have told Alex she'd been in love with a married man. What must he be thinking – that she'd had an affair with David? Her heart felt like a lead weight in her chest.

Alex was the laird and had a standing in the community. Any suggestion of her having been another man's mistress would not be acceptable. His response had made clear his disapproval. He'd said 'I see' when she'd told him about David's wife and child, and soon after that he'd asked her when she was leaving Craiglogie.

She'd begun to see a future for herself with him in her life and now she realised it was an illusion.

They sat in silence for a while. Then Alex pointed through the window to a castle perched on a cliff overlooking the sea. He told her a little about it and they began to chat again, although it didn't seem as natural as before.

'Next stop, Edinburgh,' called the guard, passing down the corridor.

Alex glanced out of the window. Why did he not say anything to her when she'd exposed her past to him, told him about that other man? And to make it worse, he'd gone on to ask Christina when she was leaving.

He didn't care that she had been engaged to a married man. All he cared about was that Christina was now free. Free to marry him, if she'd have him.

She had been brave and told him about the loss of the man

she'd loved. He'd wanted to open up, too, and tell her about the nightmares and the flashbacks. But he'd faltered at the last moment, and he knew that she was wondering why he'd suddenly gone quiet. He felt her eyes on his.

'This is our station,' said Alex, grateful they had reached the capital. 'If you look out of the window to your right,' he found himself saying, 'you'll see the castle looming up.' The sight never failed to please him.

Christina had to crane her neck to look up, as the railway line was so close to the craggy grey rock.

'It's quite something, isn't it?' he said. 'To think that in the fourteenth century, twenty men scaled that wall and recaptured the castle from the English.' He could barely believe his ears; he was behaving like a tourist guide.

'Is there anything you don't know about Scottish history?' She gave a hesitant smile.

Her smile warmed him and he suddenly felt more confident again. 'Not much.' He laughed. 'Of course that isn't true – there is much I don't know – but most Scots are proud of their history and know the bits that reflect well on them.'

She held his gaze. 'I'm sure that's true of every nation.'

The light in her eyes was mesmerising and he swallowed. 'We're here,' he said, as the train pulled into the station. He stood and reached for his hat. 'After this, the train goes on to London.' He didn't want to think of her on the train back to London one day soon. He wouldn't think of it; he didn't want anything to spoil this day.

At the end of the platform a man with the empty sleeve of his threadbare jacket folded and pinned at his shoulder, sang 'The White Cliffs of Dover'. Trying to hide from Christina the wretched look he felt on his face, Alex dropped a bank note into the man's tin.

He cleared his throat and said to Christina. 'It's a quarter to one, so time for lunch. The hotel has its own entrance from the station.'

When they passed from the hotel lobby into the restaurant, Christina stopped to take it all in. 'Oh, Alex,' she breathed, 'it's splendid.'

Her eyes widened as she looked round the circular room of the Palm Court, at the pillars and exotic palm trees, the idyllic rural scenes painted on the walls and overhead a cupola that allowed natural light to bathe all below.

Her pleasure was irresistible. 'I'm glad you approve.'

'How could I not?' Her mouth lifted at the corners. 'It's nothing like the Lyons Corner House on Lower Regent Street, where I used to eat in my lunch breaks from the studio.'

The restaurant was bustling with diners and waiters, and full of murmured conversation. The maître d' approached. 'Do you have a reservation, sir?'

'Yes. MacDonald.'

'This way, please.'

They were shown to a table, where the waiter pulled out her chair and draped a crisp linen napkin across her lap. The sparkle of the cutlery and glasses on the white tablecloth seemed to be reflected in her bright eyes.

She lifted her face to the minstrels' gallery. 'And a harpist. Vivaldi's "Spring". One of my favourite pieces of music.'

She turned and threw him a worried glance. 'This is too much,' she said, her voice low.

'I thought you liked it.' His voice was soft, to match hers.

'Of course I do.'

'So it's not *too* much, then?' he said.

She smiled and shook her head. 'But it must be dreadfully expensive.'

'Think of it as a treat for both of us. I've not been to Edinburgh for some time.' He'd had no desire to visit – until now. 'I wanted to come here for lunch. It holds some good memories for me in the past, and it's time I made a new one.'

He saw her relax as she placed her clutch bag and gloves beside her on the table.

'What is the occasion?' she asked.

The waiter returned and handed each of them an open leather-backed menu.

'The occasion?' Alex said, as if considering the question. 'Just our being here is sufficient.'

Christina held his gaze for a moment before she looked at the menu. 'It's as if rationing has completely ended. *Cornets de Jambon Lucullus. Gratin de Poisson…*'

He lowered his menu and glanced at her across the table. The soft natural light through the cupola caught the honey tones in her fair hair.

Perhaps aware that he was watching her, she looked up from her menu and caught him in her enquiring gaze. He smiled. 'Have you chosen?'

Her brow wrinkled. 'There are no prices.'

'They are on my menu. Please choose whatever you would like.'

'Oh.' She hesitated. 'That hardly seems fair.'

'If a couple are dining, they give the man the price list.'

'Because they expect that he'll be the one paying?'

'Don't you like the idea?'

'What if lunch had been on me?'

'We'd probably have gone somewhere else.'

Still she hesitated to choose from the menu.

'Ask for a priced menu if you like,' he said with a smile in his eyes.

'I'm not sure that I'm brave enough. Have you seen the imperious expression on the face of the maître d'?'

Alex twisted about in his chair and spotted the man standing by the entrance to the restaurant. 'I wouldn't risk getting in his bad books either,' said Alex, turning back to Christina. 'We'd better keep our opinions to ourselves, don't you think?' He winked at her and was pleased when she laughed. It felt like a blessing. 'Have you chosen?'

'I'd like the fish, please.'

The waiter appeared, took their order and went away.

It was almost one o'clock. Alex knew what was coming and steeled himself as a muffled boom penetrated the dining room.

'What was that?' Christina said, startled.

The other diners didn't even pause in their chatter.

'It's the One o'Clock Gun,' he said. 'I mentioned it earlier, but you'll hear about it when we get to the castle.'

'It's very kind of you to go to all this trouble.'

'Really, it's no trouble.'

With the sound of cutlery and bone china clinking in the background, he kept the talk between them light. They chatted about the farm, photography and family, and the time passed far too quickly.

As Christina placed her coffee cup back on its saucer, she caught his eye. 'Vanessa was right.'

He raised his eyebrows. 'About what?'

'The locals *are* friendly.'

He laughed. 'I'm glad you like them.'

She touched each side of her smiling lips with the table napkin. Alex wished he could stop noticing her mouth. Not just her mouth, though she had perhaps the most kissable lips he'd ever seen, but those too-blue eyes…

She placed the napkin at the side of her plate. 'I can't thank you enough for the meal, Alex.'

'My pleasure,' he said, and averted his eyes before his gaze became embarrassing to both of them. 'I think it's time we moved or we'll see nothing else of the city.'

He lifted a hand to call over the waiter and in minutes the bill was settled. He ushered Christina towards the main door. She sent him a delighted smile at the sight of the doorman in full Highland outfit. The man tipped his bonnet and opened the door for them to emerge into the Princes Street sunshine.

Alex put on his hat, offered his arm to Christina and they descended the hotel steps. He felt a wave of pure pleasure, to have this lovely woman on his arm. Adjusting his pace to hers, they turned left, crossed the road and strolled into Princes Street Gardens.

CHAPTER 16

*C*hristina loved the feel of her arm in his, the closeness of his strong body. She glanced at Alex and thought how handsome and kind he was. Did he really want her to leave Craiglogie? She was so happy when she was with him.

Forcing away these thoughts, she admired the colourful flower beds as they wandered along.

'We're now in the valley between the old and new towns,' Alex said. 'A loch was drained to make the gardens.'

'That almost sounds a shame, to drain a loch.'

'Not really – the Nor' Loch was a stinking, polluted piece of water, used for a couple of hundred years by the residents for their rubbish and worse. It was later flooded to strengthen the castle's defences. Look ahead – there's the castle again, up on the rock, towering over the city.'

Alex was right – it dominated the skyline, an impressive ancient fortress soaring above the castle walls. Christina felt the pull of Scottish history, as he did.

In the gardens, shop girls wandered along, arm in arm, enjoying the sunshine in their lunch break, while men in business suits sat on the benches reading newspapers. Small children skipped along the path, their mothers calling to them not to go too far.

'What's this?' Christina asked as they approached an immensely tall and thin Gothic structure with a spire on top.

'That's the Scott Monument, built in memory of the writer Sir Walter Scott.'

They stopped and she gazed up at it.

'Just over two hundred feet high,' he said. 'Sixty-eight figures are depicted, plus Scott and his dog. And there's a pig.'

'Who are they all?'

'Well, the people are Robbie Burns, Lord Byron, Queen Mary, King James, Robert the Bruce, characters from Scott's novels…'

She quirked an eyebrow. 'And the pig?'

'From Ivanhoe.'

Alex placed his hand over hers on his arm and drew her closer. 'I told you we Scots know our history.' A slow smile tugged at his lips, the dimple appeared and her pulse quickened.

They strolled on and emerged at the end of the gardens.

'This,' he told her, gesturing to a magnificent building in the style of an ancient Greek temple, 'is the Scottish National Gallery.'

'I had no idea there were so many wonderful places so close together,' she said, giving it a lingering look.

'We can visit that another day,' he said.

She threw him a glance. Perhaps he did intend they should come here again, after all. It was confusing, the way he went from asking her when she was leaving, to speaking of the future as if they had one together. She didn't know what to make of him. But she was determined to enjoy this day.

Soon they were climbing up the long sloping forecourt to the castle. Behind a cluster of tourists, Christina and Alex passed under the Gatehouse and through the Portcullis Gate. They climbed further, peered through the battlements, marvelled at the miniature people below.

They moved on to the Argyle Battery, where a soldier stood by a large gun on wheels.

'Is this the One o'Clock Gun?' she asked the man.

He nodded. 'It's a time signal, fired every day at precisely 1pm, excepting Sunday, Good Friday and Christmas Day.'

'Poor little Greyfriars Bobby,' she murmured to Alex. 'He must have had no dinner on those days.'

The soldier heard her, smiled and continued. 'It was established in 1861 as a time signal for ships in the harbour of Leith and the Firth of Forth.'

'I suppose you must get bored with people asking you the same questions,' she said.

'Not at all. On occasion I've been asked some strange questions.'

'Really?' she said, curious. 'What is the strangest question you've ever been asked?'

The man's face split in a grin. 'What time does the One o'Clock Gun fire.'

They all laughed, and Christina thought how pleasant it was to see Alex so relaxed and happy.

They made their way down the steps to the Royal Palace and admired the Birth Chamber, Crown Room and Great Hall with its wood panelling, suits of armour and swords fanned out high on the walls. Christina was delighted with it all, but she couldn't help noticing that Alex had become quiet and withdrawn.

At the Military Museum, he drew her away from a party of American tourists making their way round the castle. 'Do you mind if we don't visit this?'

She was startled by the look of pain in his eyes. 'Not if you don't want to,' she said.

He rubbed the back of his neck.

'Would you like to talk about it?' she asked softly.

He shook his head and her heart plummeted. He was telling her to mind her own business.

'Not here,' he said.

Alex had watched her, the entranced look on her lovely face, as she explored the castle. He remembered the first time he'd seen her and felt regret at the way he'd treated her. She'd been walking on the beach and had bent gracefully to play with his dog. How had he responded? By addressing her in an abrupt manner. He'd been wary of this stranger in his quiet and ordered world.

He wanted to apologise for being so rude at that meeting, and to explain why a week ago he'd walked away after the tender kiss they'd shared. He needed to tell Christina about his past and this was the right time.

'There's a tea room in Jenners,' he said. 'Would you like to go there?'

She nodded. 'Yes. It's a little chilly this high up and with the wind off the sea.'

The breeze lifted loose strands of hair around her face and she pushed them away. It was a casual gesture, but the concern he could see in her gaze almost unmanned him.

He forced himself not to think of what he was about to do, to reveal himself to her. She might turn away from him, disgusted by his weakness, but to let this relationship go on any longer without speaking out felt intolerable and dishonest.

Alex guided her through the crowds along Princes Street, through the huge doors of the department store and into the lift. In the tea room, he chose a table in the corner, as far as possible from the other customers, and waited until after the waitress had brought their tea.

'Tell me, Alex,' Christina said, her voice soft. 'I want to understand.'

He drew in a steadying breath, but felt the involuntary jerk of his leg and was grateful for the long tablecloth which hid it.

'In 1940 the British Expeditionary Force was sent to France to try to halt the German advance through Europe.'

'I was nine then, but I remember my parents talking about it,' she said, her voice low. 'A dreadful time.'

Alex nodded. 'The Gordon Highlanders were part of the BEF and we ended up in Dunkirk. I remember thinking it was June and how beautiful it would be at home then. But it was very different at Dunkirk.

'There were mortar bombs and machine gun fire flying past us and we were heavily outnumbered. I knew I had to give the other soldiers time to evacuate. With a handful of my men, and only rifles and a Bren gun, we held off German fire for five hours.'

'You were awarded the DSO for that action,' she murmured.

'Who told you? Never mind.' He gave a grim smile. 'When the house we were using had been set alight and all our ammunition gone, I was fortunate to be able to lead the men to safety, wading up to our chins in water for almost a mile.' He shrugged. 'There were many acts of bravery to keep the enemy back during the evacuation.'

'Even so–'

'I was lucky not to be captured at Dunkirk, as others were. In the UK, I was diagnosed with shell shock and not sent back to active theatre. Again I was lucky, as what remained of the regiment was sent to Singapore. I was put in charge of the ack-ack guns, to try to prevent German planes from reaching Aberdeen. The guns were huge things, bolted to the ground in cement and each gun took eleven men to work. One man stood on the platform, two turned the handles and the other eight loaded the shells. Underneath there were bunks to sleep on during a lull.' His voice was mechanical, but he felt the bile rising in his throat.

'The guns were often moved around the area, but on that day we were positioned on the emplacement known as Miser's Hillie. It was called that because if you stood on the hill you could get a free view into the football stadium.'

He gave a hollow laugh, and gripped his cup.

'On the night it happened, we were on alert. The guns were sighted and ready for action when a German bomber was caught in the searchlight. Its target must have been the Russell shipyard.' He swallowed hard. 'As we fired, the plane dropped a bomb and it exploded. Two of the loaders were killed outright. I was lucky. I keep saying that, don't I? I was thrown into the air, landed in the crater that had been our underground bunker and the rubble fell on top of me.'

A wave of nausea gripped him.

'I was buried alive for twenty-four hours…'

As his words fell into the space between them, he felt her hand slide over his. He turned his gaze to out of the window and across the Edinburgh rooftops.

'The war was bad for everyone, of course,' he said quietly. 'My experience was no worse than that of others.'

Christina said nothing, just squeezed his hand gently, and he was grateful for that.

He dropped his gaze to the cup clenched between his hands and stared at the dark-brown liquid. Dealing with this memory was something he did in private. He thought he could talk to Christina about it, but now he was unsure.

Alex felt the sweat beading on his forehead and a tightening of his scar. He was about to rise, to escape, when he felt her hand stroking his wrist.

'I'm so sorry,' she whispered.

He lifted his head and his heart soared at the understanding in her steady gaze.

'Go on,' she said.

He drew a breath. 'That's about it, really. The plane got away. I remember seeing pieces of metal – our gun and ammunition – flying through the air, and the reek of cordite in my nostrils so powerful that I haven't shot anything since. Imagine, a laird who can't hold shooting parties.'

'Sounds like a good thing to me,' said Christina.

His gaze flicked up to see if she was making fun of him. She wasn't. He went on with the things he needed to say.

'There was a ludicrous moment of denial as I lay in the deafening silence of that grave and then the dark realisation. I was going to die there, so close to home and yet so far away. I must have slipped into unconsciousness; I was uncertain if I were alive or dead. Sometimes there came the smell of yellow gorse, or the memory of dancing Strip the Willow… At other times, the pain told me I was still very much alive, but for how long I had no idea. I couldn't move, couldn't dig myself out. I'd never felt so helpless in my life.

'After a while, a beam of light – moonlight, sunlight, torchlight, I didn't know which – appeared through a gap in the rubble. There were frantic cries of my name, but I couldn't move or speak. I could feel myself being pulled out of the rubble, hear the men talk as if I were dead, felt the desperate need to cry out that I was alive, then the pain before slipping back into unconsciousness.'

Alex's tongue was thick. It was hard to speak. He took a gulp of cold tea. 'These images haunt my dreams. Always the explosion, the sickening hurtle upwards before crashing to earth, the deep, dark silence of being buried. And panic overtakes me when I remember that I nearly died there.'

He forced himself to breathe, to focus on the sensation of Christina's fingers tightening on his wrist. Gradually he became aware again of the sounds of the tea room.

When he was calm enough to speak again, he said, 'The explo-

LINDA TYLER

sion sent me back to Dunkirk and the shell shock I got there. Now, when I'm in a confined space, I feel what I don't want to feel and remember what I don't want to remember.'

'I'm sorry for what happened to you,' said Christina, wiping her wet cheeks with the back of her hand. 'Thank you for telling me. Have you spoken to anyone about this?' she said quietly, 'since you've been back home?'

Alex shook his head. 'Fiona knows everything, of course. But I've not discussed it with another person.' He raked a hand through his hair. 'Craiglogie is a small community. I didn't want people to know how I felt, to see their curious looks, their subtly-loaded questions.' He gave a short, bitter laugh. 'For the sake of the family's name and the estate, I know I need to pull myself together.'

He grimaced. 'I did try to tell Helen once but she cut me off, said it was better not to talk or even think about it. She's right, of course, that we do need to look forward and leave the past behind. But here I am telling you, making a mockery of that philosophy. I'm ashamed of this weakness in me.'

'Weakness!' Christina kept her voice low. 'No one in their right mind would believe that of someone who had been through such an experience.'

'You're wrong,' he said, his mouth tightening, his hand unconsciously going to the scar on his forehead. 'Folk don't want to be reminded.'

'Alex, not talking about it might not be the best idea.'

'I'd thought it was the right thing to do.' He shrugged, and looked into her blue eyes. 'But when you told me this morning about David and I saw how much he'd hurt you, I wanted to repay your trust and share my story with you.'

'I'm glad you did.'

Her eyes filled with a soft light and he felt a familiar tug of longing, to hold her in his arms. 'I wanted you to know that I had

220

a reason for my erratic behaviour,' he said. 'I didn't want you to think that the fault lay with you.'

'There is no fault,' she said, searching his face.

'You need a better man than I.'

Her smile was gentle. 'You are a good man, Alexander MacDonald. Never doubt it.'

He couldn't stop his eyes drifting to her mouth. That kiss. He couldn't shake the memory of it and he knew she felt it too.

'This isn't the wonderful day I'd promised you,' he said.

He needed to revert to a polite, detached self before his emotions overwhelmed him. 'Shall we have a look at Greyfriars Bobby? He's only a fifteen-minute walk from here.'

She pushed away her untouched tea. 'What time does our train leave?'

'Twenty past five.' He drew his watch from the waistcoat pocket. 'In about forty-five minutes.'

'It's a bit late now, I think. It would be too much of a rush.'

'We could catch a later train,' he said. 'There's one at twenty past six.' Despite everything, he didn't want the day to end.

Christina saw the lines at his temples and the dark circles beneath his eyes. He was exhausted. The events of yesterday, coupled with today's revelation, had been too much for him. As it was, they wouldn't be back in Aberdeen until just after nine and then there was the drive home. Home... Craiglogie already seemed like home to her.

'That's kind of you to suggest it,' she said, 'but I think we should stick to our original plan. Fiona would be worried if we were late.'

He slipped the watch back into his pocket. 'Now I feel bad. I know that you wanted to visit Greyfriars.'

She smiled. 'Next time – as you said yourself.'

Oh Alex, she thought, as he returned her smile, *I have lost myself to you.*

'Then there is just time for us to visit the perfume counter downstairs,' he said. 'It's Fiona's birthday in a fortnight. You can help me choose.' He rose, held out his hand and drew Christina up.

'First come and see this,' he said, leading her down a flight of stairs. They came to a huge open gallery in the middle of the store.

'It's marvellous,' she said as she leaned over the balcony. It ran all the way round the floor and from it she could see yet more galleried floors above and below them. 'It's like peering into an Aladdin's cave.'

He laughed. 'Come on.' His grip on her hand was firm as he led her down the stairs to the ground floor.

Alex had unburdened himself, told her his secret, the fear he didn't want others to know. Perhaps now she could help him recover. He didn't want her to leave, she was sure...

'Would you like to try a fragrance, madam?' A beautician carrying a little bottle in each hand approached Christina as they reached the perfume counter.

'Oh, no thank you,' she said, hurriedly. 'We're here to buy for someone else.'

'Try it,' said Alex.

'I would like to.' She held out her wrist for the young woman to spray a scent.

Christina breathed it in. 'I like that very much,' she said to the beautician.

The young woman smiled. 'It's Moonlight Mist by Gourielli.'

Christina remembered seeing the advertisement in a magazine, showing a pair of scales with flowers on one side and a scent bottle in the other. '*Worth its weight in romance*,' she murmured, repeating the words in the advertisement.

Alex shook his head. 'It's for my sister,' he told the woman, 'so I can't give her perfume advertised with those words.'

'Perhaps this one?' The assistant raised the other bottle. She looked at Christina again. 'It's Bellodgia by Caron. Designed for the elegant woman.'

'I don't know about Fiona being elegant,' said Alex.

'She is when she's given a chance,' Christina said, remembering how Fiona had looked on the night of the dinner party. It wasn't so very long ago, but she felt as though that intimidating Laird of Craiglogie and the awkward young Christina belonged to the past.

She sniffed the scent on her wrist. 'Yes,' Christina said. 'That's the one for Fiona.'

The beautician returned to her counter to wrap a box of the perfume and Alex followed to pay. Christina wandered a little distance away to admire all the exquisitely packaged perfumes for sale. After the years of war-time austerity, it was a delight. She breathed in all the scents and closed her eyes.

'Ready?' Alex stood beside her again and she opened her eyes.

'I wish I could stay here,' she said.

'You prefer the life of a pampered lady?' he asked with mock severity, narrowing his eyes.

She quirked a smile at him. 'Not really. It's just that it's nice to be indulged every now and again. And you have done just that today.'

'The day isn't quite over,' he said.

She felt his arm sliding around her shoulders and she tilted her head to look up at him, her heart beating quickly.

They wandered down Princes Street, with the long rays of the afternoon sun stretching over the people and the buildings.

'The evening golden hour,' murmured Alex.

'You remember.'

'Yes, but what I didn't remember was our cameras. They're still in the back of the Land Rover.'

'Oh!' Christina said. The absurdity of it brought laughter spilling from them both. 'How could I have not noticed that?'

His voice softened. 'Because you were too busy enjoying the day?'

'Yes,' she said. 'Yes.' She slid her arm around his waist and felt the warmth of his body as he drew her closer.

Perhaps it had been because of the way she'd tenderly stroked his hand, the way she'd listened, the way she'd shared her own grief, or perhaps it had been there from the beginning, when he'd seen her on the beach. From the moment she'd looked into his eyes, he'd felt something shifting inside his heart. Like a small ray of light in his darkness. Now he recognised that light for what it was.

He was in love. As ridiculous and wonderful as it seemed to him, as they strolled towards the station, her petite frame snuggled under his arm, he'd fallen in love at first sight. Christina made him feel whole again. She was clever and kind. He'd been afraid of letting her into his heart and of her knowing the whole truth, but she made him want to live a normal life again. Being with her made his heart sing.

He glanced down, saw a glow on her face and it matched the warmth inside him. He liked the touch of her arm around his waist, her softness pressed against his side.

On the train Alex reached up and placed the Jenners bag in the string luggage rack. He took a seat next to Christina and she leaned against him. Lulled by the rocking of the train and the dim lighting above each seat, she soon fell asleep. Carefully, so as not to disturb her, he loosened his tie.

He felt a wave of protectiveness building in his chest. She looked sweet and vulnerable nestled against his arm like that.

Sighing softly, she clutched his hand for a moment, and he wondered what she was dreaming about.

He moved a lock of hair away from her face. It felt strange to be here, in the low light of this intimate carriage, swaying through the dusk as they drew further north.

He felt desire filling his body and was suddenly glad she was sleeping. He closed his eyes. Could he really be this happy?

CHAPTER 17

*C*hristina opened sleepy eyes to find herself snuggled against Alex. He looked down at her and smiled.

'I'm sorry,' she said, sitting up, 'I didn't realise how tired I was.'

'What were you dreaming of?'

She blushed and touched his lips with her finger. 'Never you mind,' she said mischievously.

He laughed. 'Are you hungry? We should have dinner on the train as we won't be home until late.'

'Now you mention it, I am hungry.' She lifted a hand to tidy her hair back into its chignon. 'Ravenous, in fact.'

'Then let's away to the restaurant car.'

'Will there be a free table?' she asked as they made their way along the corridor.

'A waiter came to our compartment a few minutes ago, to say if we wanted a table there was one available now. I expect that's what woke you.'

She slid into the seat in the dining coach and Alex sat opposite.

'Oh,' Christina said with sudden realisation, 'what are we going to tell Helen about not taking any photographs today?'

'Helen?' He frowned. 'What has Helen got to do with it?'

'Nothing,' Christina said, hiding her relief. 'Absolutely nothing at all.'

'Next time we come,' said Alex, 'I will bring my camera. With any luck, it will be raining.'

She smiled. 'With any luck?'

'A rainy evening in Edinburgh to capture the reflections of city lights on wet streets.'

'I'm glad you remembered that conversation.'

'I remember them all.'

She held his eye. 'It was nice of you to take me out today.'

'I couldn't let you come to Scotland and not see Edinburgh.'

The waiter arrived, they placed their order and he went off again, weaving down the aisle of the coach.

'Do you like dancing?' Alex asked.

'Of course! Although I'm not very good at the foxtrot.'

'Will you come to the village dance on Saturday?' he said. 'I doubt there will be a foxtrot to worry about.' His eyes crinkled with amusement.

'I'd love to. So what sort of dancing will there be?'

'The usual Scottish dances – The Dashing White Sergeant, Strip the Willow and so on.'

Her eyes widened. 'I don't know any of those. It will be worse than the foxtrot!'

He laughed. 'Not at all. One of the band will probably call the dances, but if not I'll be there to guide you.'

'I don't want to embarrass you or step on your toes…'

'You won't,' he said. 'And you had better dance only with me, as there are some men who delight in whirling their partners around so that the girl's feet leave the floor.'

The waiter returned with their drinks and a basket of bread.

'I remember one year,' said Alex when the man had gone, 'some of the men stamped so hard when beating time that their feet went through the hall floor.'

'Goodness,' she said, 'this is beginning to sound dangerous.'

He grinned. 'You'll be safe with me.'

She coloured, glanced down and took a slice of bread from the basket. 'Who else will be there?' she said, putting it on her side plate.

'Pretty much everyone in the village, from the youngest to the oldest. It isn't just a dance, there will be singing, storytelling and all sorts. Something for everyone to enjoy.'

Helen would be there, of course. Christina spread butter on her bread. The community was small and she couldn't avoid Helen. But there would be other, and good, company. Vanessa and her family were going, and Fiona, and Fraser. There would be no need to feel awkward.

'I want you to come,' he said.

He looked sincere and she wanted to believe that he wished for her company. She didn't think she could bear it if he didn't mean it, that he was only being polite. Or – her heart thumped at the thought – that he felt the need to keep her close now she knew his secret.

They looked at each other in silence for a moment. In his eyes she saw gentleness and something else...

She curled her fingers round her glass. 'Yes, I'll be there.'

'Good,' he said with a wide smile. 'You'll enjoy the evening, I promise.'

She enjoyed seeing him smile. Christina wished she could reach out and trace his dimple with her fingers.

The train drew into Aberdeen with a hiss of steam. Alex stood and retrieved his hat and the perfumery bag from the overhead rack. Christina pulled on her beret and they stepped down onto the platform. The sun had disappeared a while ago and by the time they reached the station entrance with its closed news stand, she shivered a little in the chill air. Alex drew her towards him and danced her round.

'What are you doing?' She laughed.

'Getting in some practice for the dance.' He placed his hand on the small of her back and hummed a waltz. She surrendered her body to him as he guided her round the deserted station forecourt, her heart racing.

He ended the dance and looked down at her. 'We'll soon be home.'

Home, she thought, as Alex tucked her into the Land Rover. She felt as if she really were going home. Craiglogie and the family that lived in it had become so dear to her.

Alex slipped a package from the bag he carried and handed it to her. She looked down and saw pretty wrappings tied with a bow.

'Fiona's birthday present?' Christina frowned.

He shook his head. 'Open it.'

She carefully removed the packaging as Alex slid into the driver's seat. It was the scent she'd admired, Moonlight Mist.

He smiled. 'I couldn't wait any longer to give it to you.'

'Oh, Alex.' She looked up at him. 'That was so thoughtful of you. Thank you.'

He took her hand in his strong, warm clasp. Then he started the car and they drove along the dark roads, home to Craiglogie.

The following morning there was no one around when the telephone rang, so Christina went into the hall and answered it.

'Oh, hello,' came Helen's voice. 'It's you.'

'Hello, Helen. Did you want to speak to Fiona? I'm afraid she's at work.'

'Not Fiona, no. Did you enjoy Edinburgh?' she asked.

'Yes, thanks.' Christina didn't feel the need to answer any further.

'Did Alex manage to get any good pictures?'

'We forgot to take any. There was so much to see and do–'

'You *are* a busy little person, aren't you?' Her voice was cold. 'But I've noticed you're looking quite worn out as a result. And you seem to have lost weight since you arrived. I hope you're not *regretting* anything.'

Christina drew in her breath. Was there no end to Helen's spiteful comments?

'No,' Christina said. 'I can't say I am. It's kind of you to ask though. In fact, I'd say I'm extremely happy.'

'You couldn't very well say anything else, of course, working for the laird. I understand... and I do *admire* loyalty.' Helen sighed. 'Do you intend to stay here for a while longer? You have no roots, I suppose.'

'I've agreed to work for Alex for a period of time–'

'You mean you want to go home, but feel you can't? Oh, you poor little thing!'

Suddenly, Christina felt that she couldn't stand Helen for another moment. 'Not at all. I'm *very* fond of Craiglogie and *all* who live here. But if you'll excuse me, I will find Alex for you.' She set the receiver on the hall table and, her teeth clenched, strode off towards the garden where she'd arranged to meet him.

She found Alex, wearing his work jacket as the morning was cool, throwing a ball for Tess.

'Telephone call for you, Alex. It's Helen.'

Alex frowned. 'What does she want?'

'I'm afraid she didn't tell me,' said Christina.

Alex must have seen a flash of annoyance on her face, for he said, 'What did she say?'

Christina gave a small shrug. 'Nothing of any importance.'

He nodded and moved towards the house with his long, measured strides.

Christina would not allow Helen to spoil this feeling she had. She smiled to herself. Alex had found a home in her heart and nothing had ever felt so perfect. Happiness tingled in her veins every time she thought of him.

The garden sparkled in the morning dew and the scene warmed Christina's soul. Craiglogie had a sense of quiet completeness, which didn't need the outside world. She was happy to be here. Her wish to leave had disappeared.

Something soft dropped at her feet. Christina glanced down to see a ball, and Tess sitting and looking at her expectantly. She laughed, bent and scooped up the ball. 'Ready?'

Tess rose and her tail wagged. 'Fetch!' Christina threw the ball as hard as she could and the dog bounded across the lawn after it.

Alex returned from the house and his face was a little pale.

'Is everything all right?' Christina asked, her eyes widening.

He nodded and reached for her hand, rubbing her fingers gently in his. 'Helen wanted to know if we had any plans for tomorrow.'

'Do we?' Was Helen once again to accompany them?

'Well, I've just been wondering…' He looked up, uncertainty in his eyes. 'Would you like to come to the mart in the morning? I'm thinking of buying a few more cattle. It won't be as dramatic as Edinburgh, but you might find it interesting.'

She nodded and smiled.

'Good.' He released her hand and traced the line of her jaw with his thumb. Then he pulled her to him and his warm mouth was on hers. His lips were tender, exploring. As she responded, the meeting of lips turned into a fevered urgency. The intensity of the kiss was a shock to her, but it felt right. He kissed her until her heart was thudding, then released her mouth. She slipped her hands to his face and drank in the light in his eyes.

He sighed and said breathlessly, 'Let's see if we can make up for yesterday's lapse of work.'

He stepped from Christina and turned to the dog as she ran back with the ball. 'Tess, off you go. We have work to do.'

Tess plodded a couple of steps away, then looked back to see if Alex had changed his mind. 'Off you go,' he said more firmly, trying not to smile, and she wandered off with the ball in her mouth.

'Look at the cobweb on this bush,' Alex said. 'I thought it might make a good image.'

Christina examined the lacework. There was no sign of the spider, but covered in dew the web looked like strands of delicate pearls.

'It's a little work of art,' she said, straightening. 'Try taking the photograph from an angle, sideways on, with the sunlight shining through the web.'

Alex plucked his camera from the bench. He pushed up his sleeves and squatted. His thigh muscles strained against his trouser legs.

'Is this all right?' He glanced up at her.

'Oh, yes,' she breathed, and swallowed. Hastily, she shifted her gaze to his camera, but not before she had seen his lips curving into a smile.

He pressed the shutter, changed the angle slightly and took another photograph. As he stood, Tess came lolloping back over the lawn, thinking this was a new game. The dog sat, pricked up her ears and looked hopefully at Alex.

'She wants to know what to do next,' he said. 'I could take a photo of her.'

Christina smiled. 'Let's try that.'

'Stay,' said Alex to the dog. He walked backwards a few paces, then crouched down.

Tess immediately jumped up, bounded over the grass to him and licked his face.

'Never work with children or animals.' Christina laughed.

'So they say,' he spluttered. 'Clearly she's more of a pet than a working dog.'

'Really?' She raised her eyebrows. 'So the telling-off you gave me on the beach that day…'

She saw his eyes cloud and immediately regretted her teasing. 'It's okay. It doesn't matter.'

'But it does.' He pulled her into his arms and kissed her hair. 'I've never apologised for that, have I? It wasn't meant to be a telling-off. I'm sorry, Christina, for behaving in such a boorish way.'

She lifted her face to look at him. 'Apology accepted.'

'Thank you.' He rested his forehead against hers.

Tess barked.

'I know,' he said to the dog, as he released Christina. 'I still haven't taken any photographs of you. Christina, would you take the first one?'

'Of course.' She took the camera from him and bent her head to adjust the settings.

He came up behind her. She felt his arms around her waist, the warmth of his chest against her back. He brushed his warm lips against her ear.

'I can't concentrate if you do that,' she said, pretending to be stern, twisting round to look at him and being struck by the heat of his gaze.

He lifted a hand to her face and kissed her again with a hunger she had never experienced.

'I can't resist you,' he murmured, drawing back to look at her.

'I don't want you to try,' she said.

He laughed delightedly and pulled her towards him again.

Preoccupied with his thoughts, Alex took pictures as if he were an automaton. He was happy that Christina wanted to come to the mart and seemed genuinely interested in farm life, but he'd been shaken by the anger in Helen's voice on the telephone. Who did Christina think she was, coming here and breaking up their friendship? she'd demanded.

With a chill, he'd remembered Helen's sultry glances, her clinging comments, the possessive way she would place her hand on his sleeve, and he realised that Christina had been right. Helen did anticipate marrying him. The suitors in London – did they exist? – had blinded him to Helen's expectations.

Alex knew he must speak now, so he'd gently but firmly made it clear to Helen that he liked her as a friend, but there could be nothing more than that between them. There had been a long silence before she put down the telephone.

Alex had stared at the receiver for a while. He'd fallen for Christina, but he wasn't ready to share it. When he did, it would be his sister who'd be the first to know. The thought came to him that Fiona probably already knew, as she knew about everything else in his life. She would be happy for him, he was sure.

Alex brought his thoughts back to the photographs he was trying to take. He wanted to get a good shot of Tess, but she had other ideas and began to search under the shrubs.

'Good girl,' Christina was saying as the Labrador reappeared with the ball in her mouth. He attempted to take action shots of the dog as she pounded across the grass, but realised at best he'd probably only caught her tail.

Alex adjusted the viewfinder and watched Christina stroke the dog's broad head. Tess dropped the ball at Christina's feet and stood alert, quivering with excitement.

'Tess, fetch.' Christina tossed the ball in a high arc over the grass and the dog shot after it. As the ball curved downwards, Tess jumped up, all four legs off the ground, and caught it in her mouth.

Christina applauded and laughed. Encouraged, Tess returned and dropped the ball at her feet again.

'I should warn you this could go on for some time,' said Alex.

'I don't mind. She's enjoying it so much.'

'Why don't we do some training with her?' he said. 'It's good for her mentally as well as physically. She's still young enough and eager to learn.'

Christina gently tugged the dog's ear. 'What sort of training?'

'She's good at a number of commands – sit, stay, come and so on. She can also fetch well, as you have seen.' He grinned. 'I'm currently working on the command to find. Shall I show you?'

She smiled. 'Yes, please.'

He placed his camera on the bench. 'Can you let me have something of yours? A handkerchief would do.'

She pulled a folded white square from the pocket of her skirt and held it out. 'It's got a little of my new perfume on it,' she said with a slight flush. 'Is that all right?'

'Yes,' he said, taking it with a smile. 'Now, I'm going to hide it under one of the bushes.' He looked around. 'Under the holly. That has no scent, so it will make it easier for her to find your handkerchief. Can you distract her while I hide it?'

As Alex strode towards the bush, he heard Christina laugh. 'It doesn't take much to make you happy, does it?'

He glanced back over his shoulder to see Tess had rolled onto her back and stretched out her legs as Christina rubbed the soft pink skin of the dog's belly.

He ducked under the holly bush, carefully slid the square of cotton under the straggly lower branches and returned to stand beside Christina.

'That's done,' he said, looking down at the dog, her upside-down face stretched in what looked like a gleeful smile, her pale-pink tongue lolling out the side of her mouth. 'Tess, behave yourself and sit.' The dog shot up, onto her feet, and did as instructed, nearly toppling a startled Christina onto the grass.

Alex held out his hand to the dog and she sniffed it. 'Tess, find.'

The dog set off eagerly, sniffing along the row of shrubs as she went. All at once, she dived under the holly and came up with Christina's handkerchief in her mouth. Pleased as punch, she trotted back to him and dropped it into Alex's waiting hand.

'Well done, Tess!' exclaimed Christina.

'We haven't finished yet,' said Alex. 'Let's see if she can find it under a bush with its own scent. Labradors have a particularly acute sense of smell, so any scent in competition with your perfume will be a real test for her.'

He gestured to a magnificent shrub with white flowers hanging in heavy clusters. 'The spirea will be perfect. Can you distract her again?' *As you distract me*, he thought, his eyes straying to her lips.

Forcing himself to concentrate, Alex strode towards the spirea. He bent and laid the handkerchief on a lower branch of the heavily-scented white flowers.

Tess set off again, sniffing strongly as she made her way around the shrubs, intent on her task. She came to the spirea, hesitated and moved as if to pass on.

'Oh.' Alex heard the disappointment in Christina's voice.

'Patience,' he said, his voice low.

Tess stopped, turned and teased the fabric from within the branches.

'She's got it!' Christina cried.

Tess ran back across the lawn, beside herself with joy as Alex praised her. Christina stroked Tess's soft, light-brown ears.

'Tess, drop,' said Alex. The dog did so.

Alex held Christina's handkerchief, damp from the dog's gentle mouth, and grimaced. 'Sorry.'

The quirk of Christina's mouth was almost too much for him as she looked up at him. He restrained himself as he bent and grazed her lips with his. 'I'll get it laundered for you.' He slipped it into his jacket pocket. 'It's time for lunch.'

He picked up his camera, replaced the lens cap and slung the strap over his shoulder. 'Let's go indoors.' He took her hand.

≈

Christina was wearing the serviceable jumper and trousers Fiona had lent her, and was waiting for Alex in the courtyard when he came striding towards her. Hens squawked out of his way as he caught her by the waist and pulled her to him, and she laughed.

'Where on earth did you get those clothes?' he said, nuzzling her neck, his breath warm on her skin. 'They're too big for you.' He lifted his head. 'Don't tell me! Fiona.'

'She said these would be best for the mart. I've rolled up the sleeves and the legs,' Christina pointed out.

'Well, you're nice and early.'

'We don't want to miss the train, not if you want to get to the market before the bidding starts.'

'We can probably spare five minutes,' he said, looking down at her.

The dimple appeared in his cheek and she felt her knees weaken. 'If you're certain…'

He took her in his arms. 'You wouldn't believe how much I've missed you.'

She slipped her hands under the old tweed jacket to circle his waist, and felt the delicious heat of his body radiating through his shirt. 'I would, because I've missed you too. But it's only been eight hours or so.'

'Yet how they have dragged.' He smiled slowly, making the breath catch in her throat. 'Maybe I did something right, once upon a time, to deserve you,' he said, as he took her face into his hands and the warmth of his fingers made her head reel.

He lowered his head to hers and kissed her until she was breathless. Then drawing away, he took her hand and said, 'Come on, we have a train to catch.'

Alex sat next to Christina as the train wound through the countryside. He told her how the mart operated and she listened with interest, asking questions here and there.

Suddenly, he got up and moved to sit on the seat opposite.

'What's the matter?' she said.

'I can't function properly when you're so close, Christina, and I must think about work sometimes.' His mouth lifted into a smile.

She returned his smile, revelling in the knowledge of the emotion she produced in him.

All at once he was serious again, leaning towards her, his arms on his knees. 'I want to build up the farm, to own a beef herd,' he said. 'I intend to start small and increase year on year.'

'Does that mean you're giving up dairy farming?' She was surprised to hear the dismay in her voice. 'I like the cows and their babies...'

'No,' he said, sending her a smile. 'I enjoy dairy farming and won't give it up, but it is hard work with less help available these days. Beef is easier to manage and it pays well. Aberdeen Angus produce good quality beef. They're also well known for their docile nature and the dams have great maternal attributes.'

Christina looked at Alex and felt a surge of happiness. She loved the enthusiasm he showed when talking about his farm, and it was infectious. 'That's all right, then.'

He laughed. 'I'm glad I have your approval.'

The train drew into Kittybrewster, stopping with a hiss of steam. They alighted and made their way through the busy station, where a porter loaded the suitcase of an older woman onto a trolley, men stood gossiping and small children ran around their harassed mothers.

Once across the road, the size and noise of the mart building took Christina by surprise. Farmers sat and chatted in tiered benches that rose almost to the ceiling, arranged in a semi-circle round the ring. Alex led her up a steep flight of steps and they squashed into a space on one of the packed benches.

Before she had time to ask Alex any questions, a white-coated auctioneer appeared from the back of the ring and a hush fell on the expectant crowd.

'Taking bids for lot number one,' he said in a sing-song voice. 'Half a dozen Aberdeen Angus dams.'

Six red beef cattle were herded into the ring and paraded round for viewers to decide whether or not to bid.

'What do you think?' she whispered.

'Not bad, but let's see what else there is,' Alex said as the auctioneer called the bids in one long, indistinguishable babble.

Twenty lots of cattle were introduced and sold, while Christina took in everything around her. Here were real people doing a real job, she thought. The farmers' role in society was so important and yet others barely thought of it and how hard the men worked. She liked that Alex was focused on his estate, his farm and his workers.

She glanced sideways at him, and felt pride in the warm, strong man seated next to her. As if aware of her scrutiny, he turned his head and smiled at her, and she lowered her gaze in embarrassment.

Soon she became aware of Alex's interest quicken in the bidding.

'Taking bids for these four dams,' sang the auctioneer.

Alex almost imperceptibly raised his hand. Christina held her breath, willing Alex to be successful. The bidding increased and the tension mounted. Then the other two buyers dropped out and the cows were his.

'MacDonald.' The auctioneer banged on his desk, nodded at Alex and a young man in a brown coat bent over a ledger to record the sale.

'That's what I came for,' said Alex to her, his voice low. 'They're handsome animals and I know they are splendidly bred.'

They made their way to the office, with Alex greeting some of the men as he passed, and he paid his bill.

'Is there anything else you'd like to see?' He raised an eyebrow at her.

'I'd like to look at the chickens, if there's time. I saw a sign pointing to them earlier.'

'The fancy breeds? This way.' He led her to another building, with rows of cages each containing a breeding pair of poultry.

'I like these,' she said, stopping to peer at two fluffy white birds with matching legs and feet. 'They look like they're wearing bathrobe and slippers.'

'They're Silkies,' he said.

'And these?' Christina pointed to a pair of small, dark-grey, speckled chickens with very short legs.

'Scots Dumpies, a traditional Scottish breed.'

'They're appealing,' she said, 'all of them. Perhaps I'll live on a farm and breed chickens one day.' She smiled, meaning it as a half-joke.

'Perhaps you will,' he said softly.

There was such quick passion in his eyes that her heart thumped.

CHAPTER 18

Christina opened the door to the postman when he knocked on Saturday morning.

'Package for the laird,' he said, thrusting the thick buff envelope into her hands and, whistling, jumped back into the red van and disappeared down the drive.

She looked at the package and saw along the top the words *Lizars, Optometrists and Suppliers of Photographic Equipment.* Alex's photographs. She went into the kitchen and placed the envelope on the table, just as Alex walked in.

'Ah, my photographs,' he said, spotting the envelope. 'I thought I heard the postman.'

He took a knife from the drawer and slid it into the top of the package.

'I guess this is the moment of truth,' he said.

'I suppose it is.'

'Don't look so nervous.' He laughed at her serious expression. 'It's my work, not yours.'

She raised an eyebrow. 'But my reputation.'

'Come here and look at them with me.'

She did as he asked, moving to stand beside him. Alex slid the contents onto the table. He spread the photos out and there was the image of her in the studio, laughing at the camera.

He drew in his breath, picked up the picture and looked at it. 'Almost as good as the real thing.'

He slid his arms around her waist, turning her to stand in front of him.

'I thought you wanted me to look at the prints,' she said.

He leaned over and grazed her forehead with his lips. 'Mmm...'

The feel of him was too distracting. She pulled his mouth to hers. Her hands tangled in his dark hair as he took her lips, kissing her in a tormenting, seductive rhythm. Her heart was racing, her legs trembled.

He drew her closer against his chest. 'I've never felt like this before,' he murmured, his breath warm on her neck, his voice oddly hoarse.

Christina relaxed against him. He rested his forehead against hers.

'Alas,' he said, with mock seriousness, 'I can see this is not the time nor the place.'

'Yes,' she said, slipping out of his arms. 'We hardly know each other and must take things slowly.'

He looked a little lost, standing there in the kitchen. She took a step, leaned forward and pressed her lips against his.

'Back to work,' she said softly against his lips.

Alex groaned. 'Damn.' But he smiled.

She seized on another photograph. 'This is good.'

'Is it?' said Alex, his eyes fixed on her.

She picked up the photo and held it in front of his face. 'You will see how good, if only you'll look at it.'

He took it from her and considered the image.

'See how well you've captured the spider web glistening in the morning dew,' she said, 'like a splendid lace collar.'

He nodded, put down the print and lifted another from the collection on the table. 'Oh dear. Look at this one.'

'You did manage to capture only Tess's tail. Never mind. Practice makes perfect.'

She plucked another photograph from the pile. 'I don't remember your taking this one.' It showed a field of sheep being herded by a collie.

'That's my friend's dog working his sheep. I took it in Perthshire.'

'And this one?' She was staring at a grand house and the woman walking towards the camera was unmistakably Helen.

Alex gave it a cursory glance and stepped closer. 'Also taken when I was in Perthshire,' he murmured into her hair, as he slid his arms around her once more.

Christina continued to stare at the photograph in silence.

'I know it's not very good,' he said. 'More of a snap, really.'

'Did Helen enjoy the occasion?' She kept her face lowered.

'Helen?' He laughed. 'She wouldn't dream of watching a dog work sheep.'

'But she was in Perthshire with you?' Christina persisted, her face growing hot.

'Good Lord, no. That is, she appeared at my friend's house down there one afternoon – they have a loose acquaintance, it seems.'

Christina twisted round to look at him, felt the warmth of his smile and knew the truth of his words.

He lifted a hand to her face and tucked a strand of hair behind her ear. 'Will you save me all the dances this evening?'

'I'll need to check my dance card first,' she said with a mischievous smile.

∾

'Thanks for giving me a lift to the dance,' Christina said as Vanessa pulled open the doors of her oak wardrobe and rummaged through the hangers. 'Alex and Fiona have to be at the hall early, before the doors open.'

'Of course, the laird and his family have to welcome everyone as they arrive,' said Vanessa. 'And it's our pleasure to take you. George is much better, but he's decided to stay at home and rest – without the boys. Ah, here it is.'

She held up a sleeveless silk dress in cornflower blue, embroidered with tiny white stars.

Christina stepped closer. 'It's gorgeous.'

Vanessa held it out at arm's length and sighed. 'Blanes of London. To think this fitted me once.' She held it up to Christina's slim frame and smiled. 'Try it on.'

Christina pulled her sweater over her head and slipped out of her skirt. The fabric was deliciously soft as she drew the dress into position and carefully eased up the side zip.

She turned to look in the full-length mirror and caught her breath. The dress was exquisite, with its V-neck, fitted bodice and pleated from the hip.

She smoothed the silk of the skirt. 'Oh, Van.'

Vanessa smiled as her eyes met Christina's in the reflected image. 'You'll break a few hearts tonight,' she said.

There was only one heart she was interested in.

'Shoes,' said Vanessa. 'You don't want high heels if you're dancing, but I have some strappy sandals. They're not blue, I'm afraid, but they're cute.'

Vanessa searched among the boxes in the bottom of the wardrobe. 'Here they are,' she said, standing up and producing a pair of dove-grey, peep-toed sandals.

Christina sat on the edge of the bed, slipped them on and tied the ribbons with a bow at each ankle. She stood.

'How do they feel?' said Vanessa.

'Perfect.' Christina couldn't resist the impulse to twirl.

Vanessa laughed. 'You'll put all the other women in the shade.' She began searching through the dressing-table drawer. 'One more thing… Ah, here we are.' She pulled out a flat blue box, opened it and held it out to Christina.

Christina stared at the contents of the box. A short chain with a pendant of a single white pearl and matching pearl earrings. 'I can't possibly.'

'Of course you can.' Vanessa took Christina by the shoulders. 'My dear, you *shall* go to the ball.'

As Christina watched Vanessa's reflection in the mirror, drawing the chain round her neck, she had a sudden image of Helen in pink pearls the first night she'd met her. 'Vanessa, what do people say about Alex and Helen?'

Vanessa frowned as she fastened the clip. 'Well, it seems that the belief in the area is that Alex will marry her, but that he's taking a long time getting round to it. As far as I can tell, though, it's nothing more than friendship – whatever she might want to be the case.'

'Helen's going to the dance tonight. Stewart is giving her a lift and she's staying afterwards at Craiglogie.'

Vanessa smiled at Christina's reflection in the mirror. 'Never mind about Helen.'

'But I do mind,' Christina said, and coloured. 'Alex and I have been… getting on very well.'

Vanessa stared at her. 'You and Alex? But I thought it was Fraser you liked?'

'I do like Fraser,' she said, 'only not in that way. But Alex–'

Vanessa laughed. 'That was quick work, Chrissie! Well, I'm delighted and I hope it means I will have my dearest friend living nearby.'

Embarrassed but happy, Christina turned from the mirror.

≈

The road outside the village hall was filling up with vehicles when they arrived. Squashed in the back seat with the boys, Christina managed to spot Alex's Land Rover as Callum slowed the Morris down, looking for a place to park.

It was the first time she'd seen the village in the evening. Each of the cottages had left a light burning, ready to welcome back its occupants at the end of the night. The church and manse sat on one side of the green, and on the other side was a grocery shop, the Boat Inn and the hall. Tonight, the hall doors were flung wide open and light poured out onto the pavement.

Callum pulled into a space and parked the Morris. They all climbed out and Callum removed a couple of bottles of beer and one of wine from the car boot.

'It's Bring Your Own Bottle,' he said to Christina. 'The beer is for me, the wine for you and Vanessa. There'll be juice provided for the children.'

Each twin took one of Christina's hands and she was tugged along by them, swept into the crowd of excited people pressing towards the hall. She found herself laughing with them as they emerged into the throng.

Alex froze the moment Christina stepped through the door. She looked wonderful and elegant in a stunning blue dress, her golden hair swept into a stylish chignon. She was glancing down at the twins and laughing at something they'd said.

She took his breath away.

Before he had time to collect his thoughts, she and the rest of Vanessa's party were being welcomed by their little reception committee. He watched as Vanessa and Callum were greeted by Fiona, and the reverend and Mrs Greig, while the boys skipped off to look for their friends. And then Christina stood before him.

Almost without thinking, Alex drew her aside. The blue of her dress was the same shade as her eyes. For a moment he stood in a kind of daze, staring at her, trying to fix her image so firmly into his memory that he'd never forget this moment.

'You look beautiful.'

She smiled and her eyes travelled over him. 'And you look handsome.'

He laughed. 'You like my Bonnie Prince Charlie jacket and waistcoat?' He indicated the kilt he wore of heathery blues and greens with a red stripe. 'The MacDonald tartan.'

He leaned forward and his lips brushed her ear. 'Keep the first dance for me.'

He pulled her back to the little group. 'Welcome, Christina,' said Alex formally, grasping her hand. 'I hope you enjoy your first dance in the village – and that it's the first of many.'

'Hear, hear,' said Reverend Greig.

There must be about a hundred people here, thought Christina, as she moved away. The large hall was warm, with electric heaters high up on the walls. Groups of tables and chairs had been set round the edge of the floor and people were laying claim to them by setting out their bottles of drink.

'I'll go and find a table,' said Callum.

'Oh dear,' Vanessa murmured in Christina's ear and nodded towards the door. Christina followed her gaze.

Helen stood in the open doorway, one arm in Stewart's and the other in Fraser's. Both men looked impressive in their kilts, jackets and waistcoats. And Helen looked supremely confident in a purple satin frock with a white belt and flared skirt. She held the pose as if expecting to be photographed. As Christina gazed, Helen began swaying unsteadily, and she immediately under-stood Vanessa's concern.

247

They both watched as Helen let go of the men's arms and made her way towards Alex and the rest of the welcoming committee. She smiled at the minister and his wife, kissed Fiona on the cheek – and Alex full on the mouth.

Christina stood rooted to the spot, too shocked to speak. She glanced at Vanessa and saw her friend staring at the little group. Christina reluctantly turned back. She couldn't hear what Alex was saying, but Helen shook her head and her smile grew larger.

There was a burst of applause as the band arrived on stage. The leader, carrying a fiddle, introduced himself and the other two men, one on drums and the other on the accordion. As the band tuned up, more people spilled into the hall and the hum of conversation was terrific.

Christina turned her attention again to the reception committee. It had broken up. The minister and his wife were now mingling with the other guests and Fiona's arm had been caught by another woman.

Alex made his way towards where Christina stood with Vanessa. Helen followed behind.

'Hello,' Helen said, her speech a little slurred.

Alex turned and took her elbow. 'You're drunk, Helen,' he said, his voice low. 'You should leave.'

'I'm not drunk. I'm merely happy.' She smiled. 'I hope you'll dance the first one with me, Alex.'

'Helen–'

As Fraser and Stewart joined them, she flicked her gaze towards Fraser. 'Oh, and you the second one.'

He flushed and tried unsuccessfully to hide a look of delight. They stood in a little uncomfortable circle.

'Anyway,' continued Helen, but no one heard what she intended to say as the band struck up with 'Scotland the Brave'.

'The Gay Gordons!' shouted Helen. She grabbed Alex's hand and pulled him unwillingly into the middle of the floor where couples were forming a circle.

Stewart led Christina and Fraser to where Callum waited at their table. She sat and watched as the pairs set off round the room; forwards, backwards and forwards again, the men's kilts swinging out. Helen laughed loudly and twirled, her right hand grasping Alex's held above her head.

To Christina's astonishment, Mrs Morrison gave her a cheery wave as she flew past in a dress of red and yellow, her husband laughing at her side.

As soon as the music finished, a stony-faced Alex led the flushed Helen to their table. He pulled out a chair for her and took one himself next to Christina. Stewart excused himself and went to find Fiona.

'We'd better make sure the boys aren't getting into any mischief,' said Vanessa. She glanced at Christina as she got to her feet and raised an eyebrow, linked her arm with Callum's and they strolled off in search of the children.

The band struck up again.

'Would you like the next dance, Helen?' Fraser asked hopefully.

'Actually, perhaps not, Fraser,' said Helen above the general din. She opened her beaded clutch bag, removed with unsteady fingers a violet Sobranie Cocktail from her box and inserted it into her cigarette holder. 'But I'd love a glass of wine.'

He coloured. 'Did you bring any?'

She sent Fraser a haughty glare. 'Do I look like the sort of woman who has to bring her own drink?'

Fraser flushed more deeply and reached for one of his beers. 'I'm afraid I've only got pale ale.'

Helen gave an exaggerated sigh and pulled a face, disarranging her lovely features. She pointedly waved the slender silver holder. Alex produced a small box of matches and leaned forward to light her cigarette.

'Thank you.' She sucked in a breath of smoke and eyed with

distaste the matchbox. 'When will you buy a lighter? They are so much more chic.'

'I don't smoke, remember, Helen? I carry the matches as a courtesy to you.'

She smiled and seemed to purr. 'Darling Alex, do *you* have anything a girl could drink?'

Alex gestured to a bottle of red and another of white wine on the table.

'Angel,' she breathed, putting out her hand and stroking his cheek. 'I'll have the red.' She drew again on her cigarette, tilted her head back and blew smoke out of her mouth.

Christina sipped her drink without tasting it and watched Alex. How much longer would Alex endure this? And what on earth made Helen think her behaviour was acceptable?

She felt powerless to intervene as, wide-eyed, she stared at Alex. He caught her look and gave an almost imperceptible shrug. Helen tugged on his jacket, he turned to her and poured her a glass of wine. Helen chatted about nothing in particular, and the villagers whirled about on the dance floor.

Time stretched as Christina sat, nursing her drink. She felt like a fraud. And maybe she was. She thought of Alex, of Helen's familiar handling of him, and knew she'd upset the balance. That once again she was getting involved with a man who wasn't truly free. Helen may not have a ring or a marriage certificate, but that was surely where their relationship was headed before she arrived.

The band struck up a reel and announced the next dance would be the Dashing White Sergeant. Christina was relieved when Helen addressed Fraser.

'We can do this one, if you like.' Helen held her cigarette, sizzling, in the dregs of a glass of wine on the table.

Fraser offered his hand to help her up. She ignored it and got to her feet.

'Helen,' said Alex, half rising from his seat.

'What?' Helen glared at him. 'I'm fine and it's Fraser's turn.'

Alex sat again. 'Look after her, Fraser,' he said softly.

Fraser nodded and followed Helen, still slightly unsteady, onto the dance floor. They joined a group of four waiting for another couple to complete their circle of six. Again the music started, and the circles of dancers moved round in one direction, then in the other and separated into two sets of three facing each other.

'Do you know this one?'

Christina turned her gaze from the dancers to Alex and shook her head. 'I don't know any of them. They look so complicated.'

'They're quite easy,' he said. 'Watch and you'll soon get the idea.' He lowered his voice, although there was now no one else at their table. 'Christina, I'm sorry about Helen.'

'It's all right,' she said. 'Let's just enjoy this evening.'

Alex turned back to watch the dancing. She stole a look at him and saw his jaw tighten. He hadn't asked her to dance, despite his earlier request. Was he regretting their intimacy now? He seemed to be mesmerised by Helen as she skipped around the dance floor with Fraser.

At once Christina was cross with Alex and with herself. She felt a fool as she turned her gaze away and wondered what to do. Should she leave the dance at the earliest opportunity, hoping she could find someone to give her a lift back to Craiglogie? Or should she stay here and be made to feel miserable?

Christina took another sip of her white wine and glanced at Alex, still staring at Helen. She choked back the sob building in her chest. She'd leave Craiglogie first thing on Monday morning and take a train back to London.

His eyes turned towards her and she realised he'd heard her muffled choke. Before he could speak, Helen and Fraser returned to the table, his face red and shining with exertion, hers glowing with alcohol and pleasure.

'Not dancing, Christina?' she asked sweetly. '*Really*, you should, you know. It's not difficult.'

The band struck up again. 'Strip the Willow,' said Alex with a smile. 'My favourite.'

He shrugged off his jacket, untied the bow tie and dropped it into his sporran. 'This does have its uses,' he said, sending Christina a grin.

He undid the top button of his shirt and she had to drag her gaze from the pulse in his throat. Rising, he held out his hand. 'Christina.'

'I couldn't wait any longer to dance with you,' Alex said, his hand on the small of her back as they weaved through the crowd of people and onto the floor.

'Is this dance really your favourite?'

He laughed. 'They are all my favourites.'

'But I have no idea of the steps,' she said as he drew her into a double row of four couples, men on one side and women facing them on the other side.

'I'll teach you.' He slid the sporran around his waist to let it hang on his hip. 'It's an energetic dance and we're the first couple, so pay attention. Here we go!'

He linked her arm in his and, before she knew what was happening, spun her round and round. The room flew past in a blur to the sound of clapping and cheering. He stopped, shouted to her above the noise and pointed to the man standing opposite. 'Now you swing round with him.'

She was grabbed by the other man and round they danced, her head spinning. Alex snatched hold of her again and spun her. 'Now my turn!' he yelled.

Down the line they danced, Christina's pleated blue skirt swirling round her legs, her hair coming loose from its ivory clip.

'What now?' she shouted, blowing strands of hair from her forehead.

'We do the same again!' He pulled her into his arms and once more spun her. As the background blurred, she saw only his laughing face above her.

By the time the dance came to an end, they were gasping for breath and laughing.

'What a dance! It's thrilling and scary and completely mad. It's my favourite!' Christina felt ridiculously happy, on top of the world.

'Mine, too, after all.' He winked.

Breathless and dizzy, they returned to the table and tumbled into their seats. Alex threw an arm around her shoulders and kissed her cheek.

Vanessa and Callum came back from chatting with friends and pulled out seats to join them, a sleepy twin on each of their laps. Vanessa glanced over at Helen, dozing in her seat, her head falling onto her chest, and sent Christina a worried look. Alex caught it and raised his eyebrows at the empty bottle of red wine.

'Fraser, would you mind taking Helen home?' he said.

'Don't anyone touch me, or I'll have you for assault.' Helen raised her head and stared glassy-eyed at Christina. 'I'm staying here until the end,' she slurred, 'and then I'm going back to Craiglogie.'

CHAPTER 19

$\mathcal{A}$lex's thoughts were in turmoil. A group of young men were singing bothy ballads, telling of working conditions on farms. With unseeing eyes, he stared at them.

He loved Christina, there was no doubt in his mind. But it was now obvious, as Christina had said, that Helen expected to marry him. He couldn't marry Helen; he didn't love her. But she'd been a family friend for a long time and he was concerned for her. She was drunk and she was unhappy. It was his fault for not seeing all this earlier.

'This song is charming,' Christina whispered. 'What is it?'

He knew the haunting tune. '"Eriskay Love Lilt",' he murmured. He found himself joining in softly with the chorus, *Sad am I without thee.*

She turned and held his gaze for a few moments, then moistened her lips. 'It's been a strange few weeks, don't you think?'

He nodded slowly, not daring to speak.

'Alex, man!' called one of the men, sounding deep in his cups. 'Give us a tune.'

Alex looked up and shook his head. A chorus of villagers

joined in with the demand, banging their hands on the tables to increase the tumult.

'They're not going away,' said Fraser, with a smile. 'You could play one piece.'

Helen raised her head. 'Go on,' she muttered. 'Go and do your tricks, just like a performing monkey.'

She sat up, reached for her bag and took out a compact. In the little mirror, she touched up her lipstick with an unsteady hand.

'You know I really have no choice but to play,' he said to Helen, his voice low.

He stood to a huge cheer. Loud clapping accompanied him to the piano in the corner of the stage. Taking the seat, he called out, 'Any requests?'

Various suggestions were made, not all relating to pieces of music, but he laughed. He made a decision, flexed his fingers in a theatrical fashion and played 'The Entertainer'. A hush fell as people listened to the piano rag. After a few minutes, the twins woke and sleepily clambered down from their parents' laps. With the other children still in the hall, they were all soon running around, delighted to have the floor to themselves.

Christina's attention was brought back to their table.

'Someone should stop those children,' hissed Helen. 'They're spoiling Alex's performance.'

'It's the village dance, Helen,' said Vanessa. 'No one minds, least of all Alex.'

Nicholas came running back. 'Aunty Chrissie, will you dance with me?' He took her fingers in his small hands and pulled.

Helen tutted and glanced away.

'I'd love to.' Christina stood. 'Lead the way, kind sir.'

Delighted, he tugged her onto the dance floor and she joined in with the jumping around of the children.

Alex finished playing the lively piece of music and stood. Raising his hands, he said with a grin, 'Alas, I'm not good enough to hold their attention.'

'Too bad,' called Callum. 'You need more practice.'

To the sound of laughter in the hall, Christina watched Alex stride back to the table. Tall and strong, his throat bare, his kilt swinging, she knew she loved him.

But there was his relationship with Helen. What was she to make of it?

She held his gaze for a few moments as he took his seat at the table.

'These people have no culture,' said Helen, laying her hand on his arm.

'I disagree,' he said, carefully sliding away his arm. 'The village dance is part of the rich culture of Scotland.'

'You know what I mean,' said Helen, frowning.

'Yes, I believe I do,' said Alex.

Mention of the culture of Scotland brought a memory back to Christina's mind. When the attention of the others at the table was distracted, she said, 'Alex, you didn't finish telling me about the MacDonald–Campbell feud.'

'Did I not?'

'You said the Campbells had slain the MacDonalds because they were enemies.'

'Yes?' There was a twinkle in his eye.

'It's true the soldiers who carried out the killings were commanded by a Campbell,' she said, making her voice stern. 'But he was acting under the king's order and had no choice. And only a few of his men were Campbells.'

His mouth twitched. 'Now where did you learn that?'

'Fraser told me.'

Alex's face widened into a grin. 'Och well, it was worth a try.'

She couldn't suppress a peal of laughter.

'Christina,' he said, his voice at once urgent. 'Will you come with me tomorrow to a place along the coast? At the dinner party I promised you a trip to Bullers of Buchan.' He reached across the table and took her hand. 'Please,' he said softly. 'I want to talk to you, alone.'

She watched his mouth, caught the memory of his warm lips on hers, and smiled. 'I suppose I could take some photographs.'

Before he could say anything further, a halt was called to the entertainment for everyone to eat supper. Stovies were served from large cauldrons carried in from the kitchen and oatcakes were piled up on huge plates on the trestle tables. Christina found herself talking to a number of people, all curious to learn how she knew the laird, and she heard nothing but good about him and his sister. Yes, she thought, she had known him for only a short time and already he had brought so much happiness into her life.

She pictured his teasing eyes when they'd first met at Craiglogie, his pleasure in working on the farm, their kisses – tender, feverish, languid. She ran the tip of her tongue over her lip. Then she thought about their day in Edinburgh, how he'd confided in her about his terrifying experiences and the nightmares.

Surely it hadn't all been for nothing?

Alex watched her pass the tip of her tongue over her upper lip and his pulse jumped. He wanted to take her in his arms, but could do nothing, not with all these people here. Tomorrow, he thought, with the wide sky and pulsing sea about them, he would tell her he wanted her to stay forever.

Vanessa's voice broke into his thoughts. 'We have to go,' she said. 'The boys need their beds.'

He joined with Christina in wishing the family goodnight. The children were so tired they had to be carried from the hall. Older children still ran around, some of the adults were the worse for wear and the dancers on the floor were beginning to flag. Alex saw all this, but barely took it in. His thoughts churned as he looked over at Helen, her head resting on her folded arms on the table. He wanted her to be happy – but a marriage between them was impossible.

He took Christina's hand and as she turned to him, he longed to trace the line of her mouth with his thumb. 'Come outside,' he whispered.

He drew her through the doors of the hall, past the revellers on the pavement and into the shadows around the corner.

Out of sight of prying eyes, he wrapped her in his arms, bent his head and lowered his mouth to hers. Her lips rose to meet his. Her arms slid round his neck. She wanted him as much as he wanted her, he could feel it. Heat pulsed through him. His fingers tangled in her hair, her lips were soft and searching. Tenderly, he pulled her closer, felt her body warm against his, her lips opening as he deepened his kiss.

Everything was spinning out of control. Such a sweet kiss, such a soft, yielding body.

When he lifted his mouth at last, she said breathlessly, 'Thank you for a lovely evening.' Her eyes were luminous.

He laughed softly. 'Chrissie, you are delightful.'

'You know,' she said, 'you are different from how you were when we first met.'

'Different in what way?'

'Not so… autocratic.'

'Autocratic?' He tucked a lock of hair behind her ear. 'Maybe it's because you've stopped being so cross.'

'Well, you deserved it. You could have told me politely not to throw the stick for Tess.' She examined his face before speaking again. 'You'd come striding along the sand, casually confident, and I'd been nervous, meeting a strange man on an empty beach.'

'What I said to you on the beach could have… should have… been phrased differently.'

'And on the landing that night, when I was lost?'

He grinned. 'That, I admit, was to see the sparks fly in your eyes.'

'So you deliberately provoked me?' She spoke sternly, but there was a soft light in her eyes.

The door of the hall must have opened and closed, as for a brief moment the sound of a man singing floated out into the night.

Catching the song, Alex said, suddenly serious, 'You won't, will you?'

'Won't what?'

'... *go, lassie, go?*' he sang softly.

He saw the smile on her lips, felt her small hand squeeze his fingers. 'Do you think you could see a future at Craiglogie,' he said, 'with me?'

Christina hesitated and his heart thudded.

She shook her head.

'No?' he said, his voice throaty.

'I mean, it's too sudden, too much to believe,' she whispered.

He took her face in his hands and kissed her. 'There is nothing in the world I want as much as I want you.'

She slid her hands up his chest, over his shoulders and buried her fingers in his hair. He pulled her close and felt her tremble in his embrace.

Christina pulled away from him, her breath coming quickly. 'I'm sorry. This isn't possible. You have a previous understanding with Helen.'

He took her hand and studied her face. 'I'm fond of Helen, but only as a friend. It has never been anything more than that.'

Alex hesitated. Should he tell Christina now how she had stolen his heart and that more than anything he wanted to marry her? This wasn't how he'd planned it, standing in the shadows outside the village hall, the muffled sounds of music and thumping in the background. He wanted the wild and romantic scenery of the rugged coastline.

Their eyes met and she shivered. 'I'm getting a little cold out here.'

'I'm sorry,' he said. 'We should go back inside.'

They walked hand in hand to the front of the building. A group of men standing there smoking paused in their chat and nodded to Alex, before their curious gazes shifted to Christina.

As Alex pushed open the hall doors, the Reverend Greig was standing on the stage, trying to get the attention of everyone. 'Ladies and gentlemen, lads and lasses,' he called. 'It's approaching midnight. Sadly, we've come to the end of the evening.'

Alex groaned and laughed along with everyone else in the hall. Christina's eyes were wide with exhaustion and something else… uncertainty?

He caught sight of Helen across the room, still asleep with her head on the table, and he sighed. 'We need to get Helen home,' he said.

Christina nodded. 'Of course.'

When they reached the table, Helen's head jerked up. 'Is it finished?' she said, bleary-eyed, lipstick smeared across one cheek.

Alex felt suddenly very weary and wished he had never agreed to Helen spending the night at Craiglogie after the dance. 'I'll drive you back.' He lifted his jacket from the chair, hooked it over one shoulder and put his other arm around Christina's waist.

Helen stared at Christina as her eyes came back into focus. 'You're still here.'

'Come on, Helen,' said Alex, releasing Christina and taking Helen's arm. 'Time to go.'

They emptied out of the hall with everyone else and into the night. Car doors slammed and overexcited children were carried home to bed.

Helen hung back, standing in the street, swaying slightly, and regarded Christina through half-closed eyes. 'I suppose you think you're very clever, catching Alex?'

'There's no need for that, Helen,' Alex said. 'You're tired and it's best you say as little as possible at present.'

'She's a gold-digger, you know,' said Helen, 'just after your money.'

'Helen—' Christina began, shocked.

'It's all right, Christina,' Alex said. 'She's not herself.'

'*Not herself*?' mimicked Helen. 'Then whose self am I?' Her face crumpled. 'I thought you were going to marry me.'

Christina turned away.

'Where are you going?' he said, reaching out a hand.

'To get a taxi.'

'You won't get one. There's only Albert Lowe and he'll already be booked for the rest of the evening.'

She paused.

'Christina,' Alex pleaded.

She heard the soft, intimate voice he had used earlier and suddenly she could see that it was always going to be this way. She'd lowered her defences, believed that she could have a relationship with someone, but she'd been a fool.

Christina longed to be home, in her mother's flat, to climb into bed and pull the covers over her head. She'd done it again – misjudged Alex, just as she had David. How could she have made the same mistake twice?

She turned to look at Alex. Helen was hanging on to him. Tears spilled onto Christina's face. There was a bond between them. She imagined Alex leading Helen into her bedroom, taking her in his arms and pressing kisses to her throat, her head thrown back, lids half-closed. Like her portraits. No, there could be no mistake.

'Get in the car, Christina, please,' she heard Alex say. 'It's late. We can talk tomorrow.'

Christina turned, looking for Vanessa. Surely she could stay with her tonight? But Vanessa and her family had left some time ago.

Alex stood holding the front passenger door open, looking at Christina. Helen stumbled into the seat.

'Here you are!' Fraser appeared, his face beaming. 'What a wonderful evening it's been.'

Christina had no choice but to go with them. She slipped into the back seat and Fraser climbed in the other side.

A wonderful evening?

This had been one of the best nights of her life, but no longer.

Alex started the car and they drove out of the village.

Christina felt wretched as Alex drove in silence. How could she stay? She'd foolishly persuaded herself that Alex loved her.

Within a few minutes Helen was snoring, her head fallen forward.

It seemed this nightmare journey would never come to an end. But at last they were turning onto the estate. The car stopped at Fraser's cottage and he climbed out, bidding them goodnight.

Alex put the Land Rover back into gear and soon its head-lights were picking out the tall stone pillars at the entrance to Craiglogie House.

A light burned in the porch. As soon as the car drew to a halt, Christina threw open the door and jumped out. She heard Alex call, 'Christina!' but she ran into the house.

'Christina, wait,' he said, striding into the hall after her.

She stood self-consciously, her eyes not meeting his.

'Goodnight, Alex.' She turned to climb the stairs.

'I can't bear the evening to end like this,' he said.

She heard the catch in his breath and paused, then slowly turned towards him. In that moment, she saw confusion and longing in his eyes.

His arms drew her back and she felt the heat of his body pulsing through the soft silk of her dress. With his fingers, he lifted her chin and she was forced to look into his face. The urge to touch him was overwhelming, as she felt the glimmer of tears in her eyes.

'It's not what you think about Helen,' he said, his voice low.

Christina pulled away, trembling. 'My coming here was a mistake. I will leave on Monday morning. I don't want to trouble Vanessa on a Sunday for a lift to the station—'

'No. Please, I want you to stay.'

Her heart hammered against her ribcage. She shook her head, too wretched to speak.

'Is this anything to do with… David?' Alex asked hesitantly.

'No.' Her voice came as a whisper.

David had been her first love, with all its intensity, but it had been a puppy love. Had he lived, no doubt her feelings for him would have passed as she matured. And, she had to admit, he had been growing tired of her, the lack of real physical contact in their relationship. She'd told him she was saving herself for marriage and had chosen to ignore the annoyance that crossed his face. It could never have worked. He was no longer the hero of her imagination – quite the opposite.

Suddenly, she could not remember why David had meant so much. She no longer cared about him, only Alex.

Tears seeped out. She felt she couldn't breathe.

He took her face tenderly in his hands. 'Then what is it?'

She caught the warm smell of him and it stirred the memory of his kisses, the delicious heat of his body crushed against hers. Her cheeks burned with humiliation. 'I must leave here.'

'Please, don't.'

'Don't what?' slurred Helen, as she wandered into the hall.

Alex groaned.

Helen leaned towards him and gave him a clumsy kiss on the mouth. 'Stop that, Helen,' he said, his voice curt, as he grabbed hold of her arms and steadied her.

'Goodnight,' Christina said again and sped up the stairs, her heart pounding. *I love him, I love him, I love him*, she thought. *I am a fool.*

She reached her room, slammed the door shut and leaned against it. The way his mouth had felt on hers, the way he'd buried his hands in her hair, his deep warmth.

Then she thought of Helen's lips on his; how that cheapened things, changed them.

But Alex had never said he loved her. She drew a shaky breath. Perhaps what had happened to him during the war meant he would never heal, never be able to truly love someone. She'd go back to Surrey, taking her dignity with her.

Christina felt a tear slide down her cheek and wiped it away with the back of her hand. She loved Alex. She loved this place. It would be hard to go. There was so much she would miss. The scent of Alex, the tall strength of him, the smile that warmed his tanned face...

'Oh, what am I going to do?' she whispered as she finally allowed the hot tears to spill over onto her cheeks.

Alex didn't see Christina at breakfast the next morning and guessed she was keeping out of his way. Helen no doubt was sleeping off the previous evening's excess. Fiona had gone with

Stewart to his house after the dance last night and she wouldn't be home until sometime tomorrow.

He washed his plate and mug and dropped back into the chair. Closing his eyes, he forced himself to remember his happiness working on Home Farm, doing something useful after the terrible waste of war. If there was a way forward, it had to be through hard work.

Christina's face slid into his mind.

He pictured her teasing eyes, her delight when she'd fed the calf, the way she responded to his kisses, how she'd listened when he told her about his nightmares.

He'd been an idiot, waiting for that perfect moment to tell Christina exactly how he felt.

A spark of hope flickered in his breast. He hadn't died at Dunkirk or during that explosion. Many soldiers had lost their lives in the war. He owed it to them to live his life to the full.

Alex drew in a slow breath. He felt strangely light-headed, caught in a surge of pure happiness. It wasn't too late. He would find Christina now. Suddenly, he wondered why he was still sitting in the kitchen. He jumped to his feet.

There was an urgent knocking on the back door and with an oath he wrenched it open.

His dairyman stood there. 'One of the heifers has been trying to calve for the last three hours,' said Joe. 'Her calf isn't presenting right. She's going to need some help and it'll take the two of us.'

Alex's heart sank, but he nodded. 'You did right to call me.' He snatched his work jacket off the peg and followed Joe outside. When he got back, he would find Christina and ask her to marry him.

As Christina walked through the woods, she thought yet again of what Alex had said to her last night. How he wanted to take her to that place along the coast. He'd added, his voice soft, *Please, I want to talk to you, alone.*

What had he wanted to tell her? Surely there could be nothing left to say. Didn't he know how much he'd already hurt her?

She stopped on the woodland track. She couldn't spend the day avoiding him at Craiglogie, so she would go to Bullers of Buchan on her own. It wasn't far – he'd told her where it was – and she was sure she could cycle there in a little over half an hour. It would be better than hanging around, waiting until she could take the train home tomorrow. She blinked back tears at this last thought.

Christina hurried back to the house. She slipped indoors, hoping she wouldn't bump into Alex, ran softly up the stairs and in her room grabbed her camera.

Fiona had told her she could borrow the bicycle whenever she wished, so Christina crept down the stairs and out to the barn at the back of the house.

'Sorry, Tess,' she said as the dog padded hopefully round the corner of the building, 'you can't come on the bike.'

Her camera in the basket, Christina pedalled furiously along the empty road, concentrating on pushing Alex out of her mind.

The sky was as moody as she could have wished for dramatic photographs, but a hand seemed to grip her heart and squeeze it.

She cycled past the ruins of Slains Castle, perched on the cliff edge, gaunt against the sea and sky. *Yes, Alex*, she thought, *it is a suitable place for Dracula.*

At last she reached Bullers of Buchan and turned off the road. She bumped along a rough path to the grassy clifftop and dismounted. Her camera strap over one shoulder, Christina set off along the cliff edge. The sea was grey and turbulent, and startled seabirds rose and shrieked around her. She could barely hear her own thoughts above the roar of the waves and the salt wind dashed her face.

She saw an enormous rock below, where a high arch met the force of the raging tempest. It really did look like a huge pot with the water boiling inside. The sea rushed in so violently that it sent up a torrent of white foam and spray.

Christina moved back from the edge and sank onto the tussocky grass. Lifting her face to the wind, she closed her eyes. She could hear the sea surge against the rocks. It was wild and beautiful here. She could see why it attracted Alex.

Would she ever stop thinking about him? She forced his image from her mind and rose wearily. Slipping her camera from her shoulder, she took photographs of the sea surging through the cauldron.

The crashing of the sea appeared to be growing louder and the gulls' cries more fearful. She should visit the cave now, she thought, in case it's not safe later, and she set off along a track leading down to a shingle beach.

As soon as the heifer had calved and Alex could see mother and baby were fine, he washed in the barn, pulled his jacket back on and returned to the house with a spring in his step.

'Christina!' he called, pausing in the hall. There was silence.

He pushed open the kitchen door. Helen looked up from her magazine, the smoke curling from her cigarette. 'She's not here,' she said.

The realisation struck him like a bolt of lightning. He'd promised to take Christina to Bullers. Had she gone there anyway, on her own, to take photographs? His mind raced. He'd intended to take her there this morning and now it was afternoon. She knew nothing about that part of the coastline, about how fast she could find herself stranded on the beach. It wouldn't be long until high tide.

'When did you last see Christina?' He forced himself to speak calmly.

'Let me think.' Helen tapped cigarette ash onto the saucer. 'It must have been round about lunchtime. Why?'

Alex left the room and ran up the stairs two at a time. On the landing he knocked on her door. 'Christina, are you there?'

There was no reply, so he threw open the door. The room was tidy, her bed made.

Alex turned on his heel and ran back down the stairs.

'Helen,' he said, bursting into the kitchen, 'do you know where Christina has gone?'

She ground out her cigarette and said, her voice sulky, 'She told me she was going to skip lunch and take some pictures at Bullers.'

For a moment he stared at her, unable to believe his ears. 'How could you have let her go?' he said, his anger barely controlled. 'What if she's gone down to the beach there? The tide will be in soon.'

'I'm sorry,' she said with a shrug. 'I didn't think.' She put a hand to her forehead. 'This damn head...'

'Helen,' he said, barely controlling his temper, 'you were kind to me when I came home from the war, but there never was and never could be anything between us other than friendship. I don't love you and I have never said or done anything to make you believe otherwise. There can be no future between us. Christina has nothing to do with you and me not being together.' He turned towards the door. 'I'm going after her.'

Helen called, her voice plaintive, 'She doesn't deserve you, Alex, not the way I do.'

Alex turned and looked at her. 'You don't know what it means to love.'

'And I suppose you do?' she retorted.

'You are selfish and deluded, Helen,' he growled, taking a step towards her. 'If you stopped wasting your time on an imagined love, you wouldn't be so blind as to how Fraser feels about you.'

'Fraser?' she said, startled.

'Or does the man you choose to marry have to fund a London lifestyle?' He didn't wait for an answer, or expect one. 'Listen to me, Helen. I am going to marry Christina, and only Christina.'

Her face paled. He turned and in a few strides had crossed the room.

'Wait,' called Helen, her voice shaky, 'I'll help you find her.'

Alex wrenched open the back door and ran to the Land Rover, aware that every word he'd thrown at Helen was a moment he'd wasted getting to Christina in time. As he pulled open the driver's door, Tess came bounding as if from nowhere and took a flying leap onto the seat.

'Sorry, girl, but you can't come,' he said brusquely. She stared up at him.

'You want to help find Christina, too? Okay, move over.'

Tess jumped into the front passenger seat, just as Fraser in his Land Rover pulled into the yard.

Alex paused in the act of climbing into the driver's seat.

'Afternoon, Alex,' called Fraser, as he stepped out of his car and walked towards him. 'Got time for a quick word about the planting?'

'Christina's missing, Fraser,' said Alex, his voice grim. 'Helen thinks she's gone to Bullers. I'm on my way there now to find her. I hope to God I'm in time.' He jumped in, slammed the door shut and started the engine.

'I'm right behind you,' shouted Fraser.

In his rear-view mirror Alex saw Helen come running out of the house, Fiona's gumboots on her feet. The thought crossed his mind to stop, but he was already driving away. He'd wasted enough time as it was.

CHAPTER 20

*C*hristina followed the curve of the cliff, treading carefully down a rough track. At the bottom was a narrow shingle beach and she made her way along it, looking for the cave. She found the opening in the rock and eased herself through.

The ceiling was just high enough for her to stand upright. The hiss and rush of water betrayed the sea's constant bombarding of the arched rock outside. The light had almost gone; she wouldn't be taking any photographs here.

Cautiously, she stepped further in, grateful for her ankle boots to keep her feet dry. The floor was damp from the wash of the sea and there were loose pebbles. As she walked, the narrow cave grew wider, the ceiling higher, until it opened out into a lofty cavern. Christina paused, pleased with the momentary image of a boisterous Edwardian party enjoying a picnic.

Now she'd reached the back of the cave, she saw there were a number of passage openings leading away into darkness. She peered into a couple of them but could see nothing.

Christina shivered. The cold and damp were beginning to penetrate her woollen cardigan and skirt. She turned away, and as she did so her foot slid on a loose stone. Her ankle turned, her head grazed the rough wall of the cave and a pain shot through her temple. She gasped, unable to move for a moment, tears springing to her eyes.

When the pain in her temple had subsided, she tentatively touched her right foot to the floor of the cave and tried to put weight on it. Immediately, her ankle burned and throbbed. She bent and carefully pulled down the side zip on her boot. Her ankle was already swollen, there was a small cut above it and her nylon was laddered.

As she bit her lip to stop the hot tears falling, Christina realised the roar of the sea was louder. Was the tide coming in? No, it must be the pulsing in her temple from the knock against the wall. Her thoughts were less clear than before. Should she try again to put her weight on her foot or should she have a rest and move on afterwards? The rest sounded like a good idea.

There was a ledge of sorts near her, where the rock jutted out. That must be where she'd banged her head. Wincing, she eased herself onto it, set the camera by her side and lay down on the ledge. Pulling her cardigan tighter and tucking her skirt about her legs, she closed her eyes. It's just for a little while, she thought.

As he drove, Alex thought again and again how he'd intended to tell Christina today that he loved and wanted her. Why had he waited so long?

The car skidded to a halt on the loose gravel at Bullers and Alex jumped out. Fraser's car pulled in beside him.

'You two search up here,' Alex said, seeing Helen sitting in the passenger seat. 'I'll take the track.'

He ran down the rough path, stones skittering beneath his feet. Tess followed, the sense of urgency coming from Alex keeping her close and ready for action. At the bottom of the track, he paused. The cliffs were silhouetted against the grey clouds and the chill in the air struck him. It was late. Please God, not too late.

'Christina!' he called. The sound of her name blew back at him on the wind.

He sprinted along the shingle, calling her. The tide was coming in. If she was down here, she'd be cut off soon. He saw the dark, narrow opening of the cave. Surely, she wouldn't have gone in there? He ran to the end of the shingle beach. There was no sign of Christina.

Had she fallen into the icy North Sea and been swept away? No, he wouldn't think of that possibility.

He turned and saw the dog running around happily. 'This is not a game, Tess,' he said abruptly. His voice shook.

A game. All at once he remembered. He pushed his hand into his jacket pocket. Yes, thank the Lord, it was still there. Christina's handkerchief. He'd forgotten to launder it after the training session with Tess.

Alex pulled it from his pocket and held it out to the dog. 'Tess, find. Find Christina.'

Tess sniffed the scrap of cotton. With a wag of her tail she set off, back across the shingle beach, nose to the ground. She stopped at the mouth of the cave and barked.

Alex's heart thudded. Had Christina entered the cave? The roar of the sea was loud in his ears, matching the surging of his blood.

Her tail wagging, Tess looked at him for further instructions.

Christina must be in there.

'Tess, go up there and stay.' Alex pointed to the path leading from the sea and was relieved when she bounded away.

The tide was rushing over the pebbles and into the gloom of the cave. He stood at the entrance and called.

'Christina.'

There was no reply.

As he faced the dark cave, fear threatened to overwhelm him. He felt light-headed, dizzy, the fierce sound of the waves seeming to fade away. Putting out a hand, he leaned against the rocky entrance, his head down, forcing himself to breathe deeply. You must conquer this, he told himself. You must, for her sake. Christina was alone in there, scared and perhaps hurt.

Close by, he heard the sound of the angry sea. Time was running short. He clenched his jaw, ducked his head and squeezed through the entrance. There was no sign of Christina, but he was sure she had to be in there somewhere. His body felt cold, but sweat gathered on his brow as he pushed forward, deeper into the cave. He splashed through the ankle-deep water, painfully aware that the sea level was rising. Let her be alive, he prayed.

The glistening surface of the rocky walls and ceiling seemed to close in around him and he almost cried out. The roof level was so low that he had to keep his head bent. Soon it must become higher and the cave wider, he thought, his heart thudding.

The relentless flow of water sucked back and forth, tugging at his trousers, and reached his knees at a frightening pace. The tide was threatening to shut them into this tomb.

He must be calm, for her sake. He must get her out.

His heart in his throat, he reached the cavern and straightened up.

She was lying on a narrow, rocky ledge, just above the water line, her eyes closed. He waded forward, his breathing deep and uneven. Reaching her, he saw her eyelids were still closed, long lashes resting on pale cheeks.

'Christina,' he said, his voice soft, his hand shaking as he reached out. Her cheek was cool under his touch.

She stirred and her eyes flickered open. 'Alex?' she whispered.

There were violet smudges of exhaustion under her eyes. 'I'm here,' he said.

She struggled to sit up on the ledge. Quickly, he sat next to her, stripped off his jacket and pulled it round her. Holding her close, he drew her head onto his shoulder. She shuddered.

He held her tight. 'It's okay, I've got you.' He pressed his lips to her hair. They could not stay here.

'Christina,' he said, keeping his voice calm, 'we need to leave. You'll be safe once we get out of here.'

'It's just that I banged my head and my ankle is a bit painful,' she said, her voice low. She saw the water and her eyes grew wider, her face more pale.

'Everything is all right now,' he said softly, tightening his arm around her waist.

She sobbed with relief against his chest. 'How did you find me?'

He felt her tremble. 'I guessed you'd come to Bullers, because we'd intended to do that today. But it was Tess who led me here. She followed the scent on your handkerchief.'

'Dear Tess,' she said, her voice shaking a little.

'Now, come on, we must go.' Alex stood, hung her camera strap over his shoulder and lifted Christina from the ledge. He held her close to him; she needed to draw warmth from his body. Carrying her, he pushed through the icy water as it swirled about his thighs, through the low passage and out into daylight.

He waded across the beach, pebbles shifting under his feet, waves slamming into his legs, the powerful force threatening to send him sprawling into the surf. She clung to him and the wind caught at her hair, whipping it round her head.

Alex climbed the track, the sea crashing on the rocks behind them, his arms around her, her face buried in his neck. From the top of the track, Tess barked joyously as she caught sight of them.

Christina lifted her head. 'I must thank Tess.' She gave him an unsteady smile. 'I can walk now.'

He frowned. 'Your ankle…'

'Let me at least try.'

Reluctantly, he set her on her feet, but kept his arm firm around her waist.

'Thank you, Tess,' she said, reaching down to stroke the dog's ears.

'It's all right, I've got her,' Alex called as Fraser and Helen came into view.

'Thank goodness,' said Fraser, hastening forward, relief clear on his face.

Helen's face was white and her breath ragged, as she came up to stand next to Fraser. 'Christina, I'm so, so sorry. I should have stopped you. I never gave it a thought when you said you were coming here. I've been too wrapped up–'

'It's okay, Helen.' Christina managed a smile. 'This wasn't your fault; it was mine for being too impatient.' She glanced up at Alex. 'Too unwilling to trust in a good man.' She turned back to Helen and Fraser. 'I'm all right.'

'And I will make everything all right from now on,' said Alex, smoothing her hair back from her face. 'Fraser, can you put Fiona's bike in the back of your car, and take Helen home to her aunt's?'

'I've left a few things at Craiglogie…' Helen began. 'Oh.' Her eyes lighted on Fraser's meaningful glance. 'But nothing I can't manage without for a night.'

She gave Fraser a smile, took his offered arm and they made their way back to his car. Alex helped Christina as she limped along the path to the car park. By the time they reached his Land Rover, the other vehicle had gone.

He helped her slide into the back and he lifted her foot to place it along the seat. 'Are you comfortable?'

She nodded.

'No, Tess,' he said, seeing the dog ready to jump in after Christina. 'Not in the back.'

'It's all right, Alex,' said Christina. 'There's room for both of us. Oof! On the seat, Tess, not my lap.' She gently pushed the dog off, made a space and Tess sat facing forward, looking pleased with herself. Christina smiled and leaned forward to fondle the dog's head.

'Try to rest,' Alex said to Christina. 'We'll be home soon.'

As he drove, Alex could hear Tess on the back seat panting with delight at Christina's attentions. Goodness, he thought, glancing into the rear-view mirror and seeing that Tess had worked her way back along the seat and was now nuzzling Christina's cheek, he was envious of his dog.

They drove along the clifftop in the fading daylight. Christina was surprised how quickly they reached Craiglogie. Alex stopped the car, turned off the engine and went round to her side. She began to ease herself out of the seat.

'Wait.' He leaned into the car and gathered her into his strong arms.

'You're not going to carry me again!'

'I already am. Now, hold on.'

She slid her arms around his neck as he swung her up.

He adjusted his hold slightly. 'Okay?' His body against hers felt hard and warm.

'Yes,' she said, her voice suddenly husky.

She was vaguely aware of Tess bounding out of the car and going in search of another adventure as Alex carried her across the courtyard. She leaned against him and felt his fast-beating heart against her own breast.

He nudged open the kitchen door and set her carefully onto a chair.

'Tea and toast,' he said firmly.

'I'm not an invalid,' she said with a smile as she slipped off his jacket. For the first time, she noticed his wet trousers and shoes. 'But you're soaked. You must change your clothes.'

'In a moment. First I want to make sure you don't have concussion.' He held up one hand. 'How many fingers?'

'Three,' she said confidently.

He nodded. 'Do you feel sick?'

'No.'

'Show me where you banged your head.'

She touched the spot above her temple. 'Here.'

He gently felt her head and examined it. 'I can't see a cut or any blood.'

'It was mainly my ankle,' she said, looking down at her right foot. 'It was swollen, but it seems to be okay now. There was a cut, too.'

Kneeling, he eased off her ankle boot and gently took her stockinged foot into his hand. 'It would be easier if you were not wearing nylons.' He looked up at her from under his dark lashes. 'Are you able to remove your stocking or shall I?'

She moistened her lips and coloured. 'I'll do it. Turn around.'

He remained kneeling, but removed his hand and turned his head away. Quickly, she raised the hem of her skirt, unhooked the torn stocking from its suspender and rolled it to her ankle.

'Okay,' she said, a little breathlessly, as she smoothed down her skirt.

He turned back and gently slid the stocking from her foot, his hands firm and cool on her hot, throbbing ankle. He lifted her foot clear of the floor to get a better look at the wound.

'It's only a small cut, but it should be cleaned. You don't want to risk an infection.' He lifted his jacket from the back of her chair, laid it on the floor and carefully placed her bare foot on the warm material.

She watched as he took an enamel bowl from a cupboard, filled it with warm water and returned with soap and a fresh towel. He set the things down on the floor, knelt again, moved his jacket out of the way and put the bowl in its place.

'Ready?' His large hands cradled her foot as he looked at her, a crease on his forehead. 'It may sting to start with.'

'Yes.' She held her breath.

He eased her foot into the bowl of warm water and shot her an enquiring look. She bit her lip at the sharp pain, but nodded. He soaped his hands and tenderly cleaned the cut. She felt breathless and dizzy as his hands gently circled her skin. She gazed at his bent head and had an urge to touch his tousled hair, to stroke the skin at the back of his neck. She gave a soft sigh.

He looked up quickly, concern in his eyes. 'I'm sorry, did I hurt you?'

She shook her head, not trusting herself to speak. He looked down again and with gentle hands lifted her foot out of the water, dried her skin and smoothed an antiseptic plaster onto the cut.

He stood. 'Stay there while I make the tea.'

Christina looked down at her bare leg and foot. 'My stocking is ruined. I need to put something else on,' she said, starting to rise.

'Then allow me.' Alex's eyes sparkled, as again he swept her up into his arms. She felt the movement of his muscles, heard the smile in his voice.

Laughing, she slid her arms around his neck and settled against him, as if she belonged there. Their faces were inches apart and she tightened her grip, nestled her head into the crook of his neck, the clean, musky scent of his skin filling her nostrils.

He carried her out of the kitchen, across the hall and up the staircase. He kicked open her bedroom door and gently lowered her onto the bed.

'Is there anything else I can help you with?' He looked at her and lifted an eyebrow.

'No, thank you,' she said firmly, pulling down the hem of her skirt.

Alex grinned and left the room.

She slid off the bed, unzipped her skirt and threw it onto the eiderdown. She removed the other stocking and her suspender belt, made her way over to the wardrobe and eased on woollen slacks, socks and a pair of soft canvas shoes which wouldn't rub against the cut. After she'd brushed her hair and put on a touch of lipstick, she sat on the edge of the bed.

Christina shivered with pleasure at the memory of his strong, warm body against hers as he'd carried her up the stairs. Had David ever made her feel like this?

'I don't think so,' she whispered, knowing for certain that he had not.

Dusk had fallen when, freshly bathed and changed, he heard her soft footsteps on the tiled floor. Christina came to stand beside him at the open main door.

He glanced at her foot. 'How is your ankle?'

'Much better, thanks.'

He pointed to the ghostly white dots appearing in the darkening sky.

'Look up,' he said. 'The first stars tonight.'

She tipped her head back to look and Alex saw the glimmer of her white throat.

'Superb,' she breathed.

They stood for a moment in the quiet darkness.

When she glanced at him, he was caught in a surge of longing. What is it that binds one person to another? he wondered. He knew only that he loved her.

Alex took Christina's face in his hands. 'I find it impossible to keep away from you, Christina.'

'What makes you think you need to?'

His lips were on hers, all thoughts gone as the chill of the evening mingled with the heat of their kiss. He pulled her closer, felt her tremble, and was lost in the sensation of her perfect mouth, her perfect body.

Heat surged through his veins and he forced himself to pull away, concerned she would be shocked by his passion, his lack of self-control. He leaned his forehead against hers. 'You are good for me, Chrissie. I hope I am for you.'

'You are,' she whispered. 'You've made me live again.'

Alex felt the softness of her hand as she touched his rough cheek.

'You came into that dark cave to find me,' she said.

'I feel like a swimmer who has at last dived up to meet the air.' He took her hand. 'Come indoors.'

He led her through the house, past the kitchen with the sound of Tess snoring, and into the small sitting room where a fire burned. He softly closed the door behind them and turned the key. When he switched on a side lamp, in its soft glow he saw light dance in her eyes.

Pouring whisky from the decanter on the sideboard, he handed her the glass. 'This will put a little colour into your face.'

'I could say the same is needed for you.'

'I intend to join you,' he said, pouring another for himself.

She swallowed a mouthful of whisky and coughed. He put down his glass, took hers and placed it next to his.

Alex had been taken aback by the intensity of his relief when in the cave he had pulled Christina into his arms. Until then, he had never fully realised how much he loved and needed her. His heart thudded at the memory of Christina lying on the ledge, his belief for a moment that she was no longer alive. He'd thought his own heart would stop.

He moistened his lips. 'Christina, there's something I must tell you.'

'Yes?' she said and slowly lifted her eyes to his face.

'You stole my heart the day we met on the beach.' His eyes searched hers. 'Although I didn't realise it then. And every moment I've spent with you since, you have managed to steal more and more of me.'

Alex reached his fingers to the curve of her cheek. 'You're trembling. Are you cold?'

She shook her head.

'Here,' he said, pulling the blanket off the back of a chair and wrapping it around her shoulders.

'Oh, my darling.' His voice broke. 'You make me whole again.' He pulled her against his warm body, no longer worrying that she would feel his longing. He lowered his head and kissed her burning lips as she reached up to him.

'I love you,' he said, kissing her forehead, her eyelids, her slender throat. 'I love you and I need you, Chrissie,' he whispered into her ear. 'I can't imagine a future without you.'

She pulled back a little and looked at him from under her lashes. 'I didn't know for certain what your feelings were for me.'

'I wanted to tell you,' he said. 'So many times I came close. But always fear of what you might think prevented me from speaking out. And this abominable scar–' He lifted his hand to touch the thick line on his forehead.

Christina raised her own hand to his face and traced the wound. 'In truth, I had stopped noticing it. But now that you mention it, I like it. It's part of your history, part of you.'

Alex took her hand, turned it over and kissed the palm. His eyes met hers. 'Will you marry me?'

For a moment she didn't speak and his heart beat faster.

'Yes,' she said, laughing through the tears. 'I will.'

She slipped her hands to his waist and the blanket slid from her shoulders. He felt the heat of her fingers through his shirt. Gently, she pulled the fabric out from under his belt and slid her hands up his back. He drew in a sharp breath. Swiftly, he tugged his shirt over his head and dropped it on the floor, seeing her watch the muscles ripple in his chest.

Trembling, she pressed her lips against his skin. He closed his eyes, let the delicious sensation wash over him.

When he opened them again, her eyes held his. He smoothed his hands down her arms, then slowly undid the buttons on her soft cashmere cardigan. He slid the pale-peach wool over her shoulders and let the garment fall to the floor.

He swallowed at the sight of her, and tentatively brushed the curve of her breasts with the tip of his finger. 'You are so warm and soft,' he murmured.

Carefully, he unfastened the clip in her hair and uncoiled the glorious, golden tresses until they fell about her face in a tumble. Her scent filled his nostrils as she sank against him, skin to skin, and sighed softly. His heart beat faster.

Dizzy with longing, he tilted her chin and brushed her lips with his. She moaned faintly. Stroking the lacy edge of her bra, he said, his voice deep and hoarse, 'May I take this off?'

Shivering a little, she stepped back and held his gaze as she slipped it off, her body glowing in the firelight. He wanted to kiss every ravishing inch of her.

She stepped closer, running her hands up his arms, over his shoulders, to cup his face. He wrapped his arms around her, covered her mouth with his. Her lips were warm, tender and filled with longing.

He drew her down onto the blanket, the heat from the fire matching that in his body.

CHAPTER 21

TWO MONTHS LATER

*C*hristina woke to the sound of Alex's gentle breathing. Daylight streamed through the curtains. She turned over and looked at him, his head on the pillow beside her, his dark hair tousled.

He sighed softly, and momentarily in his dream his lips curved into a smile.

She remembered the way he'd touched her just hours ago, his honey-brown skin showing darker against her paleness. She shivered with pleasure at the memory of his slow kisses trailing over her body.

Reaching over, she moved a lock of hair away from his forehead, the light catching on her gold wedding band. She lightly traced his wound with her fingertips, let her hand wander to the tight scar on his biceps, and wondered if she'd soothed his spirit, as well as his body and heart. He'd had no nightmares since the wedding ceremony.

Christina smiled at the memory of that day. Her gown had been simple but elegant. White satin fitted to the bodice, accentuating her slender waist, before the long skirt gently flared. Most of the estate workers' families and half of the village had massed outside the gate, waiting for the bride to arrive. She'd felt like the newly-crowned Queen Elizabeth, calm and serene, even though a rogue gust of wind almost took her short veil.

The church looked wonderful with its profusion of pink roses, the same roses she carried in her bouquet. Fraser escorted her down the aisle, Fiona as bridesmaid following in a pale-blue dress. The congregation was small because of the short notice, but she could see that almost all of those who mattered most were present. Vanessa's boys waved and shouted out her name as she passed down the aisle, and Christina laughed to see the frown on her friend's face as she brought the twins under control. Alex's mother had been forced to send her apologies. They were all disappointed, but a bout of ill health had kept her away. Christina's own mother, arriving by train that morning and terribly flustered, was instantly charmed by Alex. Helen had volunteered to look after Mrs Camble for the day. Fraser sent Helen a warm smile in the church and Christina was pleased when she saw it returned.

Christina conjured up the image of Alex as he stood waiting at the altar, flanked by his best man, Stewart. As she approached, Alex had turned, so handsome in his short dark jacket and kilt, and the expression of love for her she saw on his face made him the most desirable man in the world…

As if he could hear her thoughts, he opened sleepy eyes. 'Good morning.' He shifted closer and pulled her into his arms.

'It is.' She followed the outline of his lips with her finger. He smiled slowly, the dimple appeared and she leaned forward and kissed it. He laughed and the breath caught in her throat.

'Seven days married already,' he said. 'And now the first day of our life together at Craiglogie. Let's start by walking Tess and going to see how your calf is getting on.'

'My calf? You mean the one I've been feeding? Is she really mine?'

'Of course she's yours. You should give her a name, you know.'

'Betty.' It came out immediately. 'I think she looks like one.'

'On second thoughts, my wife,' he said, his eyes studying her face, 'I think Betty will have to wait.'

It was a bright morning and the air smelled fresh and clean. Everything had burst into new life. She heard the distant crow of a cockerel, caught the smell of the newly-mown lawn. Blue forget-me-nots looked gay in their tubs, scented wisteria drooped above the back door and the birds sang as they gathered twigs and moss for their nests.

'Off you go, Tess,' said Alex and the dog ran ahead of them.

'Do you know why I wanted to marry you?' he said as he took Christina's hand.

'Of course I do! You needed someone on hand who is good at naming calves and has an aptitude for walking the dog.'

His eyes were bright with laughter. 'No, that wasn't it, but it is useful to have a willing slave to lend a hand on the farm.'

She pulled her hand from his in mock anger and he laughed, but quickly grew serious as he caught it up again. 'I'm thankful for everything you've done since you came here. Teaching me about photography, helping on the farm – and above all showing me how love really does conquer all.'

'You talked of conquering, by the fire pond that day,' she said.

'You remember? Yes, I did.'

She stopped walking and looked up at him, her eyebrows raised.

'I was desperate to conquer my fears, so I could gain your respect and love.'

'So, are you saying that love is the conqueror in our modern MacDonald–Campbell feud?'

'You have every right to laugh at me,' he said. 'I was, I confess, a pompous ass.'

'I think you'll find you still can be.'

Alex let out a laugh. 'Maybe so, but we're both different for being with each other. You're no longer the same girl who arrived here a few short months ago,' he said, moving closer to her. 'You were shy and prickly, but so very pretty in that cream dress.'

Then she was in his arms, the sparkle of tears on her lashes. 'My self-confidence was low, and I felt lonely and very uncertain about the future.'

'I know that now, but I didn't at the time. All I could think was I didn't want to make a mistake.'

'You thought I might be a mistake?'

'No. Lord, no.' He held her tight and pressed his lips into her hair. 'I thought you didn't particularly like me and I was afraid of falling for a girl who didn't return my feelings.'

'I didn't like you at first, it's true.'

'When did that change?'

'Probably the very next day. When Vanessa and I came to dinner.'

'That soon?'

'I was completely against coming that evening, you understand, but–'

'Love must have its way.'

She leaned back so she could see his expression. His eyes held such tenderness. A wave of happiness washed over her. 'I know that it does.'

'With you beside me,' he said, 'I'm overcoming my fear of dark, confined spaces.'

'Working in the darkroom must have been a real challenge for you, but you passed. Would you like to continue the photography sessions?'

'I would, very much. And I have a suggestion. How does

having your own business sound? Perhaps Craiglogie Photography?'

'Mmmm,' she said, 'but I don't have enough of a portfolio to impress clients at the moment. Maybe though' – she let out a long sigh, glancing up at him from under her lashes – 'I could start with the photos I took on our honeymoon.'

He grinned and bent his head closer to hers. His breath tickled her ear. 'Some of those are private.' He straightened, his eyebrows raised, and looked down at her.

'Just as well, then, that we are doing our own developing and printing.' She gave him an impish smile.

'You could take on commissions – respectable ones,' he said. 'I'll convert one of the outbuildings into a gallery for you to exhibit and sell your work. I'll be your willing assistant.'

'And I'll be yours on Home Farm.'

He drew her close again. 'Once we've walked Tess, Mrs MacDonald, there's an attractive and extremely secluded spot in the woods I'd like to show you.'

Christina wound her arms around his neck. 'Should I get my camera?'

'You won't be needing it,' he murmured.

THE END

ACKNOWLEDGEMENTS

I must first thank the team at Bloodhound Books.

I am very grateful to Michael Hendry for his invaluable advice on the photographic studio and dark room. I am indebted to two senior guides at the Gordon Highlanders Museum in Aberdeen: Sandy Edwards for discussing ideas with me for my hero's military background and Marcus Hartland-Mahon for showing me round the museum.

Thanks also go to my friends Frances Jaffray for setting me right on the Doric and Vicki Singleton for her knowledge of birds, my book group for their enthusiastic input on farming issues and my writing friends who read the early draft of this novel. In particular, huge thanks to my writing buddy Julie Perkins, for her cheerful and wise comments - I couldn't have done it without her.

Some liberties have been taken with the geography of Bullers of Buchan. Any mistakes are my own.

Printed in Great Britain
by Amazon